IN STRANGERS' HOUSES

A Lena Szarka Mystery

ELIZABETH MUNDY

Constable • London

CONSTABLE

First published in Great Britain in 2018 by Constable

1 3 5 7 9 10 8 6 4 2

A CIP catalogue record for this book
is available from the British Library.

ISBN: 978-1-47212-636-8

Typeset in Bembo by Photoprint, Torquay
Printed in Great Britain by Clays Ltd, St Ives plc

Papers used by Constable are from well-managed forests and other
responsible sources.

Constable
An imprint of
Little, Brown Book Group
Carmelite House
50 Victoria Embankment
London EC4Y 0DZ

An Hachette UK Company
www.hachette.co.uk

www.littlebrown.co.uk

Elizabeth Mundy's grandmother was a Hungarian immigrant to America who raised five children on a chicken farm in Indiana. An English Literature graduate from Edinburgh University, Elizabeth is a marketing director for an investment firm and lives in London with her messy husband and baby son. *In Strangers' Houses* is her debut novel and the first in the Lena Szarka mystery series.

For Susan and Roger

CHAPTER 1

The fish were staring at her. Mouths agape. Lena Szarka breathed in their salty scent and found herself to be hungry. There weren't fish like this back in her landlocked country, only bony perch and other muddy river fish. These fish were in neat rows on their bed of crushed ice, their scales catching the cold November sunshine like shards of a broken mirror. She blinked the glare away.

Lena continued through London's Chapel Market towards Angel station and Timea followed. Plastic boxes full of cheap men's boxers were next to wooden crates of delicatessen salami. A man whistled as he laid out his organic cheeses on to beds of wood shavings, sticking toothpicks with price labels in ornate calligraphy on each one. He had good reason to be cheerful, thought Lena. A pound of that Normandy camembert cost the same as a three-course meal where she came from.

Lena turned back to her friend. Timea's face was pale and glistened with a slight sheen despite the cold of the day. She reminded Lena of a shelf freshly sprayed with Mr Muscle.

'Coffee?' said Lena. 'You have not eaten yet today. Perhaps we share some toast?'

'*Kávé*,' said Timea, in Hungarian. 'It's too early for English.'

'*Oké*,' said Lena. She pushed the door open for her friend. 'Coffee first,' she said, breaking into her native tongue. 'English practice later.' She ordered at the counter for them both while

1

Timea sat down. Lena watched her friend for a moment. Timea was sitting at a table near the window, staring out and seemingly fascinated by a Sainsbury's bag bumbling through the air as if it had ambitions to become an orange balloon. Her fists were clenched.

Lena sat down opposite, giving her friend one of the double espressos and placing a plate of toast between the two of them. She picked up a slice and bit in, enjoying the melted butter on her tongue. Timea picked at a crust.

'If you're not well you can go home,' Lena offered. 'I don't mind covering.'

'It's OK,' replied Timea. 'I'm just tired. I didn't sleep well last night.'

'Any special reason?' Lena was looking at Timea's fists, still tightly balled, as though she was trying to crush an insect in her palm.

Timea released her hands, picked up her coffee cup and took a small sip. 'No,' she replied. 'I will feel better after my coffee.'

'If you're sure.'

Lena followed Timea's gaze into the street and caught the eye of a man in a hoodie. He broke eye contact immediately and sauntered off. Both women sipped their coffee. Timea reached for the final piece of toast and smiled at her friend. 'I feel better now,' she said, biting in. 'I think that maybe Tomek's *kielbasa* did not agree with me last night.'

Lena smiled back. 'You're a delicate petal,' she said. 'All it takes is some Polish sausages to finish you off.'

'I still can't believe Tomek ate five *kielbasy*. Even your mama would be impressed. She does love a boy who can eat.'

'Don't say that,' said Lena. 'Surely I can't have picked someone my mama would like!' She gulped the dregs of her coffee.

2

'Perhaps you're more like her than you thought,' teased Timea. Lena spluttered and coffee spurted over her friend. Both women laughed.

'You deserved that coffee shower,' said Lena, passing her friend her napkin. 'Make yourself decent and let's get going.'

They emerged from the market bustle on to the wide expanse of Upper Street. It was the beginnings of Monday morning's rush hour on this London artery; cars and buses trundling from Islington to the City and West End, taking blank-faced commuters to their livelihoods.

'*Szar*,' said Timea, as they walked across the road. 'Tracy's there.'

Tracy was easy to spot, even in the crowd outside the station. The other faces were blurry and anonymous from over the road, but Tracy had painted over her features with thick make-up. She was clinging on to Faisal, staring at any woman who took the copies of the free London paper he was handing out.

Timea turned away. 'Can we go?' she said. 'I can't face her. Not today.'

'Wait.' Lena watched as a man with black jeans and a loose leather jacket circled a woman with a mass of ginger curls. The woman jabbed at her phone. There was something predatory about how he moved. Like he was stalking her.

'Lena, let's go.'

Lena ignored her friend and got closer to the man she was watching. She didn't like how she couldn't see his body under those baggy clothes. He managed to look furtive and focused all at once, glancing around and then back to the woman. Lena felt as if she was watching a nature programme, where she wanted to shout out to the gazelle to warn it that a lion was approaching.

She looked around to see if she was alone in her concerns. A man in a well-fitted suit was inspecting something sticky on the bottom of his shoe. A gaggle of school children shrieked at each other like excited monkeys. A homeless person snuggled in a sleeping bag, oblivious to the hubbub around him. Someone had left a cup of Starbucks coffee and a small box of Danish pastry next to him.

The lady looked expensive. Her ginger hair was big and curly, probably professionally blow dried, and matched the orange of her ballet pumps. Her handbag was a deep shade of purple, like the half-drunk glasses of Burgundy that Lena poured down the sinks as she cleaned for her clients. The lady was engrossed in whatever the phone had to offer. She gave it hectic little taps and never took her eyes away.

'Faisal has seen me,' said Timea. 'Look. But he will not speak to me, not with Tracy there.'

Lena looked at Faisal. He either hadn't noticed them or was doing a good impression of it. He was wearing his regulation blue jacket and a sleazy smile as he handed out copies of the morning paper, singing to himself and tapping his foot. Tracy gave out glares. Her hair was scraped into a tight, high ponytail, a hairdo that must mimic the feeling of someone pulling your hair. Constantly. No wonder she was always in a bad mood.

Lena put her arm around Timea and gave her a quick squeeze. 'I am glad you have got rid of him finally,' she told her. 'He's no good.'

Tracy's eyes looked as if she'd outlined them with felt tip. She was staring at Timea. She spat on the ground, before pulling Faisal's head down to hers and giving him an exaggerated movie kiss. Their mouths interlocked as if it were a competition, where the loser would be devoured. Lena felt a little sick. Evidently the toast she'd just eaten was keen to see the display. She turned away before it had the chance.

'Do you think she is prettier than me?' said Timea, still staring at the couple.

Lena's answer was halted by a surprised yelp.

4

Lena turned. The phone woman was on the ground. For a moment the lady looked confused. Then she looked to her empty hands.

'My iPhone!' she said. 'My handbag!'

Lena knew. Her eyes scoured the crowd for the leather jacket. The suited man tutted at the disturbance, the school children started to giggle, the late arrival of the 73 bus distracted the others. No one moved to help.

'My Mulberry handbag,' she heard the woman say. 'I've been robbed.'

The woman's voice got louder with the lack of response. 'Stop thief!' she shouted, as if trying out words she'd heard in a film. 'Help!' A few people looked at her, but still no one moved. This is what happens in London, thought Lena. No one cared.

Lena looked at Faisal, who had broken free of the hungry kiss and was staring at something with more intensity than he normally mustered. She followed his gaze and saw the leather jacket man, dodging traffic as he weaved his way across the road.

'There he is,' Lena shouted, her English words sounding foreign and loud in her own ears. 'The thief. Stop him.' People glanced at her and then away again, like she was a rabid dog who might attack if you made eye contact.

Lena launched into the road in pursuit.

The traffic lights were red and she made good time. It felt good to run. She took deep breaths of the bus-fume-infused air, and felt the power in her thighs as she pushed away from the uneven pavement. The man scuttled along Chapel Market in front of her, then darted past the fish stall around the corner.

Lena jumped to avoid a crate of fluorescent cigarette lighters. She took the corner.

She collided with something and was on the ground, a mess of arms, legs and the chemical aroma of fake leather.

Lena realised what had happened before the man did, and she wiggled around so that she straddled him. He blinked up at her in confusion.

The man was dark with black hair like her own. His body felt scrawny and fragile underneath her, as though she could snap him in half with her thighs.

She drew the purple leather handbag out from his jacket and dangled it over his head. 'Thief,' she told him.

'Be careful,' called Timea, approaching. Lena twisted round. As she did so the man began wriggling beneath her thighs like a puppy that didn't want a cuddle. She turned back to him. He'd extracted an arm and she felt a sudden pain. His fist. The metallic taste of blood filled her mouth. Before she knew what was happening she was on the ground, the man scrambling to freedom.

'I call ambulance,' shouted Timea.

Lena sat up. Her mouth was throbbing. She touched it, feeling the hot wetness of her blood. She wiped at it with her sleeve.

'I'm fine,' she told Timea, who'd already started to dial. She got to her feet, and for a brief moment was unsteady. Then she came to herself. 'We must return the handbag,' she said, starting to walk back to the station. 'I do not want to be late for Liberia Road.'

Back at Angel, the red-headed woman's mascara had left little trails down her cheek where she had mourned her handbag. A woman pulling a battered wheelie shopping cart was comforting her.

'They come over here to steal you know,' she told the ginger lady. 'I saw a documentary about it on Channel Four last week. I bet he was from Romania.'

'Yes, I read something about that,' replied the victim. 'These awful gangs promise the world to people and then they force women into prostitution and men to steal.' She sniffed and looked a little more cheerful. 'Gang crime. That's what's happened to me,

6

right outside Angel station. It's not what you expect on Upper Street.'

'Islington isn't what it used to be,' agreed the old woman. 'Muggings in broad daylight since we started letting in all these immigrants. Did you see the headlines yesterday? No wonder that police sergeant said they should all be sent back. I don't see what all the fuss is about. He's quite right.'

The ginger lady muttered something noncommittal, looking a little uncomfortable with the un-PC turn the conversation had taken. Lena stepped in.

'I got it back.' She passed the bag to the woman, who hugged it to her chest, cradling it like a baby. The woman looked Lena up and down, then opened up the bag and had a quick rummage.

'Thank you ever so much,' she said, a little too late for Lena's liking.

'All there?' said Lena. She was beginning to wish she hadn't got involved. The old woman was eyeing her suspiciously.

'Did you get my phone?' said the redhead.

'*Szar*,' said Lena. 'He must still have it.'

'He still has my new iPhone? The contract's just started. You're kidding me!'

'You're not from here,' the old woman informed Lena. 'You're foreign.'

'He hit me and ran,' said Lena, reaching her hand to her face, checking the injury was still there to verify her story. She looked at the women, suddenly angry at them. She didn't need this hassle. No wonder no one else had tried to help.

'I have to go,' she told them.

'You're Romanian too, aren't you?' said the wheelie cart lady. 'I know your type. You come here to beg.'

'I am Hungarian,' replied Lena with dignity. 'And I need to go to work.'

'No, wait,' said the redhead. 'The police are coming; they'll be here any minute. You'll need to tell them what happened.'

'Come on,' Lena said to Timea, starting on her way. 'Let's go.'

'Did you see handbag?' said Timea, in English at Lena's insistence now they were fuelled by coffee. She swept petals dropped from the enormous bouquet on the table. 'Leather was soft, and colour . . .'

Lena was balanced with one foot on the mantelpiece, the other on the bookshelf next to the *Penguin Book of Love Poetry*. She stretched up with her duster to the cobweb clinging to the white coving. It felt good to stretch her tall body. She couldn't see the spider responsible for the mess. Lucky for it.

'The colour,' she corrected, without turning her head from the task at hand. 'And that bag cost her more than we make cleaning in a week, put together,' said Lena. 'More than the doctor in the village earns too.'

'It was beautiful. I like to have bag like that,' she said. 'The bag,' she corrected herself.

Lena smiled at her friend. 'One day I will buy you one. I will work all through the day cleaning houses and all through the night cleaning offices,' said Lena, jumping down and landing with bent knees before straightening, perfectly balanced. 'And in five years you will have the bag and a very tired Lena.'

Timea laughed. 'OK, perhaps I do not want it so much. Instead I bring Laszlo to this country and send him to good school. He will work hard and become lawyer.'

'Then he can buy us both all the handbags we desire,' joked Lena. 'In the meantime, we clean for this cheating man.'

Timea looked up from the petals she was sweeping. 'Why you think he is cheat?' she said.

8

'Flowers mean guilty conscience.'

Timea bent down to the flower petals and gave them a deep sniff. 'These are lovely. Beautiful roses.'

'Roses are for funerals. Like chrysanthemums.'

'Not in this country,' said Timea. 'But I like more daisies. Daisies remind me of fields back home. I miss the fields.' She paused for a moment. 'Maybe these are not guilt flowers, maybe they are love flowers?'

'*Képtelenség*,' humphed Lena. 'Nonsense. There are empty Calvin Klein underwear boxes in the bin. I fished them out for recycling. Purple. Men do not buy new purple underwear for themselves to impress their wives.'

'Perhaps wife buys them for him as present,' said Timea. 'Because she was pleased with flowers.'

Lena laughed. 'I wish everyone was as sweet as you,' she said, ruffling her friend's hair. 'You should live on the flying palace – where children come from apples, and flowers are not just from men who cannot keep their *fasz* in their trousers.'

'I know life is not fairy tale,' said Timea.

Lena patted her friend's shoulder. 'It is not too long till Christmas now,' she said, inspecting the vase. 'You will go home to Laszlo for a visit. And you can walk through all those cold snowy fields you like together. Build snowmen.' She sniffed at the vase and pulled a face. The water was rancid, and the flowers dropped their petals faster than Timea collected them. She could throw them away, and risk an angry 'where are my beautiful flowers?' text message, or leave them and get a 'why have you left a mess?' text message. She'd have to put more credit on her phone to reply. All because this man was a dirty cheater. She grabbed the vase and took it into the kitchen, leaving a trail of petals behind her like a flower girl at a wedding. She dumped the whole bunch in the organic waste caddie and felt better.

'Faisal was not much use today – not that he ever is,' said Lena, going into the bathroom. It was tiled in travertine, the beige stone giving it the atmosphere of a luxury cave. 'He saw the thief, did not even shout. Just stood there tapping his feet and singing like he always does.'

'He has beautiful voice,' said Timea. 'He will be famous pop star one day.'

'So he always says,' said Lena. She paused to look at her face in the mirror. Her lip was cut, and a scab was starting to form. She turned away from her reflection and splashed some floor cleaner into a bucket. A synthetic citrus smell filled the room. 'I hate the lemon-scented one,' she said, lugging it back into the living room. 'Reminds me of Mama's sour calf-foot soup.' She put the bucket down next to Timea; water sloshed over the sides on to the hardwood floor. 'Watch your feet.'

'I am sorry. I will help in minute,' Timea said, remaining where she was. 'I just feel tired.'

Lena broke into Hungarian. 'Timea, I am worried about you. Something is wrong. I can tell.'

Timea smiled at Lena. 'You are so good to me. I don't deserve you. Not at all.' Timea squeezed her hand but looked straight ahead towards the blank television screen. Lena glanced at the grandfather clock, its copper pendulum swinging.

Timea was tearing the sweaty flower petals in her hand into tiny pieces of confetti. 'You can watch television, if you like,' said Lena. 'Istvan will be on.'

'We're not allowed,' said Timea.

'I know clients hate it,' said Lena. 'It doesn't matter how spotless the place is, if they knew we had the TV on they'd fire us. But we have had a tough morning. Let's treat ourselves to some *Heroes of Law.*'

'I don't feel like watching Istvan today.'

'Of course you do, you always do.' Lena put the television on. 'Let's see what he is up to. It will cheer us up.'

Istvan was flashing his CID badge at a pretty girl who was giving him unmistakable come-to-bed eyes. 'Not much acting needed for him to be the lady's man,' said Lena, with a laugh. 'He has not changed.'

'Do you miss him?' said Timea.

'He left us,' replied Lena. 'He doesn't deserve to be missed.'

Lena turned to look at Timea. She was sobbing into the petals.

Lena balanced the mop in the bucket and sat down next to her. 'What is it?' she asked her. 'Is it Faisal? A client?' She put her arm around her, pulling her towards her. 'I can fix it, whatever it is.'

'I know something, only I don't know. It's happening again. And I don't know what to do.' The macerated rose petals fell to the floor as Timea put her head in her hands. 'I'm sorry,' she said. 'I'll clean them up.'

On screen, Istvan was busy kissing the girl.

Lena waved away Timea's attempts to gather the petals and hugged her closer. 'Tell me. I can make it better.'

'I don't know what to do. And I am so scared of what will happen.' Lena looked into her friend's eyes. Timea was so pretty, like a china doll. And just as fragile.

'Is it man trouble?' said Lena.

'Yes. No.'

'Someone I know?' said Lena.

Timea paused. 'No,' she said.

'You're lying to me,' said Lena gently. 'Why?'

'It's . . . it's a client. Sort of.'

'A client is bothering you? Tell me who – I will sort them out for you.'

'I don't feel like anything good will happen in this country,' said

Timea. 'It is not safe.' Timea looked earnestly at Lena. 'I feel like there is danger, following everywhere I go.'

Lena couldn't help but laugh a little at her melodramatic friend. 'Has the mugging upset you?'

'It is not the mugging,' said Timea, putting her head in her hands and starting to cry again. 'I want to go home. I want to go back to Hungary. I want to get away from him. From what he is doing to me.'

'Your client?'

'Yes. My client.' Timea didn't look up.

'Which one?'

Timea emitted another sob. 'I cannot tell you. Not yet. Not until I know what will happen. Please do not ask me again.' Timea shrugged off Lena's arms and stood up. 'I am done with men,' she said. 'Have you changed the sheets in the bedroom yet?' She sniffed, and wiped the tears from her eyes.

'Forget the sheets,' said Lena.

'I'll do it. It will only take a minute.' Timea disappeared into the bedroom.

Lena began taking the cushions off the sofa and banged them with her fist until little clouds of dust emerged and danced in the sunlight. Underneath the cushions was a handful of change and fragments of poppadum. Lena collected the coins and put them on the table and went to get the vacuum cleaner for the poppadum shards. As she was changing the attachment head, Timea's phone emitted a double beep from inside her handbag. Lena opened the bag and removed the phone. Timea charged from the bedroom. She swiped the phone away.

'Do not touch my phone. Do not read my messages!' shouted Timea, angrier than Lena could remember seeing her. 'It is private!'

'I'm sorry,' said Lena, stepping back. 'I was just going to pass it to you.'

Timea took the phone to the bedroom with her and closed the door. Lena watched the door for a moment, wishing she could see through it. Timea emerged, flashed Lena a smile and grabbed her handbag. She went back into the bedroom. Lena followed her.

'Timea, who was it? What is going on?'

'Sorry for the fuss,' said Timea. 'I'm just a bit on edge. It was my two o'clock. She wants me to come early, she has guests for tea and needs it clean.' Timea had pulled her powder from her handbag and was dabbing her face to cover the signs of crying.

'Say no. We need to talk.'

'I want to go,' said Timea, pouting as she applied her lipstick. 'It will take my mind from my problems.'

'From what? What has this *fasz* done?'

'I will tell you later. This evening. I will know by then.' Timea ran a brush through her hair and squirted herself with the perfume on the dresser. 'I love you.' She gave Lena a quiet peck on the cheek and left the room, leaving little sock prints on the wet wooden floor.

Lena watched through the window as Timea hurried down the street. Lena couldn't keep up with her friend's moods these past few weeks.

Lena put a hand to her lips and felt the clotted blood forming what would be an ugly scab. She looked around the room. It had two bay windows, a grand chandelier and an open fireplace. She felt a moment of pride. It looked good. Clean. But there was more to do. She heaved the sofa forwards and set about hoovering up the dust bunnies that had found refuge underneath. Every week she did this. Every week they came back. It was these old houses that rich Londoners liked to live in with the exposed floorboards that held all the dead skin that had built up there since the Victorians. Spitting it back up to gather as dust under the sofa. People would never look under the sofa, she'd learnt, unless they'd hired a cleaner. Then they'd be checking every week. Lena couldn't understand it. If they didn't want dust in their houses, they shouldn't live in places built a hundred years ago.

Lena put her fob to the scanner at the entrance to their building and waited while it decided whether to work. Lena and Timea joked that they'd found a little patch of Eastern Europe in Haringey. Even the greenish glare of the hall lights, when they worked, gave your skin the same unhealthy pallor as a day-in, day-out diet of watery cabbage and potato soup. She pushed open the door and pressed the lift button. The light didn't come on. Nonetheless she could hear rumblings from the shaft that suggested it was on its way.

When it arrived she took a deep breath of air before stepping in. Trying to avoid the inevitable stench of urine. There must be something about the change in altitude that messed with men's bladders, but the rudimentary drawing of a penis on the wall didn't shed any light on her hypothesis. The lift pinged open at her floor. She took a relieved breath in. Her lungs were getting practised at this: twice this week she had managed to get all the way to the ninth floor without a cheating little unsavoury intake.

'I'm glad you're home,' called Tomek from the sofa as she opened the door to their flat. 'I have not felt right all day again. Come kiss me better.'

The living room was small, with faded brown patterned carpets that did little to camouflage the stains left by previous tenants; try as she might, Lena could not scrub them out. The light let in through the red curtains gave the room a pinkish hue, offset by the green tint of the television. But at least it was clean. Tomek was stretched along the length of the brown two-seater sofa, with the blanket from their bed draped over his ample body.

'You look like a slug,' she said, smiling at him.

'A sexy slug,' he replied. 'Kiss me.' She leaned in. He smelt of sausage rolls and she could see pastry crumbs on the floor in front of him.

'What happened to you?' he said, seeing her mangled mouth. She explained. 'You're a hero,' he told her. 'Have another kiss.'

'Where's Timea?' she asked, taking off her coat.

'She was here earlier but then went out again.'

'I thought she was going straight to a cleaning job?'

'She'll be with some man, I expect. Come have a snuggle before dinner. I've recorded *Doctors*.' Tomek shuffled an inch over, and Lena sat half beside, half on top of him. She felt her muscles relax in response to the warmth emitting from his body.

'She said she was done with men,' said Lena, pulling the blanket over herself.

'That's like me saying I'm done with cheeseburgers,' said Tomek. 'I can mean it all I want, but if you were to put one in front of me right now . . .' Tomek leaned in and nibbled at Lena's neck.

'So why are you not working today?' she asked him, putting her arm over his shoulder. It fitted comfortably.

'Everything. My poor sore belly.' Tomek gave her a look full of melancholy. 'I cannot drive my Uber taxi around while I have a sore belly.'

'You Polish men,' she replied, giving his soft stomach a pat. 'Too sick for work but not too sick for dinner, I suppose?'

'I need to keep my strength up. Let's have kievs. The chicken of champions.'

'We will wait for Timea,' said Lena, settling back to watch the show.

She ignored Tomek's objections, but by 9 p.m. she gave up, put the oven on and took the packet out from the freezer.

'She's pushing it now, delaying dinner!' said Tomek. His stomach emitted an odd sound, full of longing.

'She is not answering her phone,' said Lena. She dialled yet again.

'She's a grown-up.'

'I still need to look after her.'

'She's lucky to have you. We both are,' said Tomek, taking Lena's hand and planting a wet kiss on it. 'Can I have her kiev?'

CHAPTER 2

Lena opened her eyes. She glanced at the clock on the bedside table. It was 8 a.m. already. *Szar.* She'd overslept. Lena lay in bed for a moment anyway, listening out for the sounds of Timea going about her morning ritual. No sounds of a shower, no patter of her friend's feet on the kitchen lino, not even the little trumpeting sound that Timea made when she first blew her nose in the morning. Lena turned over and reached for her phone, knocking it to the floor in her morning haze. She leaned out of the bed and stretched to grab it. No messages from Timea.

Lena got up, shivering a little. Wrapping her dressing gown around her, she went to Timea's room and knocked. There was no reply. She opened the door. The bed was unslept in. She went into the kitchen and put the coffee on while she phoned her friend. It rang out. '*Basszus*,' she cursed.

'What is it?' Tomek called out, his voice full of sleep.

'Timea is not back yet,' she said.

'Big night,' said Tomek. 'Give her a few hours. Let's have bacon sandwiches for breakfast.' He came into the kitchen in just his boxers, scratching his bedhead.

'How many times have I told you not to walk around half dressed,' said Lena. 'It is not fair on Timea.'

'You just said she wasn't here,' replied Tomek, giving her a kiss on the top of her head. 'We should take advantage. Come back to bed.'

'Where do you think she is?' Lena gulped down her coffee and gasped a little as it burned her throat. She needed the caffeine.

'Doing what we should be, most likely.'

'But she does not have a boyfriend. She split up with Faisal months ago.'

'She's not exactly a nun,' said Tomek. 'She'll have found someone.'

'She would text me. She would know I worry.'

'She is fine. Come,' he said, tugging at Lena's arm. 'I'll make you forget all about her.'

'No time,' said Lena. 'I will have to cover Timea's jobs this morning or the agency will fire her.'

Tomek rolled his eyes at her. 'I'm going back to bed,' he said. 'Leave the butter out.'

She tried Timea's phone again but there was no answer. She went to the rota on the fridge and saw that Timea just had one job for the day, in Stoke Newington. She was booked for five hours so it would be one of those big sprawling Victorian family homes overrun by children undoing your cleaning as soon as you thought you'd finished. That was all she needed; she had two houses on her list for the day as well. Mrs Kingston liked her to come at tea time, so she decided to get Timea's job out of the way first. She scribbled a quick note in case Timea came home, and left it by the rota.

The minute Lena entered the flat she knew. It wasn't a sprawling mansion but a one-bed apartment in a neat new-build. It contained an enormous bed, its sheets still in disarray from the last activity it had witnessed. No wardrobe, no drawers, just a solitary shelf with a couple of gossip magazines propped up by a dusty vase. The tiny kitchen revealed only a small fridge with an unopened bottle of champagne and some tired-looking strawberries, gradually softening to mush.

She'd cleaned love nests before. Tiny little places with sexy knickers flung everywhere by women enjoying other women's husbands. Sometimes there were even used condoms dumped on the floor by the bed, their contents nourishing the parquet floor. She peered under the bed but saw no evidence of that here. Plenty of dust bunnies though.

She tutted at Timea's negligence and opened the barely touched bottle of multi-purpose cleaner. This was hardly five hours of work for Timea, even if she had scrubbed it spotless. It was a bit of a gift really: most people allocated much less time than was needed to get somewhere clean, and then complained at the tasks left undone. This would be a quick job for Timea, a bit of easy money. If a bit seedy.

There was an abundance of men's cosmetics in this flat: anti-ageing face creams, a specialist tube for de-puffing the eye area, several pots of miscellaneous gels and hair waxes, a nasal hair trimmer and an electric razor with so many widgets it looked as if it could have flown to the moon. Lena laughed at this man's vanity. Only one woman's lipstick sat by the sink, looking lonely and out of place.

Lena dusted the shelf, picking up a celebrity gossip magazine. She noticed with a grunt the small photo of Istvan in the corner of the cover. The caption read 'How my marriage keeps me grounded.' She picked it up to flick through, not that she really cared, she told herself, but Mama would want to know what he was up to. She flicked to page seventeen and looked at Istvan smiling, his arm resting around a blonde woman with abruptly cropped hair. Lena peered at her. Well maintained and glamorous, she had a good fifteen years on him nonetheless. She was smiling too, but when Lena looked more closely she saw that the smile didn't extend to her eyes. Small and cold. Lena smiled back at her. This was not an easy woman to live with, she thought. Just what Istvan deserved in a wife.

As she reached up to dust the top shelf, she knocked a small square plastic thing on to the floor. Lena tutted at her clumsiness as she bent to retrieve it. She saw her face reflected in the round glass, and it flashed a tiny red light at her. Some gadget or other and not broken. Good.

Lena was just putting the bucket back under the sink when she heard the key in the lock. It couldn't be Timea because Lena had taken the only key. She didn't much want to bump into the cheater that lived here, or his girlfriend. But it was best to make yourself known straight away. Otherwise, no matter how many times you've met them, people always think you are a burglar.

'Hello, cleaner here,' she said, in her best sing-song voice.

'You are not Timea,' the surprised woman's voice told her. 'That is impossible.' Lena replaced the bleach where it had been and withdrew her head from the cupboard.

'I am her colleague, Lena Szarka, from the agency. I just cover today while she is sick,' she said, trying to sound cheery.

'Sick?' The voice sounded even more surprised, but the woman didn't bother coming into the kitchen. People like her were allowed to get sick, but they couldn't abide it in the staff. Assumed they were slacking.

'Don't let me disturb you,' said the woman, retreating, her voice getting fainter. 'I just popped back for my umbrella. I'm on my way out again.'

Lena didn't have time to tell her she was finished before she heard the door close. All that was left of the woman was a waft of expensive perfume. Chanel Cristalle, she recognised, from when she'd let Timea have a go on Mrs Ives's bottle one time. Timea had loved it. 'Smells like the meadows back home,' she'd said. 'Smells like us getting fired,' Lena had replied.

As Lena made her way down the staircase she remembered the client list from the rota. Steven was the name she had put down for these keys. She expected the woman had no wish to be identified.

'Jasper has chewed the vacuum-cleaner wire again,' called Lena. She was in the sitting room of her next job, her favourite regular client. Mrs Kingston hobbled out of the kitchen and handed Lena a mug of coffee, gesturing to her to sit down.

'Nonsense,' she replied, heading back to the kitchen as Lena perched on the edge of the sofa. 'Jasper wouldn't do such a thing. He's a good rabbit.'

'He is a bad rabbit,' said Lena, holding out a carrot she'd remembered to pop into her bag from home. 'He goes to the toilet on the floor.' Jasper emerged sheepishly from under the coffee table and hopped to the carrot, sniffing it carefully before taking a tentative nibble. 'Very bad rabbit,' she scolded, rubbing his silky fur.

'That's nonsense as well,' said Mrs Kingston, coming back into the room with a plate of biscuits in one hand and her walking stick in the other. 'You know as well as I do that Jasper is house trained.' She sat down on the sofa with a grunt of pain. 'He's a perfect gentleman.'

'Then what is that?' said Lena, taking a chocolate digestive and pointing with it to a rabbit dropping on the floor. Mrs Kingston adjusted her glasses and leaned forwards to peer at it. 'Gentlemen do not poo in the living room where I come from.'

'Then I must have dropped a raisin,' Mrs Kingston declared. Both women laughed. 'Once you've been a journalist for thirty-five years, you never lose your powers of deduction,' she said. 'Not even when you reach my age.'

Lena took a swig of coffee and finished her biscuit. 'I will use a broom,' she said. 'After I have dusted. Or has Jasper eaten the duster again?'

'That was a one-off,' insisted Mrs Kingston. 'And the house is still clean from last time. Why don't you just have a chat with me instead?'

Lena looked around. The family photos littering the mantelpiece were covered in dust again, and there was so much straw, cabbage leaves and carrot ends lining the floor that it looked like the day after the harvest festival back in her village.

'I can chat and work,' she said, getting up. 'As long as Jasper does not try to trip me up again.'

'He'll be good as gold,' said Mrs Kingston. 'He likes a natter. They don't call it rabbiting for nothing!'

Lena had no idea what she was talking about, but carefully stepped over Jasper and began to dust.

The next morning Lena looked out of her kitchen window, cradling a cup of coffee to combat the cold. It was too early still on this Wednesday morning for the winter sun, and the streetlights gave the air a soft orange haze, like the remnants of baked-bean sauce lingering on a plate. Back in her village it would be pitch-black at this time, with just the stars providing little glimmers of hope that light still existed. She still wasn't used to how it never got completely dark in London. People could always be seen.

Down below, two workmen were making their way to their jobs, their reflective jackets shining in the intermittent lights. A nightshift worker hurried past them, eager for bed. It was quiet without the daytime traffic, and Lena listened to the song of a lone blackbird in an out-of-view tree, making an unlikely duet with Tomek's gentle snoring.

Timea was still not home. She had not been home when Lena had got in, and was still not there when Lena reluctantly went to bed at midnight.

Lena took a sip of coffee, but the heat seared her tongue. Last night's dishes were still in the sink. It was Timea's turn to wash and Tomek had insisted they leave them for her. Lena put down her coffee and turned on the hot tap, watching the water splatter down, washing the worst of the creamy kiev crumbs from the plate. She scrubbed and thought. Where would Timea be? She did sometimes spend the night away unexpectedly. Timea was not promiscuous, but she was someone who could fall in love in an evening. But she would always text Lena so she wouldn't worry. Always.

Lena dried her hands and rubbed her neck. She had a crick in it from a poor night's sleep. She rolled her shoulders back, listening to her muscles click in objection. She was worried. Either Timea was being uncharacteristically inconsiderate, or something had happened to her.

Lena deserved to know.

She padded softly in her slippers over the kitchen lino into the hallway, pulling her dressing gown tight. Then she pushed Timea's door open. The room was small, with a single bed in the corner, neatly made up with Timea's floral duvet cover, more pink than Lena would have chosen. The only other furniture was a dresser strewn with makeup, a wardrobe, its door half ajar, and a small nightstand.

Lena felt guilty even being in this room. She had come in uninvited once to see if Timea had any laundry and Timea had been furious. It wasn't like sweet-natured Timea, but Lena respected her for it. We all need our privacy, especially when sharing such a small flat. Perhaps she should wait before looking through her things, she thought. Give Timea a chance to wake up, kiss the man goodbye and come home. Lena dismissed the

23

thought and peered inside the wardrobe. A quick rummage through Timea's clothes revealed that there was nothing major missing. Her only suitcase remained on top of the wardrobe, gathering a thick coating of dust that made Lena sneeze when she moved it. Lena began opening and closing the dresser drawers, seeing her clothes inside were folded neatly; all present and correct. Lena moved to the nightstand.

On top was a photo of Laszlo and Timea, her arms entwined around her son. They were both smiling, squinting in the sunlight. Lena remembered taking that picture. She and Timea had been living in Debrecen, Hungary's second city, eking out a living. Lena had been selling subscriptions to a magazine no one read; Timea working as a secretary. Laszlo was visiting for the weekend and Timea scooped him into her arms as soon as he stepped off the train, barely thinking to thank Mr Kovacs for delivering him safely from the village. Even with the long hours they both worked, neither had managed to save enough to buy a car.

Lena watched them, enthralled at how engrossed they were in each other. It reminded her a little of how she and Istvan used to be, when the whole of the world could be found in each other's eyes.

'In a few years, you'll be able to live with me here always,' Timea was saying. 'Once you are old enough to be able to take care of yourself after school until I get home from the office.'

'I'm old enough now,' declared Laszlo, pulling himself up to his full height. 'I am six and three-quarters.'

'Six and three-quarters is not old enough,' replied Timea. 'Eleven.'

'That's forever away.'

'Time will fly like magic castles,' Timea had replied. 'Let's go to the Ludas Matyi Park. The spinning swans are waiting for you.'

Next to that photo was one of Timea with Lena. Lena looked at it, her friend's delicate face softly framed by her bleached blonde curls. It was a contrast to Lena's own sharp features and straight black hair. Lena put it on the bed; she hated looking at pictures of herself. Underneath the photos was a magazine, one of the showbiz ones that Timea loved to read. Lena picked it up and saw it was open on a page with Istvan's picture. It seemed like he was everywhere at the moment, pouting at the camera with his arms folded. She put it down again with a roll of her eyes and pulled open the small drawer. Timea's passport was inside. To her surprise she saw a little case underneath it. Tiffany's. She lifted it out and sat down on the bed before opening it to reveal a silver necklace with a heart-shaped pendant. Lena lifted it out of the box and held it to the light, noticing it was inset with seven sparkling diamonds. The silver felt cold in her hand.

Lena had seen Timea admiring a necklace just like this one at Mrs Ives's house – she'd even tried it on once and smiled at herself in the mirror. Lena had been furious, but now she was worried. She knew Timea would never have been able to afford this, even if she didn't send all that was left at the end of each week straight to Greta for Laszlo. Could she have stolen it? Lena hurriedly put the necklace back in the box and closed the lid. She didn't want to think about it.

As she placed the box back in the drawer, she noticed a small notebook. She pulled it out and flicked through. Only a few pages were written on, and mostly it was scribbled English words and phrases that Timea must have been trying to learn, with the odd doodle in between. One page was just covered in definite articles. '*The the the the a an the*,' Timea had written, underlining each several times. Lena smiled and turned the page. '*It is raining cats and dogs*,' it said. '*She will bite my head off.*' She turned the page again. '*There is an elephant in the room.*' Lena laughed to herself. The English were a funny lot.

One page was different. Lena read it, ready to smile at the

amusing idiom. But she couldn't find it. She read it again, then a third time.

'*I cannot lose him again. I am sorry for the hurt it will cause her. But I cannot live without him.*'

Lena put the notebook down. She had not realised that Timea still felt this way about Faisal. She felt a pang of guilt. She had known he was bad news for Timea, with his arrogance and swagger. She suspected he took drugs too. So she had made things difficult for the two of them, encouraging Timea to come around to her way of thinking. She'd been successful: with a few months and a few tears, Timea and he had broken up. Lena thought Timea seemed happier afterwards, happier than she'd been in a long time. Perhaps she had been wrong.

Faisal was leaning against a lamp post outside Angel station, hands in the pockets of his bright blue jacket. His head was bopping a little, as though he were dancing to a track only he could hear. It was still early, before the mainstream maelstrom of commuters began. Only a few sleepy people wandered through the half-light of the morning, beating the rush hour but sacrificing extra time tucked away in bed.

Even with Faisal's smug expression, Lena could see why Timea had been smitten with him. He had big dark eyes; skin the colour of caramel. Timea was such a sucker for attractive men.

'Why would he see her?' interjected Tracy. 'He has me.'

'Faisal, just tell me,' said Lena. 'She did not come home last night, again. Has she been in touch?'

'Who could blame her?' Faisal said, running his fingers over his gelled hair. 'They all want more.' He winked.

Lena suppressed the urge to gag. Both women glared at him, Tracy through her false eyelashes. They looked like mangled spiders.

26

'Faisal is joking. He thinks he's funny,' said Tracy. She spat on to the ground. 'We haven't seen her. Not since all the fuss with that ginger bitch.'

Lena reached for Faisal's arm. 'Get off him,' hissed Tracy, like an angry cat.

Lena ignored her, and pulled Faisal to the other side of the bus shelter with her. A grubby backlit poster of a muscle-bound man was looking past them into the middle distance. Advertising after-shave perhaps, or underwear. She couldn't tell and didn't care. 'Don't worry babe,' Faisal called, as Tracy went to follow them. 'This one doesn't stand a chance of making sweet Faisal Javaid music.'

'Was she with you last night?' Lena kept her voice down to placate him, but he was trying her limited patience.

'A threesome? I wish.'

Lena felt her cold hands tingling to slap his smug face, but took a deep breath. 'She is gone,' said Lena. 'I am worried about her. Did she tell you anything?'

'We broke up. I haven't heard from her. I'm focusing on my music.' He began to hum.

Lena ignored him. 'I know she cared about you. Did you still meet up, when Tracy was not around?'

Faisal looked at her, surprised. 'We used to,' he admitted. 'But there was someone new on the scene. Rich.' He made a money sign, rubbing imaginary notes between his fingers.

'She would tell me if she had a new boyfriend.'

Faisal squared up to her. 'Perhaps she was worried you'd mess it up for her. Like you did us.'

'It is not my fault that Timea saw sense.'

'You never liked your precious princess Timea shagging a Paki.'

Lena took a breath. 'You know that is not the problem I had with you.' The two of them stared at each other, priming for a fight.

A spit dart hit the ground between them, announcing Tracy's presence.

'There's more people coming now, sweetheart,' she said, dispelling the tension. 'I need your help with the papers.' She fluttered her spidery eyelashes at Faisal and draped herself over him, rubbing her ear on his shoulder like a cat marking its territory.

'I'm all yours, babe,' said Faisal.

Lena watched them walk away, Tracy gripping Faisal's waist.

Lena wasn't used to panic, but she felt it sweep over her now. Timea had been gone since 11 a.m. Monday. Now it was almost 8 a.m. Wednesday. Her phone went straight to voicemail; there were no texts. Timea had been worried. Lena tried to calm down and force herself to think logically. Timea had been going to visit a client just before she disappeared. Had she made it there?

Ronalds Road was a quiet residential street that ran from the leafy expanse of Highbury Fields through to the kebab and sex shops of Holloway Road, interspersed with the occasional coffee boutique that was waiting patiently for the road to gentrify. The amount of wholemeal sourdough bread in the windows suggested they did not have long to wait. Lena got off the bus at Highbury and Islington station and cut through the park, taking deep breaths to calm her thoughts. The park was quiet, though a number of people were taking their coiffed dogs for walks. Lena watched a well-groomed Afghan the size of a bear prance through the grass after an angry little Chihuahua. The large dog was undeterred by the yapping, and sniffed with interest at the smaller dog's bum while their owners sipped coffee from organic paper cups.

Lena reached Ronalds Road and stood outside number 138. She'd never been there with Timea, but the address was easy enough to find from the details on their rota. It was a three-storey

Victorian terraced house with red bricks and ornate stucco, like so many of the houses in these Islington backstreets. She walked up the slate front path and rang the doorbell.

Lena was just about to give up and turn away when a woman opened the door with a squirming child in her arms. 'Can I help you?' said the woman, in a way that suggested she was in no position to help anyone.

'Penelope Hansam?' said Lena, looking to the woman for confirmation. She nodded. 'I am Lena Szarka, I work with Timea Dubay, your cleaner, at the agency. I want to check that she was here yesterday?'

The small child wriggled free and ran back into the house. 'Casper, no!' shouted Penelope at the disappearing infant. 'Don't do that to your brother again.' Penelope turned back to Lena. 'You'd better come in. Take a seat while I put the baby somewhere Casper can't reach.' Lena entered the house and looked around. The hallway was an obstacle course of small wellington boots, tiny coats, a pushchair and a small blue tricycle. She stepped over the tricycle and went into the living room and stood awkwardly, not wanting to take a seat until asked. She could hear Penelope's strained voice scolding Casper in another room. Lena looked around. There was an L-shaped leather sofa in one corner, pointed at a large flat-screen TV. The coffee table was glass and chrome to match the three chrome lightshades that hung from the ceiling. It would be smart were it not for the myriad primary-coloured plastic objects strewn around the room. Lena poked the nearest one with her foot. It mooed back at her. These were people who had their dream house exactly as they wanted it. Then they had children to come and destroy it.

Penelope returned, holding a tiny baby this time. Casper charged in after her and proceeded to run laps around the room making a loud brumming noise, keeping his arms outstretched like aeroplane wings. His mother raised her voice over the din as if it were nothing and sat down, gesturing for Lena to do the same. 'Now, I'm sorry,' she said. 'Something about Timea? Be quiet, Casper, and the nice lady will play with you.' Casper continued to brum, but ran up to Lena and placed his sticky hand coyly on her leg.

Lena realised why Timea had never asked her to clean this house with her. Penelope was one of the people who would expect their cleaner to be a nanny, too. Timea loved those jobs, looking after the children and chatting to the clients. Lena hated it. If they wanted her to do two jobs, they should pay two wages. She made an effort to smile at Casper nonetheless, and rubbed his silky blond hair as if she thought he was sweet. He blew a raspberry at her.

'Casper!' his mother exclaimed. She smiled apologetically at Lena. 'He's a bit J.E.A.L.O.U.S. of his new brother,' she spelt out. 'It's playing havoc with his behaviour, which is such a pity as he was always a good boy before. Jealousy does such horrid things to people; you should see what he did when we left him alone in a room with Crispin for five minutes. It took Timea hours to scrub it off. I suppose that sort of thing is very common though, don't you think?' She looked at Lena pleadingly.

Lena made an indeterminate noise of sympathy. This was a client who was lonely and wanted to tell her woes to a captive stranger. Again, Timea, with her endless bank of sympathy, was better suited for this.

'He'll soon grow out of it,' Penelope continued. 'He's very good in nursery and the teacher says he is well ahead of his peers. Don't eat that, Casper. Put it in a tissue and in the bin.' Lena felt a little sick.

'I am sorry to disturb you,' said Lena. 'I need to know if Timea came here yesterday?'

'I don't want to get her into trouble, but no, I'm afraid she didn't. She didn't even call. I had to miss my two p.m. Pilates class at the movement studio and I do look forward to that. I always treat myself to a nice coffee afterwards, and a natter with the other ladies.'

Lena sat forwards on the sofa and tried to ignore whatever Casper was doing to her shoe. 'Two p.m.?' she said. 'You did not ask Timea to come earlier?'

'No, she always comes at two p.m. on Tuesdays. She knows what a relief it is for me to get out of the house. And I really do need it. Having children has done terrible things to my waistline. You should have seen my stomach before these two. Quite impressive when I used to go to the gym every day in my lunch break. I think I have a photo somewhere. Here, hold baby Crispin while I look.' She leaned over to Lena. Two small eyes peered up at her from the blanketed bundle.

'No, that is OK,' said Lena hurriedly, leaning back again. 'If you are sure that she did not come, and you did not send a text message, then that is all I need to know.'

'Has she gone missing? I do hope she hasn't gone back home to . . . remind me?'

'We are from Hungary,' said Lena, standing up to leave.

'Of course,' said Penelope. 'Budapest is such a beautiful city. The Danube is sublime. I went with my husband before we had Casper. Of course I do hope she turns up. The house is a state, what must you think of us? Perhaps if you are free now you could give it a quick once-over?' She glanced at her watch. 'Perfect timing. There's a yoga class at the Buddhist Centre in ten minutes. I could still make it.'

'Sorry,' replied Lena, gently shaking her foot free from Casper. He'd stuck some sort of brightly coloured sticker to her trainer and was grinning up at her in delight. 'I have other jobs now.' She thought for a moment. She needed to keep Timea's clients happy for when her friend reappeared. 'So not today. But I am sure Timea will be back tomorrow. I will send her here. Or I will make other plans, no need to bother the agency. You will not be let down again.' She started to leave the room.

'Perhaps you'd like some tea?' Penelope called to her back. 'Casper has really taken to you.' Lena looked at the small child. He was sitting in a corner now, pulling the leaves off a fern.

'Maybe next time,' she said, and escaped, closing the door firmly behind her. She took some long, quick strides to put distance between her and the house.

Timea had never arrived at the appointment she told Lena she was going to. Had she lied about the text message? Lena phoned her again, knowing there would be no answer. Something was very wrong with her friend. Something bad must have happened and she didn't know what more she could do. It was time to get the police involved.

CHAPTER 3

Lena decided to walk to the police station at Angel. She wanted some air and some time to think. She went down Holloway Road, pushed through the hustle of commuters swarming into Highbury and Islington Station, then turned down Upper Street.

By now it was 9.30 a.m. Although it was only a Wednesday, there were already a smattering of lonely-looking men holding pints and cigarettes outside the Wetherspoon's. Shift workers perhaps, Lena thought generously, just on a different timetable to the rest of us. Their red faces and shaking hands suggested otherwise. She walked past one of the many fried chicken shops that littered this end of Upper Street, catering to the football trade from Arsenal, before the trendy bars, expensive cafés and boutique shops took over as she approached Angel. Some pigeons pecked at a piece of chicken that someone had abandoned the night before. Lena looked away. It was like eating your cousin.

Lena walked fast through the posh end of Upper Street, eager to avoid the mothers gossiping next to their designer three-wheel prams that probably cost more than a Balaton car. She was starting to feel weary by the time she reached the police station, situated on a side road dominated by the Sainsbury's car park.

The police station was a yellow brick building, not at all like the chrome and glass affair she'd seen on *Heroes of Law*. She should have expected that. *Heroes of Law* wasn't about the truth. Even

Istvan didn't seem real to her anymore, though she could still remember how his breath tickled her ear as he whispered to her outside the bakery in the village. But that was years ago. Now he was involved in ridiculous plots and swooning victims. She had no idea what his real life was like. No one had met his wife; not even his own mother.

A harangued-looking community support officer behind the bulletproof glass screen looked at her suspiciously. Lena supposed most people this lady came across were up to no good.

'How long?' asked the woman, when Lena told her what had happened.

'Since Monday. My boyfriend saw her about one p.m., but I have not heard from her since.'

'How old?'

'She is twenty-five.'

'Take a ticket. You'll have to wait, I'm afraid.' Lena felt as though she had failed the urgency test.

'But she is missing. It is urgent.'

'It's all urgent. Here's a form to complete. Don't worry; we'll get to you as soon as we can.' The officer had already turned her attention to a worried-looking woman holding a baby behind Lena in the queue.

Lena took a ticket, feeling like she was waiting for the deli counter at Sainsbury's. She looked at her seating options. None appealed. All the institutional polyester-clad chairs, affixed to the floor, had suspicious stains. The whole place smelt a bit like her lift, but with more disinfectant mixed in. That was a good thing, she supposed. They were trying. Although it was cold outside, it was impossibly hot in the police station, and she began to feel herself sweating. Eventually she selected the chair where the stain looked the least likely to be fresh and sat down. She wished she'd come sooner. This was awful, but at least she was doing something.

Lena looked around. There was a woman a few seats along from her who was barely conscious, swaying in her chair, occasionally drifting so far to the right that she almost fell. An elderly man clutched a grey polyester bag close to his chest and eyed those around him suspiciously. An angry-looking schoolboy was kicking the leg of his chair. She could hear voices through the thin walls. Other interviews taking place, perhaps other people missing. They all looked up when the voice rose to an angry shout, and Lena strained her ears to hear what they were saying, but it was just indiscriminate muffled anger.

She took Timea's photo out of her bag, ready for when they called her. Even in the institutional light of the police station, Timea's face seemed to shine. The photograph was two months old, taken on a sunny Sunday in Clissold Park. Timea looked radiant, smiling at the camera, wearing the new pink lipstick Lena had found on special offer at Aldi. She'd printed the photo to send back home to Laszlo, but had forgotten about it; left it sitting in a drawer gathering dust.

By the time Lena's number was called, the photo was tatty from her fiddling. It looked as if it had been taken twenty years ago.

'My friend is missing,' she told the solid back of a policeman, introduced as PC Gullins, as he led her from the waiting room through one of the myriad doors.

'Tell me in the room,' he said, without glancing behind him.

The interview room was more like something from *Heroes of Law*, with a dormant recorder on the table and one-way mirror. The policeman was nothing like Istvan. He had the thick neck and cabbagy ears of someone who grew up playing rugby, and the belly of someone who had given it up years ago.

'So,' he said, when they were seated. 'Tell me what the problem is.' Lena was not good with English accents, but she thought she recognised this one from *EastEnders*.

35

'My friend is missing.' Lena pushed the form she'd completed and Timea's picture across the table to him. 'She is missing since Monday.'

'Pretty,' he replied, taking a look at the picture.

'Yes,' said Lena. 'But she is missing.' Lena looked at him. His yellowing eyes suggested that all his hydration came from sugary tea during the day and beer at night.

'Her name is *Timmy-a Doby*,' he read uncertainly.

'*Tim-may-ah Doo-bay*,' corrected Lena.

'That's what I said. OK,' he said, producing a notebook. 'Does she have a boyfriend she could be staying with?' he asked, looking as if he knew the answer.

'No,' replied Lena. 'At least, I do not think so.'

'You are not sure,' he said. 'So she could be. And how long has she been missing?'

'Since Monday,' Lena repeated, getting the feeling that was not an answer that would incite action.

'Has she stayed out all night before?'

'Yes,' admitted Lena. Gullins made a small grunt. 'But she would always send me a message,' she said, sensing his interest waning. 'It has been two nights.'

Gullins slowly wrote something in the notebook. The pen seemed too small for his large hands. 'It seems pretty clear in that case,' he said. 'I'll take some details and run the routine checks, but I wouldn't worry just yet.'

'But there was something wrong with her,' said Lena, feeling his help slipping away. 'She was acting strangely. Emotional and angry and upset and scared.'

'Drugs?' said Gullins, looking a little more interested.

'No,' Lena said quickly. 'Not that. Never. Just, she was worried about something. A client. She told me.'

Gullins raised an eyebrow. 'What type of client would that be?'

'We are cleaners,' explained Lena, colouring slightly. 'She told me she was worried about what a client would do. The more I think about it, the more sure I am that one of them is involved. I have made a list of them for you to investigate.'

Lena passed the paper across the table, laying it next to the photo of Timea. 'She said she was visiting this one yesterday, but she never arrived.'

'We'll look into that,' said Gullins. 'But there really is nothing particularly suspicious about this,' he told her. 'I'd call this one low risk. She'll probably turn up on her own, a bit embarrassed at the trouble she's caused.' He smiled at her. 'We'll do a basic custody check and the hospitals, just to make sure, and I'll record her as missing. If she isn't back tomorrow then let us know. Call round her friends and see if anyone has seen her. Most likely she is with the boyfriend,' he concluded. 'Lucky lad,' Lena thought she heard him mutter, under his breath.

Lena felt hot. He wasn't going to take her seriously. A red flush spread up from her chest to her face. She swallowed and tried to calm herself.

'She was meant to be home two days ago. We work all day, often alone, in the houses of strangers. She told me she got a text that the client never sent. And she never arrived there. She said she was scared. You need to find her.'

'Listen. I've seen lots of these cases and almost always they are with a boyfriend. Don't worry, your friend will be fine.'

'No,' said Lena, plucking the photo from his fingers. 'This is serious. I want to see your boss.' At least back home she knew how to make things happen. Oil some palms and a burly policeman would sort out your problems. She felt a wave of homesickness, the first in years.

'Where are you from?' said Gullins, as if reading her thoughts.

'Hungary,' replied Lena.

Gullins grunted. He got up and went to a filing cabinet in the corner. He produced a piece of paper and handed it to Lena.

'Here's the complaint form,' he said, passing her his pen. 'Drop it in the box on the way out. I'm sorry, but we've done what we can.'

'I do not want a form,' Lena told him, standing up. 'I want another policeman. Your boss.'

Gullins stood up. He towered over her but his voice was calm. 'I know you're worried, but there's nothing more we can do for the moment. There's crimes to deal with and our department's budget has been cut. Gangs. Muggings in broad daylight.'

She stormed out of the room and into a corridor. She glanced behind her. Gullins was shouting something at her. She ran on, colliding with an oncoming policeman.

'I'm so sorry,' the policeman said, putting a steadying hand on her arm. She could feel the warmth of his hand through her sleeve. 'Are you OK?'

'No,' she said, feeling awkward.

'Perfect,' said Gullins, catching up with a slight wheeze. 'PC Cartwright, excellent, you're just the man. Good practice for our resident graduate. Weren't you saying you wanted some more stimulating work for your stint on the beat?'

'Anything I can do to help.'

'Here's a "rising star" for you,' Gullins told Lena. 'If you're not happy with me, perhaps my colleague here will be able to help. He's got a degree, you know. On the fast track to the top, apparently, if he makes it through his time with me.' Gullins laughed, giving Cartwright a slap on the back that was too hard to be friendly.

Cartwright took this with good grace and smiled at Lena. She let him shepherd her back to the interview room, conscious of his hand gently resting on her back to guide her. As they sat, he brushed a strand of sandy-coloured hair from his forehead and looked at Lena intently. 'Tell me how I can help you,' he said. Lena felt a catch in her throat. For the first time in a while, it seemed the desire to help was genuine.

'My friend is missing.' She noticed the vivid blue of his wide eyes and a sweet aroma on his breath. Like bergamot. 'Since Monday.'

'Yes,' said Cartwright, frowning at the notebook Gullins had passed him. Lena saw across the table that there were only two lines of writing, and those were indecipherable. 'Let's start from the beginning,' he said, turning to a clean page. 'I think that would be best.'

Lena began to retell the day's events and watched Cartwright take notes in an elegant hand. She'd almost forgotten the robbery, until then. What did she care about some woman's bag, when Timea was missing?

When she finished, she realised Cartwright was staring at her, his pen paused.

'What is it?' she said.

Cartwright coughed and looked back down at the notebook. 'That's quite a day you had. Did you know that resisting a mugging increases your likelihood of being hurt by twenty per cent?'

'No,' replied Lena.

'It was brave of you, but dangerous. That's why you should let the police look after that kind of thing. It's what we're here for.'

Lena shrugged. 'No police were there,' she replied.

'Would you mind telling me a bit more about the mugger?' said Cartwright, turning over a page in the notebook. 'Could you tell where he might have been from? Did he have anyone with him, perhaps?'

'He was alone. Very skinny, like he had not eaten enough.'

'What did he look like?'

'Like someone who had nothing to do with Timea,' Lena replied, losing patience.

Cartwright turned the page back. 'I'm sorry,' he said. 'Let's focus on the task in hand.' He sat forwards again, pen in hand. 'I'll need to know what she was wearing, who saw her last, what she was doing and where she was going, plus any odd behaviour recently.'

Lena told him all she knew. 'Will you send out a search?' she said.

'I can certainly put her picture out, and we can run traces on her phone, her Oyster card and her bank card. If she's been using technology, we'll be able to track her down. We'll check on her passport records too, just in case she's left the country.'

'Her passport is still in her drawer,' said Lena. 'What about talking to her clients? One of them was scaring her. You will investigate them?' She got out the list again.

Cartwright studied it. 'I couldn't justify this yet,' he said. 'You see, it takes a lot of resource and at the moment there is no reason to expect anything untoward. In the majority of cases—'

'And if something has happened to her? What then?'

'It's amazing what we can do with DNA these days,' he said, his eyes shining. 'All we need are seventeen chromosomes for an accurate match. It's very interesting how the process works. With just a few skin cells, or some saliva from a toothbrush, we can identify anybody with almost total accuracy.'

'Body?' Lena looked at him in horror.

'I'm sorry, that's not what I meant. That's just if we need to . . . She'll most likely be back home by the time you get there, or she'll have used her card on the way to visit friends. There's no need to be alarmed yet.'

Gullins popped his head around the door. 'Is Einstein taking care of you?'

'I want to leave now,' said Lena, feeling tiredness washing over her.

'I'll show you out,' said Cartwright, looking disappointed. He didn't put his hand on her back this time.

Lena ignored the harassed woman on reception as she strode back into the sunlight. She took a deep breath in. The air seemed fresh and clean in spite of the traffic. She was sure one of Timea's clients had something to do with her disappearance. But if the police wouldn't investigate it, she would have to. She'd take over all of Timea's clients until she found something that led her to her friend. She'd start tomorrow and she wouldn't stop until Timea was home again.

CHAPTER 4

The next day Lena started with her usual Thursday client in Stoke Newington. She'd need to be quick to do both her and Timea's jobs, but she didn't want to risk the agency realising that Timea was gone and assigning her clients elsewhere. Timea would need a job to come back to.

Once Lena had finished there, she needed to get halfway to the City to start Timea's work. She stood at the bus stop at Stoke Newington Church Street, feeling the beginnings of rain hit her head like cold little bullets. Stoke Newington almost reminded her of the village back home, with its coffee shops and second-hand furniture. Until she saw the prices. The inhabitants were fiercely protective of their 'village'. She remembered when her local client had railed against a Nando's opening up there, even starting a petition. Apparently chain restaurants were not con-ducive to the village atmosphere. But the food had won over the local residents, and it was full to the brim with families hungry for peri-peri chicken.

Lena didn't want to stand under the shelter, as it seemed designed so she couldn't see the bus coming. And if she wasn't on the case with holding her arm out in plenty of time, the bus driver would take the opportunity to hurtle by without stopping. Eventually the bus approached, and Lena stood, arm outstretched, in its path: a game of chicken with the driver. It was close, but she won.

Once aboard, Lena hauled herself up the staircase. As if bitter at having to stop, the driver sped up as she neared the top of the stairs. Lena kept her balance long enough to swing herself down and settle with a bump into a window seat at the front. She sat back to watch the pedestrians in the rain.

Clissold Park was empty save for a few intrepid joggers, their music likely loud in their ears to help them forget the rain, now pouring down. Lena watched as a woman sheltered under a tree and shouted encouragement to her playful Labrador to hurry up and poo. It ran away at a gallop, bounding to keep a surprised jogger company. Lena smiled to herself. She loved Clissold Park. Even in the rain. In the summer, she and Timea had spotted small turtles trying to sun themselves on a rock, while Timea had told Lena of her plans to bring Laszlo to London. 'Just a little while longer,' she had said, and she would be able to support him. Lena had promised to help: they would make room in the tiny flat. Of course they would. Ignore Tomek.

Timea had worshipped Laszlo from the moment he was born. Others in the village pitied her state. Seventeen, already come from tragedy, now with a child of unknown paternity. It kept the gossips of the village entertained as they speculated on the identity of the father. Timea ignored it all, taking endless pleasure from the tiny creature she had formed in her womb. Eventually the matriarchs melted, enchanted by the giggly boy and his sweet orphan mother.

Lena was never one to coo over children. And she found it hard that her friend would not confide, even in her, who the father was. She had tried to guess many times, but nothing rang true.

Lena was ashamed to admit that baby Laszlo held little interest for her. He smelt funny, he tired her friend. And by the time he could toddle, he had become a master at getting under Lena's feet.

His screams, when he was hungry or tired, physically hurt Lena's eardrums. But she had to admit it was good to see Timea, whom she had always looked after, have a little person to look after herself. And she did it so well. By the time Laszlo was five, Lena was used to him. So she made no objection when Timea insisted he accompany them on their long-planned trip to the Transylvanian mountains.

The breeze had that lightness you only experience at altitude. The elite air that has outwitted the soot, the smoke and the smog to reach nirvana. Lena filled her lungs with it, the faint aroma of pines dancing lightly around her body.

That was before pines reminded her of toilet cleaner.

'I'm tired,' Laszlo said.

'Breathe the fresh air,' Lena retorted, starting to get cross.

'It is not much further,' said Timea. 'You want to see the mountain goats, don't you?'

Laszlo grunted his assent. Lena regretted letting him come. She wanted to go higher, faster, further. And she wasn't convinced they'd find any mountain goats, or be impressed with them if they did. She didn't see how they could be so much more exciting than the farmed goats in the village. Then there would be screams and a futile insistence on ice creams from freezers miles below.

'Maybe it is too far for him,' said Timea. 'I'll give him a piggyback.' She swung him on to her shoulders.

'He's a big boy now,' said Lena. 'Make him walk. He is too heavy for you.'

'I like the feeling of him here,' said Timea. 'It means he is safe. And looked after.'

Lena took a deep breath and coughed a little. Suddenly the air wasn't so sweet.

'I think the goats are nearby, after all,' said Lena. 'I can smell them.'

They picked up the pace. 'I see the goats,' said Laszlo. He scrabbled off his mother's back and ran forwards.

By the time the women caught up with him, he was standing about five feet away from the nearest goat in a beautiful field of daisies. The two were transfixed by each other, perfectly still except for the goat's ear, casually flicking at a fly. Laszlo reached out his arm towards the animal. The spell was broken. The goat turned and ran, seeming to climb up a vertical cliff-face, its feet sure even on the loose stones.

They all watched it perform its impossible feat. 'Wow,' said Laszlo. Even Lena had to admit that the goats in the village lacked the same dexterity.

'I want one,' said Laszlo, turning to Timea. 'Let's take it home.'

'If you can catch it you can take it,' said Lena. Timea gave her a dirty look. Laszlo looked as if he was going to cry.

'We can't fit it in the suitcase, darling,' Timea had said.

'I want it,' Laszlo had told her. 'I never get anything I want.'

Lena had felt the urge to reprimand the child, but Timea had scooped him up and cuddled him.

'I'd give you the world,' she had said. 'If I had it to give.'

Clissold Park was long behind them, as were Timea's plans. Lena hated the prospect of telling Laszlo his mother was missing. She would find her first. She had to.

The bus sped down Essex Road as if the driver really wanted to be playing *Gran Turismo*. The Criterion Auction Rooms were gone in a second, and she missed Get Stuffed entirely, the taxidermy shop that had fascinated her and revolted Timea.

At Islington Green the bus ground to an unwilling halt. Traffic had slowed, with the flashing blue lights ahead suggesting trouble.

Lena peered through the window and recognised PC Gullins outside Waterstones bookshop. She strained her eyes to see if Cartwright was with him. There he was, holding an umbrella to shelter a distraught lady in a mauve coat. The lady repaid him by jumping up and down with indignation, seemingly unaware of the puddle she was splashing over his poor regulation boots. Lena smiled at him, tempted to wave. Eventually the bus passed, accelerating again until it was forced to stop at Angel Station.

She hopped out and made her way down City Road. The rain had eased a little, but Lena covered her mouth with her scarf, hoping to filter out the traffic fumes before they poisoned her lungs.

She cheered up when she saw the apartment block that Timea's client Yasemin Avci lived in. She approved. It was brand new, the whitewash still clean despite the heavy traffic on the road outside. A series of balconies towered up, one after another, most with the same box sphere plants and rattan furniture adorning them. It reminded her of the fancier apartments she'd seen on the outskirts of Budapest, the new-builds that were springing up as the city expanded. The better ones in this block would have views of the canal, the cheaper flats overlooked the busy road.

Lena swiped the key fob and entered the code Timea had written down. The door emitted an efficient beep and allowed her access first time. Lena pressed the lift button and the lift appeared immediately, as if it had been politely waiting for her. She decided that this would be where she'd live, once she had her own cleaning firm. Each flat nicely sized. Easy to maintain. No lawn to mow. The giant windows might be tricky to clean, though; you'd have to get someone in with special equipment. Probably the building would organise it for you; a man with a long window-cleaning stick, who'd clean them all from the ground. Lena admired the efficiency of those devices. Invented by a genius.

She decided to be quick. Someone who lived here would be sensible – they wouldn't want anything from her friend. An accountant, perhaps, or a smart young lawyer.

Lena slipped the key in the lock, turning it with ease. She stepped into the apartment, but it was not what she had expected.

A week's worth of half-eaten takeaway containers were strewn across the table and floor. A few were upturned, dripping sauces on to the laminate floor. It stank, too – an international aroma of chillies, cheese and soy sauce.

Lena stepped over the food remains and looked around. The apartment would be smart once she had cleaned; the furniture was chic and expensive-looking. One wall was floor-to-ceiling windows. There was a brand-new black leather sofa along the opposite wall, with a glass coffee table peeking out from underneath the pizza boxes. The floors were wooden but new, parquet, with no gaps between the floorboards – not the Victorian kind that spat up dust. There were no pictures on the white walls, no photos on the mantelpiece, no ornaments to gather dust. Once the rubbish was cleared up, this would be a quick job. Lena went to the kitchen to find a bin bag.

As she came out of the kitchen with the roll of bin bags, she froze. Something was rummaging in the containers. Clutching the roll like a baseball bat, Lena approached. The creature looked a cross between a rat and a pig.

It raised its head, looked Lena in the eye and meowed. Lena lowered the bin bags as the cat ran towards her. It rubbed its furless body against her leg and Lena bent down to investigate.

'What is wrong with you?' she asked it, giving it a tentative pat. It felt like stroking a bald man's head. 'Poor *macska*. You are so ugly.'

The cat clearly didn't understand and was delighted at the attention. It began to purr, rubbing its head against Lena's bent knee. Its body was translucent, its skin failing to disguise the bones and organs that lurked beneath. It had tiny little scratches all over it, like all cats must have and successfully conceal with fur. But it behaved just like the furry cats that Lena had loved back in her village, as if it had no idea it was so freakish-looking.

'You are lucky there are no other cats here,' said Lena, trying to ignore its prominent ribcage and giving the cat a rub behind its bald ears. 'They would soon tell you that you are not normal. Probably scratch you to death for being weird.' The cat's purr reached a crescendo, and it rolled on to its back, displaying its pink, nippled belly.

'You are skinny,' she told it. 'Takeaways are not good for you. Let's see what we can find.'

The cat followed Lena into the kitchen. Cat food and a sprouted potato were all there was in the cupboard, which was by far the cleanest room in the apartment: either Timea was a much better cleaner than Lena had thought, or this kitchen had never been cooked in. She put cat food in a bowl, which her new friend began to gobble in the ravenous way only a cat can. Like it hadn't been fed in weeks. Lena continued with her task.

The client clearly liked all types of takeaway: there were the remnants of Chinese, Indian, Turkish, plus a half-eaten pepperoni pizza. Lena quickly dispatched it all into the bin bag, and went to snoop before she mopped.

There were some white, black and beige clothes in the cupboard, all designer, all classic, all plain. Another cupboard contained rows of expensive shoes: beige, black, and all with painful-looking high heels. But there was nothing more personal than that. No photos, no ornaments, not even any clothes with a pattern or a colour. No post, which she found odd. And no Timea, of course. Lena cleaned quickly, collected the money on the kitchen counter and gave the cat a final stroke. She left.

By 5 p.m. it was getting dark. Lena looked behind her. She felt as though there were footsteps echoing her own. Someone following her. But when she looked there was nobody there. She shook her head, wondering where her paranoia was coming from. The streetlights were coming on just as her energy was waning. She looked up at the grand Georgian house, the last client of the day, and hoped it didn't need much work. Just as she was fumbling with the keys, the door swung open to reveal an ageing tanned man in a white towelling robe.

'So the agency have sent me a new girl,' he said, smiling at her. 'Good.' The man held out his hand. 'You are most welcome. I am François.' She gave him her own hand and he raised it to his mouth, planting a wet kiss on it.

Lena suppressed a grimace and followed him inside. The corridor was poorly lit, with long, old-fashioned rugs covering the wooden floor. Dark oil paintings lined the walls, and a dusty chandelier provided what light there was.

François went into the drawing room, beckoning Lena to follow him.

'I start upstairs,' she said, her heart sinking. This house needed lots of cleaning.

'*Non, non.* Start in here. You can keep me company.' He lay on a chaise longue like a Roman emperor about to dine. His hair was greying, and she noticed his hairy chest was too, like a backwards silverback gorilla. He caught her looking at his chest and smiled. Lena blushed, taking her eyes away.

Lena went to fetch what she needed, finding the cleaning materials as always under the kitchen sink. When she came back she positioned herself so she could watch him. He had the same idea, and was looking straight at her. She swallowed her dislike, and tried to see him through Timea's eyes. He wasn't a bad-looking man. Older but distinguished, with a tan that looked to be from the San Tropez resorts. Not the bottle. And he seemed rich. Perhaps he treated Timea to beautiful things, took her to fancy restaurants. Perhaps he had bought Timea that necklace.

She smiled at him for a moment and he winked at her. She came to her senses. She needed to work out if he was nothing to

Timea, just an overbearing client, or whether he had something to do with her disappearance.

'So are you French?' she asked, trying to sound interested.

'Swiss,' he replied, with a smile. 'You have the dark hair and lean body of a Slav, perhaps?'

'I am Hungarian.'

'Ahh. A Magyar. Passionate. Like Bartók.'

She sprayed some Pledge on the mantelpiece and began dusting, reaching up to clean the top of a carriage clock. She noticed his eyes on her upstretched body.

'You know Timea,' she said.

'Oh yes,' he replied, without moving his eyes. 'Another Magyar.'

'We are very close,' said Lena, watching his reaction. 'Almost like sisters.' He smiled at her. Lena swallowed, and decided to bluff. 'She told me all about you.'

'And you are here,' he replied, smiling more broadly. 'Excellent.'

Lena worked in silence for a while, trying to work out what he meant. There were two fireplaces in the room, both with mantelpieces covered in little statues that collected dust like Uncle Attila collected stamps. Houses like this were designed by people who would never have to clean up themselves. The house was big too, and old. The kind of place where you could hide things. People even.

'Your brass needs polishing,' she told him, thinking she'd like to explore the house, look for signs that Timea had done more than clean here. He winked at her again.

'I look forward to it,' he said. 'Perhaps you would care for a drink? Champagne?'

Lena agreed, breaking the agency's rule about accepting alcohol from a client. If they shared a drink he might tell her more about Timea.

'I'll just clean upstairs first,' she said.

'Good idea,' he replied. 'The bedroom is very dirty.' She was starting to wonder if his wink was a nervous tick.

She made her way up the staircase, sliding the duster up the mahogany rail. She went to the very top floor first. All three rooms were tidy and unlived in, with their beds made and dust gathering on the duvet covers. Even the bathroom was empty, save for a spider trapped in the bathtub. Feeling generous, Lena scooped it out and released it on to the outside window ledge. It scurried away, glad of its luck. She peered inside the cupboards in every room, but each was empty, bar a few hangers. They were for guests that never came. The study on the second floor was definitely lived in. A stale scent pervaded the room. It reminded Lena of her father, the scent of their house before he left them. She traced the smell to an ashtray full of cigar butts. A few half-drunk crystal glasses of whisky were scattered about. Lena ignored the urge to clean immediately, and went through the documents on the desk. On top were thick, textured, creamy papers, stamped with the European Union logo. Three pages deep she found a thin, glossy magazine. A woman stared out at her, looking full of reproach as she spread her legs and clutched her ample bosom, pushing them up so her nipples pointed at Lena.

She put it down, and re-covered it with the papers. She wouldn't find Timea on the desk. She didn't know what to do. It wasn't as if he'd leave a piece of paper on his desk, *I've buried Timea here.*

No. She wouldn't think that. She visualised the paper. *I'm keeping Timea here.* No. While she was at it, it would say, *Timea has gone on a holiday. She'll be back tomorrow. With a tan.*

This was getting her nowhere. Lena went into the bedroom and gasped.

François was reclining on the bed, looking at her. The same way he had downstairs. Except now his robe hung open, revealing his hairy chest and hairier crotch. He was excited.

51

'Sorry,' said Lena, exiting the room.

She hurried downstairs and began to run the kitchen tap, scrubbing her hands, although she hadn't touched him. She didn't know whether to get out or to stay and finish cleaning. Maybe it was an accident.

The answer was forthcoming. A hand grabbed at her breast from behind, clutching it and then squeezing. 'Don't be shy,' he said. 'We can have fun.'

Lena spun around, sending her elbow into his face as she freed herself.

'*Merde!*' he exclaimed, rubbing his cheek. 'You girls are so excitable. First Timea and now you. No more Hungarians for me.'

'Timea? What did you do to her?'

'She wouldn't let me do anything,' he said. 'Nothing. So I got rid of her.'

Lena gasped. François moved towards her, his arms outstretched. She stepped backwards and bumped into the marble of the kitchen counter. She was trapped.

'Come,' he said, his hand wrapping around her shoulder. 'You will definitely enjoy yourself, *mignonne.*'

Lena raised her knee and firmly jabbed it at his groin. He doubled over in pain and she jumped over him, grabbing her bag and rummaging through it to find her phone. She heard him whimper as she dialled. '*Non!* Don't call the police,' he pleaded. 'My wife, she will leave me if she finds out it has happened again.'

CHAPTER 5

The policeman flashed his badge at Lena, but there was no need. She recognised him from the station. She looked past Gullins's blank face to Cartwright, who gave her a smile of recognition. 'What seems to be the problem, madam?' Gullins said. She beckoned them both in and gestured to the kitchen.

Cartwright touched her arm lightly as he walked through. 'Are you OK?' he asked. 'The call-out said that there had been an assault. Do you need any medical assistance?' His eyes scanned her body, then gazed concernedly into her own.

There was a groan from the kitchen. '*Aidez-moi!*' called out François. 'Help, I am hurt.'

'What's gone on here?' said Gullins, leaning down to inspect François, who was sitting up on the floor, rubbing his crotch. 'What's happened?'

Lena hurried to the kitchen. 'He touched me, grabbed me here.' She gestured to her breast. Both policeman looked to her chest. Cartwright's eyes hurried back to her face. 'He has done something with Timea. He said he got rid of her.'

'No, no,' said François. 'Simply a misunderstanding. Then, this beast, she set upon me. Look at this injury. And my chin. It is full of pain.' He looked up at Gullins mournfully.

'Did you do this?' Gullins said to Lena. A dramatic-looking red swelling was forming on François' face.

53

'I just defended myself,' said Lena, feeling the tide beginning to turn against her. 'But you see it, on the news. Old men keeping women prisoners.'

'I am not old, no!' said François, struggling to his feet. His robe fell open in the process. Now both policemen looked away. 'Timea, I just tried to have a little fun with her. But no, no more.'

'Sort yourself out, sir,' said Gullins, suddenly interested in his own shoes. 'Put some clothes on and we'll get this resolved. Down at the station.'

'That is not necessary, surely, officer,' said François, tying his robe. 'Just a little misunderstanding. Perhaps we could open a bottle of something, have a little drink. I have a very nice bottle of—'

'The station,' said Gullins. 'Put some clothes on now or we'll take you as you are.'

'We must search the house,' said Lena to Cartwright. 'There might be a clue to where Timea is. I have not found it yet, but you can help me look.' She pulled on Cartwright's sleeve to get him to follow her.

'Not so fast, madam,' said Gullins. 'You need to come too. An allegation of assault has been made against you.'

Lena looked beseechingly at Cartwright. 'I'm terribly sorry,' he said. 'You've got to come with us, I'm afraid. I promise the house will be thoroughly searched as soon as we can get a warrant.' He touched her hand, where it still rested on his sleeve.

'Come on, Casanova,' said Gullins. 'Let's get these two back to the station and get some sense out of them.'

Lena woke to the sound of a clank and the smell of baked beans and urine. It was a moment before she remembered where she was, but the cold narrow bed she'd half slept on and lack of windows soon jogged her memory. She sat up, wincing at the pain

54

in her back. Whether it was caused by sleeping on the awful foam mattress or restraining François, she wasn't sure.

She looked around. There was a tray of what might pass for breakfast on the floor – that's where the bean smell must come from. The seatless toilet in the corner remained unused. She was going to hold out as long as was physically possible. She felt disgusting enough already without approaching that thing.

She was surprised by a polite rat-a-tat-tat on the outside of her cell. Cartwright entered.

'Good morning,' he said. 'May I have a seat?' He sounded like a guest at her house, not a policeman in her cell.

Lena felt aware of the foulness of her breath and the greasiness of her hair. She didn't feel like talking. She just wanted to go home. To brush her teeth. To shower.

'Please?' he said. Lena jerked her head towards the end of the bed, retracting her feet and sitting up to give him space. 'Thank you.' Cartwright perched on the edge of the bed. 'I'm sorry,' he said. 'With Monsieur Belladot's permission we searched his house, but we didn't uncover anything suspicious. There wasn't anything there worse than a few girly magazines.' Cartwright coughed and then continued. 'And we can't arrest everyone who has that sort of thing, I'm afraid. We'd be over-capacity pretty quickly,' he laughed awkwardly. 'This means that we can't keep him in, certainly not without any proof that he is involved with what's happened to your friend.' He looked at Lena. 'If anything *has* happened to her, of course. She could still come home at any time.'

'You kept me.'

'Yes, I'm sorry about that. We had a bit of a rush last night. Busy time around Guy Fawkes. I'm not sure what it is about fireworks that makes people commit more crimes, but there you have it.' He smiled. 'Perhaps the treacherous spirit of the gunpowder plot is to blame – 1605 and all that.'

Lena ignored him. 'But he touched me.'

'Yes, and of course we take that very seriously. But you did assault him too, with rather more force than could be considered necessary, given the context.' Lena shrugged. He'd deserved it. 'The good news is,' continued Cartwright, 'he's prepared to drop the charges if you are. He's been very co-operative. He didn't even make us get a warrant for the search of his house.' Cartwright smiled, then added conspiratorially: 'I don't think he's keen for his wife to know what he's been up to.'

'He could still have taken Timea,' said Lena. 'Just because you didn't find anything in the house yet, it does not mean—'

'We questioned Monsieur Belladot. I'm afraid he is quite uninvolved. He has been in Brussels on business for the last month, and only returned to the UK yesterday.'

'You are sure?' Lena felt Timea slipping away from her, back into the uncertain shadows.

'I'm sorry,' said Cartwright. 'He's been in EU meetings. Multiple politicians can bear witness to the fact he's been in Brussels the entire time. Not that you can trust politicians,' he said with another awkward laugh. 'So I suppose in reality he could have been anywhere.'

She reached forwards and grabbed Cartwright's hand. It felt warm and soft under her own cold, calloused fingers.

'You need to help me,' she said. 'You need to help me find her. Timea has a son, a son who needs her.'

Cartwright was studying her hand on his. 'Of course,' he said. 'Let me update you. I'm afraid we haven't been able to get a trace on her phone, she must have it switched off. No card transactions either. What I'd like to suggest is that I visit your home and collect some DNA. It's been four days now, I think we'll be able to justify ramping the investigations up a gear. There's no reason to be alarmed. We'll just need her toothbrush, or a pillow that only she sleeps on, perhaps?'

Lena dropped his hand and put her own over her face. 'Do you think—'

'There's still a good chance it's nothing,' said Cartwright quickly. 'Maybe she's just had enough of technology and needed a break. I know I sometimes feel like turning my phone off and going for a good long walk in the countryside.' He smiled at her, fiddling with his collar before looking straight into her eyes. His eyes, Lena noticed, were the blue of the summer skies above the mountains outside her village. She reached out and touched his hand again, lightly brushing his fingers.

'Thank you,' she said. 'I hope you are right.'

'Thank God!' said Tomek, when she was finally brought back to the police station front desk. He jumped up from the chair, flinging his polystyrene cup of tea away and enclosing Lena in an enormous hug that lifted her feet from the floor. 'Are you OK?'

'Smelly and tired,' she said sheepishly, trying to disentangle herself from his arms, aware of Cartwright's eyes on them both. Tomek began to cover her face in sloppy little kisses.

'I was so worried. No more cleaning. It's too dangerous. I'll take care of you.' He grabbed her again and she felt her face crushed in his armpit.

'I can take care of myself,' she said, her words smothered against his sweatshirt.

'What happened? I don't understand. Something about an assault?'

'I want to go home,' said Lena, disentangling herself.

'She's had a long night,' Cartwright said. Both turned to look at him.

'Who are you?' said Tomek.

'Cartwright helped me,' said Lena. 'Let's go.'

'Then I must thank you,' said Tomek, in his grandest voice. He shook Cartwright's hand vigorously. 'Let's get you home, sweetheart.' Tomek put his arm around Lena's waist. 'Thank you again. I will take it from here. I will make pancakes for my lovely girlfriend.' He guided Lena out through the door, into the cold glare of the November morning sunlight.

CHAPTER 6

It felt good to brush the fuzz and odour from her teeth. Lena spat the last of the night's trauma into the basin and stepped into the steaming hot shower. She raised her face upwards, letting the hot water massage her face as she explored her lip with her tongue. The scab was gone. It had healed since the last time she had seen Timea. Four days. And she was no closer to finding her. Lena scrubbed herself with the bar of soap and vigorously washed her hair, pressing her eyelids together.

Lena dried herself and wrapped Tomek's terrycloth bathrobe around her. She took a deep breath and smelt the reassuring aroma of soap and toothpaste. That was better. Lena went to the bedroom, sat on the bed and turned her hairdryer on her dripping hair, hoping the hum would drown out her worries. She felt the hot air scalding her scalp and smelt burning hair and hot dust. Where would she look for Timea next?

She turned off the hairdryer and felt tiredness wash over her. She went into the living room where Tomek was ensconced in his usual place on the sofa. He leapt up when Lena entered the room. 'The best place,' he announced to her, gesturing grandly. Lena sank down into the cushions, shaped by Tomek's ample body. He arranged himself to one side of her, and stroked her hair. 'Would you like to sleep first or have pancakes then your nap?'

'Pancakes,' said Lena, snuggling down into the sofa. She shut her eyes for a moment. 'But then I go to work.'

When Lena woke up Tomek was coiled around her. Her back was sweaty from his hot belly pushed up against her. She felt a wetness on her shoulder, where he'd dribbled a little in his sleep. It smelt of maple syrup. Lena pushed aside a little bit of disgust. There was one empty plate on the coffee table, with sticky syrup starting to congeal. She saw her plate next to it; the pancakes flaccid and cold. She struggled to get up, giving Tomek a push to release herself. 'How long have I been asleep?' she said. Tomek blinked down at her, then yawned.

'Good nap,' he said. 'Do you want your pancakes?'

Lena shook her head and looked at her watch. 'I'll be late for work,' she said. Tomek was pouring syrup on the cold pancakes and tucking in with gusto.

'You can't go in today,' he said. 'Tell the agency you're sick. I don't feel too great myself – certainly not well enough to drive around London at the whim of that app. We can stay home together.' He gave Lena a syrupy kiss. She pushed him off.

'You are not too sick to have six pancakes for breakfast,' said Lena.

'Just because I can eat doesn't mean I'm not sick,' said Tomek.

'Fat. And lazy. But not sick.' Lena struggled out from under him to stand up and began clearing the greasy plates off the coffee table.

'Lots of fat people are sick,' said Tomek, rescuing the last pancake from the plate before Lena swiped it. 'They die. Every day. Eating pancakes till the end.'

'Well I am not staying home with you,' said Lena, heading into the kitchen. 'I have to find Timea.'

'Haven't you learned anything from yesterday?' Tomek said. 'Lena, you spent the night in a police cell. You need to give this

60

up. Timea will be with a boyfriend. She'll be OK. But you have to be careful, you can't keep going round accusing people.'

'There is another client I need to investigate today: her Friday client,' said Lena. 'You should go to work too.'

'I will. Later.' Tomek pulled himself to sitting with a groan and stretched his arms out to Lena. 'Don't worry about her. Come have a cuddle instead. That will help.'

Lena stepped out of his reach. 'That will not help,' she said, laughing a little.

Tomek wriggled back down into the sofa, pulling the duvet to his chin. He looked like a comfy maggot. 'She'll be fine, you know. It's me who's suffering.'

'It is you who is whining.'

'She'll be back by the weekend. I'm sure.'

'How can you be?' Still, Lena hoped it was true. Maybe she was overreacting. The thought comforted her. She grabbed her coat. 'I'm off. Do not eat all the potato croquettes; I do not have time to go to the shops for more.'

'But they settle my stomach,' said Tomek, his voice full of indignation.

Lena closed the door behind her and waited for the lift to trundle up to her floor. Timea did like men, she had to admit. But then she liked everyone. She was so quick to see the good in people. She remembered when, as a child, Timea had befriended Tamas, the twenty-five-year-old who still could not tie his own shoelaces and used to shuffle around the village muttering his own name. Timea and his mother had been the only people who would make time for him. Most of the village children ignored him, perhaps giving him the odd kick when they passed him in the street. One day, a gang of them had collected sheep droppings to throw at him, laughing when he started to cry. Timea had comforted him, helping to pick the droppings from his tangled hair.

Lena gave up on the lift and began the long descent down nine flights of stairs. The smell of piss was weaker here than in the lift, but the exertion meant you had to breathe more deeply, take the stench deeper into your lungs. Still, the exercise made her start to feel a bit better. Once she was in the fresh air, the day would look brighter.

The first house of what already seemed a long Friday was one of a line of Georgian terraces overlooking a garden square. Lena looked up. The windows were larger on the ground floor, getting steadily smaller on each of the three floors. It was designed to make the house look taller, a trick of the eye. But it made the rooms on the top floors dark and unappealing from the inside. The price you paid for showing off.

All the windows had the curtains closed. She knocked anyway, waiting a moment before inserting the key in the lock. Lena switched on the light and made her way through the hallway. She hoped that no one would be in so she could snoop around in private. After the incident with François, she'd have to be more careful about jumping to conclusions. Lena didn't fancy another night in the cells.

'Timea!' a plaintive voice called out. 'Is that you?' Lena's heart sank at yet another client being at home. And a whiney-sounding one at that.

Lena walked towards the sound. At least the house was more modern on the inside than François' dusty mansion. There were scarves and shoes scattered around the hallway, but underneath it looked reasonably clean and recently redecorated.

In the living room, painted a pretty sky blue, Lena found a woman reclined on the sofa in a silk dressing gown, an ice pack covering her eyes. She must be Margery, thought Lena, remembering the name from the rota.

'Hello Margery,' she said. 'Timea is sick,' she told her. 'The agency sent me to clean today for you. I am Lena Szarka.'

The woman bolted upright, the ice pack falling from her face.

Lena couldn't suppress a small scream. The woman's face was covered in bruises. Deep purple. Mottled browns. Her skin was so swollen she could barely open her eyes.

'What happened to you?' said Lena. 'I call an ambulance.'

'I'm fine,' said Margery, covering her face with the ice pack again. 'I can't believe Timea didn't come,' she muttered. 'I was relying on her.'

'What happened? Have you been attacked?' Lena began to rummage through her bag for her phone. 'Do the police know?'

'Stop fussing,' replied Margery, through the ice pack. 'It's certainly nothing to do with the police. Good grief.' The woman lay back down.

'But what happened to you?' said Lena.

'Mind your own business,' said Margery. 'Just clean, please. Leave me be.'

Lena glanced around the room. A large wedding photo was mounted on the chimney, the bride and bridegroom leaning in to a posed kiss. Lena peered at the photo.

'Yes, you do recognise me,' said Margery, answering an unasked question. 'I'm a weathergirl on Channel Three. I'm taking a sabbatical, for obvious reasons. But I don't want it to get out, so please keep it to yourself. I'm on holiday in Corfu if anyone asks. Beautiful island.' Margery was quiet for a moment. 'Are you still here?' she said, after a pause. 'Stop gawking. Go on, into the kitchen. You can leave this room today. Don't worry, I'll still pay you for it.'

Lena went into the kitchen. It was adjoined to the conservatory and felt light and airy. Lena looked up at the sky through the glass, whitened by the clouds as though coated in cotton wool. The whole kitchen was fairly new, with a breakfast bar and two leather stools pushed up against the quartz worktop. It was inset with sparkles that twinkled at Lena as though it was scattered with diamonds. Remnants of several breakfasts were still sitting on it: grapefruit halves, an open jar of organic almond butter, and dried-up sourdough toast crusts. Lena began dumping the food into the bin and opened up the dishwasher to begin loading. As she leaned over the dishwasher, she wondered what had happened to the woman. Those bruises were not the result of an accident. Someone must have beaten her. Badly. Lena put her hand to her own lip and felt the scar healing. If Margery had been attacked, why wouldn't she tell the police, or – at the very least – tell Lena what had happened? Lena thought back to that photo. Her husband. She'd seen it happen in the village with Mrs Dameth, who'd walked into more doors than she had in her house.

Lena popped a tablet in the dishwasher and switched it on. It purred contentedly. Not all of the dishes would fit, so she began running the hot water to wash up the rest. The water steamed up around her and she squirted in washing-up liquid. It came out the purple of amethysts. Lena sniffed appreciatively – it was a fancy flavour. She let herself be distracted and played a game, trying to guess the scent. Lavender and ylang-ylang perhaps? She looked at the bottle. 'Arabian nights.' Lena chuckled to herself.

She left the plates to dry and opened up the oven. As she'd expected, it was filthy; covered in the myriad baked remains of dinners past. Too incinerated to identify. Ovens had not been Timea's strong point. But she was better at chatting to clients than Lena. They warmed to her, enjoying her genuine interest in their miserable lives. Lena wasn't here to do a deep oven clean, but she couldn't leave it like this. She sprayed cleaner into the oven, averting her face. All oven cleaners seemed to have the same harsh smell. No ylang-ylang here. What if Margery had opened up to Timea? Told her what her husband had done to her? Lena watched the cleaner foam up like an angry cappuccino, then reached inside and began scrubbing. What if Timea had tried to interfere, to help Margery? What if Margery's husband was the man that she was frightened of, the reason she wanted to go back to Hungary? He was a violent man. Would Margery know what he had done to Timea? Lena scraped out the debris from the oven, feeling herself break into a sweat. As she stood up to dump it in the bin she felt suddenly dizzy.

Lena stumbled to the stool. Her head was pounding and she could hear a whistling noise in her ears.

She took a deep breath. Lack of sleep and the stress and the fumes were getting to her. She couldn't go around accusing each one of Timea's clients. She needed time to think about this, to plan what she should do next. Slowly she stood back up. She wiped the counters down and took the rubbish bag from the bin. She'd finish here, keeping an eye out for any clues, anything that could lead her to Timea. Then she'd collect her thoughts, perhaps even write them down. That would help.

By the time Lena had finished cleaning she was exhausted. She muttered goodbyes to an unresponsive Margery and left, closing the door behind her with relief. If there had been any clues she'd have been too tired to see them. Timea could have been sitting in the corner of the living room and she wouldn't have noticed. Lena saw a bench in the garden square opposite and tried the gate. She needed to sit. The gate was locked; the square was for residents only. Then the rain began to fall, large drops that were cold on Lena's skin. Lena was so tired. The rain fell more heavily; it meant business now. Lena hurried to a café she'd passed on the corner but paused for a moment outside the window. She wouldn't usually go into a place like this, full of pretention and overpriced pastries. But it was cold, raining, and she needed a place to think.

A man glanced up at her from his MacBook Air as she entered, but he dismissed her and his spectacled eyes returned to the screen. Lena ordered herself a hot chocolate from a waitress with an elaborately tattooed neck and a multitude of painful-looking piercings. Deciding that she would treat herself, Lena agreed to whipped cream on the drink, and found herself adding a flaky chocolate croissant to the order. Her stomach was growling. She wished she'd eaten those pancakes now.

Lena set her drink down, the tall glass unstable on the table made from reclaimed railway sleepers. As she sipped the hot chocolate through the cream and nibbled her way through the buttery croissant, she collected her thoughts. For a moment she wished she had a notebook in her bag instead of the rubber gloves she always carried. You never knew what you would have to stick your hand into.

So Timea could have gone off with a secret boyfriend. Lena didn't believe this, but she examined the facts. To this day, no one else knew who Laszlo's father was. There had been months of speculation, years even, but Timea had kept quiet. She hadn't even confided in Lena. The village gossips had assumed Timea didn't know, but Lena knew that couldn't be true. Timea loved too easily, but she was faithful. When Laszlo arrived, villagers had peered eagerly at his face. But he was the spit of his mother, no clues to be found.

Timea would know that Lena would worry about her not coming home on that first evening, never mind for four days. If she was OK, she'd have found a way to get her a message by now.

Or could there be a link to François, after all? Was it right that he was ruled out because he had been abroad? Could they have had an affair? Had he done something to her, somehow, from Brussels? Flown her there to wait for him? Locked her up in his basement?

And Margery, the lady with the bruises. Timea could have found out what had been going on. Could Margery's husband have threatened Timea? Bribed her to get out of town? Or worse?

Then there was the love nest. Perhaps Timea had discovered the affair. If Timea had been anyone else, Lena might have suspected she could be blackmailing the flat owner – Steven, it had said on the client list. He could have got sick of her threats and made her disappear. But this was Timea. Timea, who couldn't bring herself to dust away spiders because it might injure their legs. It was impossible. She was too generous: not with money – she never had any – but with emotions. She would always think the best of people.

When Istvan had announced he was going to leave the village, Lena had mocked him, not wanting to believe he was really leaving them. Although they'd broken up again, until the moment he left she had been sure they'd get back together one day. 'So what is this big chance supposed to be?' she had asked him, with the cynicism she had relished at seventeen. The three of them had been at the old village playground, each squeezed into a swing designed for a six-year-old. Istvan and Lena were gently swinging, a few chickens clucking around near their feet. Timea was intently twisting her swing around in circles until it uncoiled itself and spun her around and around. She was eleven.

'I will be the face of *Rauch*,' he replied, swinging himself higher and sending the chickens waddling off in alarm. 'The premier fresh fruit beverage company in Hungary.' He slowed down, allowing the breeze to sweep his hair from his face.

'And what is it about your face that will make people thirsty?' she asked him, gently swaying.

'This is my break,' he said, ignoring her. 'What I've been waiting for. It starts with a print ad for apple juice, but the campaign could extend to television. It could go pan-European, my agent said.'

'Drinking juice on television? I suppose that is everyone's dream. And Klaus is not your agent. He was a pig farmer before he went to Budapest.'

'I'm so proud of you,' Timea said, getting off her swing and taking his hand. 'How long will you be gone?'

'That's more like it,' Istvan replied, glaring at Lena. 'At least someone is impressed. The shoot will take a week, then I'll need to hang around in Budapest, to be available for follow-up and television opportunities. You'll both miss me.'

Timea hugged him, almost knocking him off the swing. Istvan looked at Lena, then tentatively reached his hand up to take hers.

'Don't get too upset, Timea,' Lena had said. 'He'll be back when the money runs out. Apple juice is not liquid gold. I give him a fortnight.'

'Don't listen to her,' Timea said to Istvan. 'This is your chance. Don't let anything stop you. Nothing.'

Lena had been right, of course. The juice had come to nothing. But Istvan had stayed away, anyway, making a living somehow before he had finally started getting acting work.

Lena let the sugar from the chocolate nourish her brain. What had Timea said before she left? Her mind went back to Monday, the day she disappeared. Something had been wrong. Timea had told her that it was happening again. What did she mean by 'again'? What had happened to her before?

Lena gulped down the gritty chocolate at the bottom of her glass, and collected the last crumbs of croissant from her plate with her finger, popping them into her mouth. She would work it out.

'No, I told you, we're not getting married.' Lena balanced the phone between her shoulder and ear so she could undo her shoelaces during her mother's Hungarian diatribe. This was all she needed.

'I know he's a Pole, but if you move to London you can't be fussy. Not at your age.'

'I am thirty-one. I still have plenty of time.'

'You were nine when I was thirty-one. I had given up on ever having another child by then.'

'I know. I'm sorry.'

'And now here I am. No grandchildren. Not even one.'

'You have got Laszlo.'

'He is a blessing and I am pleased to look after him while Timea is away. But grandchildren of my own. Where is Timea anyway? I want to tell her about Laszlo's new trousers.'

'Timea is out.' That was true, at least.

'Spending the night with a man, eh? She needs to get married – that would stop all the sex. It certainly stopped your father and me.'

'Has she been in contact with you?' Lena tried to ask the question casually, so as not to cause alarm. She needn't have bothered.

'You can't keep sex a secret for long,' continued her mother, ignoring her. 'Look at Laszlo.'

'How is Uncle Attila?' Lena didn't want her mother to start on one of her sex rants again.

'His foot rot is playing up and his toenail has gone yellow again. It looks like a squashed banana. How is Istvan?'

'How many times? London isn't like the village. There are nine million people living here. I don't see him.'

'He sent his mother a beautiful handbag. Strawberry.'

'Mulberry.'

'So he showed it to you? Good. Ask him about children. Oh, my heart bleeds for his poor mother. All that money and no grandchildren. We were eating nothing but stuffed cabbage and dumplings and we still both managed children.' Lena heard Tomek come in.

'Tomek wants to say hello.' Tomek gestured that this wasn't at all what he wanted to do. Lena threw the phone to him. He instinctively caught it and reluctantly placed it to his ear.

'Not yet, Mama. But soon, I promise,' said Tomek. He mimed eating at Lena as he listened to her mother's tirade.

Lena left him to it and put the oven on for the bag of croquettes she'd picked up from Iceland. She didn't want to worry her mother and Laszlo. Not yet. She sank down on to the sofa.

Finally Tomek escaped from the phone call. He went into the kitchen and finished off the dinner, bringing Lena a plate of potato croquettes covered in melted cheese, swimming in baked beans, with some anonymous tinned meat perched nervously at the edge of the plate. She tucked in with relish. Timea wouldn't have liked this meal; it was too fatty for her. She'd been worried that she was gaining weight and she said that Tomek's Polish meats smelled like dog food. Lena had to agree with the second statement. She looked at Tomek. He had already finished and caught her eye, so she took his plate and scraped her meat on to it. Then she added one of her croquettes. 'If you're sure you don't want it?' said Tomek, already shovelling it in. Lena smiled at him.

'So I cleaned for another of Timea's clients today,' she told him. 'Her face was very bruised. I think that perhaps she had been beaten by her husband.'

'That's awful,' said Tomek, using the final piece of croquette as a mop to absorb the baked-bean juice. 'Men are pigs.' He popped the fork into his mouth, put his plate on the table and emitted a slow burp.

'I think maybe she told Timea about it,' said Lena, clearing the plates. 'The husband is clearly violent; perhaps Timea went to him to try to help, and he did something to her . . .'

Tomek sat upright. 'You didn't say anything to her, did you?'

'No,' said Lena. 'I will tell the police though.' She walked to the kitchen and popped the dishes into the sink, running hot water over them. She looked around the room. She couldn't conceive how Tomek had made this much mess on such a simple meal. Escaped fragments of cheese littered the counter, and there was a squashed croquette on the floor. Plus, how had he managed to get a baked bean to stick to the door of the fridge? She reached for the kitchen roll.

'You can't go round accusing people,' said Tomek, standing in the kitchen doorway and watching her work. 'Timea will turn up. She just needed some space.'

'From what?' Lena turned to look at Tomek. He looked uncomfortable.

'Everything,' he replied. 'It's not easy. Here. Too much work, not enough money, not enough room. It's not healthy, us all living on top of each other like this.'

'We get on with it,' said Lena.

'You do. But Timea isn't tough like you. She was struggling, and she wanted a way out.'

Lena came closer to Tomek. 'She knew I would look after her,' she told him.

He stepped back and looked down. 'She needed more.'

'Did she say that?' Lena barked at him. 'What do you know?'

'She always wanted more.' Tomek was retreating from the kitchen into the living room.

Lena followed him. 'What did she tell you? If you know something about where she might be . . .'

'I don't. But I just know she wanted more than she had, that's all. That she didn't want things to carry on like they had been. There's no reason to get angry. That's what I told the police too.'

'The police? When did you talk to the police?' Lena could feel herself getting hotter, worry creeping up her like mercury in a thermometer.

'Sit down,' said Tomek, doing so himself and pulling her with him. His voice was calm. 'I didn't want to tell you because I didn't

71

want to worry you, but I suppose you'd notice soon anyway, knowing you. They came around today and took Timea's toothbrush. Just to test for DNA. It is standard procedure when someone has been gone this long, apparently. But she will be fine, I know she will.'

Lena put her head in her hands. Tomek put his arm around her. 'This is a good thing,' he said. 'It means that they are taking it seriously. You can stop investigating, it is wearing you out. Leave it to them to waste their time. You can stay here with me, and wait for Timea to get in touch. She will.'

CHAPTER 7

Lena opened her eyes. This wasn't her bedroom. For a moment she thought she was back in the police cell, then she blinked and remembered. This was her sofa. She had been awake most of the night, trying to figure out what could have happened to Timea. When Tomek tried to make her give up and get some sleep, she had practically accused him of being involved in Timea's disappearance. She cringed, ashamed at what she'd said to him. She sat up and rubbed her shoulders, her back complaining of another night spent away from her bed. She could hear the traffic jam outside, the piercing screech of sirens. From the noise she guessed it must be after nine in the morning already.

There were crumpled bits of paper strewn over the coffee table. Lena picked up the nearest one, written in her Hungarian hand. *Margery's husband attacked Timea to keep her quiet about his wife-beating*, it read. She reached out to the next one. *François paid someone to abduct Timea and take her to Brussels. Obsessive pervert.* Lena shook her head. She sounded like a crazy person. *White slave trade*, the next note said. Lena tutted at herself and gathered the papers up into a pile, glancing at the top note, written just before she had fallen asleep. *Tomek?* Lena tore that one up into tiny pieces. She took the lot into the kitchen and hesitated by the bin for a moment before dumping them all in. She'd been overtired, upset, paranoid. Things looked different this morning.

Lena put the kettle on and went over to the window. The sky was grey but the day still managed to be bright; the sun fighting the odds to illuminate the earth. Traffic was heavy and Lena could hear the sound of a police siren frustratedly trying to battle past the throng of Saturday morning traffic. Timea had been gone since Monday. Not even a whole week had passed. There must be a reasonable explanation, one that didn't involve perverts or the sex trade. Lena would shower, she'd have a cup of coffee, and then she'd work out what it could be.

Feeling cleaner and brighter, Lena dressed quietly, being careful not to wake Tomek. She put on her jeans, and then hesitated before choosing a pale green jumper that Timea had given her. Her friend had told her it suited her, the colour bringing out the green in Lena's otherwise hazel eyes. The jumper felt comforting; soft as Mrs Kingston's rabbit against her skin.

Lena opened the notepad on to a clean sheet and went into Timea's room. She sat down on the bed and surveyed the area, waiting for inspiration. Timea had gone away for a while of her own volition. Why and where? She stood back up, and went to the dresser. She sprayed Timea's musky perfume onto her neck and breathed in deeply. It was almost like Timea was in the room with her. She felt a little better already.

She opened the drawer. Ignoring the notebook, Lena took out the Tiffany's box and went back to the bed. Today was a positive day. Saturday, a happy day after a week from hell. She wouldn't think about the chance the necklace was stolen. It had been a gift from a new boyfriend. Lena opened the box and watched the diamonds glisten in the light. They had gone away for a few days; he had surprised her with the trip and she had sent Lena a message and hadn't noticed it hadn't gone through before the phone ran out of battery. Lena looked. Sure enough, there was Timea's phone charger, still plugged in by the bedside table. This felt like evidence, and Lena breathed in the perfumed air again. She scribbled down the scenario and read through it. It sounded so sensible, so much more likely than the horror stories she had concocted last night.

Lena leaned back in the bed. She would linger here for a moment more, then she would get up and cook Tomek a proper breakfast to say sorry. She tried to visualise what was in the fridge, then decided she would have to pop down to the shop for eggs, bacon and bread. Tomek would be OK after breakfast – he found it a struggle to stay angry at her long if he had a full belly. Not like Istvan, who could keep his anger stewing like goulash in a cauldron.

Lena was passing a brush through her hair when the intercom buzzed. Gullins announced himself and Cartwright. She pressed the button to let them into the building. Feeling strangely guilty, she ran to Timea's room, grabbed the necklace and stashed it under her own bed. Tomek rolled over but didn't wake up. Lena glanced at herself in the mirror and felt glad that she'd had that shower. Then she felt ridiculous. They had some news of Timea – perhaps she had used her cash card – and here she was, busy preening herself. She put the kettle on again. It was just about to boil when the doorbell rang. She glanced around the room to make sure there were no more stray scraps of paper to evidence her craziness, and then plumped up the cushions. It wasn't a nice flat, but it was certainly cleaner than a lot that Cartwright might have seen. Smiling, Lena opened the door.

Something was wrong. Lena could see that immediately. Cartwright opened his mouth to say something, but no words came out. He closed it again.

Gullins took over. 'Can we come in, please?' he said. 'I'm afraid we have some bad news.'

Lena stood to one side and let the men in, following them into the living room where the three of them stood awkwardly. 'You might want to sit down,' said Gullins, taking a chair. The others copied him in silence, sharing the sofa.

As soon as Lena felt the sofa underneath her, she crumpled. Gullins was talking. She didn't even hear the words, but she knew what he was telling her: she'd already seen it in the blue of Cartwright's eyes.

She had known Timea all her life. Their parents had been close friends for years. When Lena had been a little girl, she used to poke baby Timea and watch her wriggle in confusion. When Timea got a little older, she would dress her up like her own little doll. Baked *kifli* together when a tearful Timea had to move in with them, stuffing the little pastries with ground walnuts and moulding them into crescent shapes like the moon. Lena had been the first person Timea had told when she had got pregnant at seventeen. Lena had been there when Laszlo had come into the world, red-faced and screaming. When Lena had decided to come to London, it was natural that Timea would follow.

Lena couldn't believe that all this was over now. It didn't feel real. She realised that Gullins had stopped talking. Both men were looking at her, as if they'd asked a question. 'Are you sure?' she said. 'Are you sure it is Timea?'

Cartwright answered. 'I'm sorry, but we are sure.'

'I saw someone who looked like her the other day,' said Lena. 'And maybe that picture I gave you, it was not such a good likeness. I have others . . . on my phone. The screen is not so good, but you can still see . . .' Lena started to get up. Cartwright gently put his hand on her arm. She could feel his fingers through the sleeve of her jumper. She stayed seated.

'It was a DNA match,' he said. 'They are very accurate. I'm so very sorry.'

'Do I need to identify her?' she asked.

'That's not necessary,' said Gullins, his voice softer now. 'You can see her if you would like, but she will not be as you remember her. Bodies change after death, especially when they've been in water. The DNA, combined with her dental records, has confirmed that it is Timea Dubay.'

'In water?' echoed Lena, blocking the rest of the information.

Gullins cast a glance at Cartwright. 'Yes, she was found in Regent's Canal, like I told you.'

'No,' said Lena, 'Timea hated the water. Ever since that time at the beach . . .' Lena turned to Cartwright. He squeezed her arm.

'That's where she was,' he said.

'But what happened?'

'As I said, it is too early to say. We'll be exploring a number of options.' Gullins cast a surreptitious glance at his watch. 'We'll need to inform the family, unless you would like to do that yourself?'

'What's going on?' A sleepy-looking Tomek stood in the doorway in his boxers and vest. 'Lena?'

'We should be going,' said Gullins. He went over to Tomek and spoke quietly to him.

'If there's anything I can do,' said Cartwright. 'Anything at all . . .' Lena managed a weak smile in reply, then put her head in her hands.

'You can go now,' she said. She wanted to be alone.

Lena felt cold. Tomek tried to hug her but she pushed him aside and went into the bathroom, locking the door behind her.

Lena sank to the floor, her back resting against the shower door. The lino was a little damp under her, where the shower had leaked.

'Can I get you something?' she heard Tomek say. 'A sandwich? Cheese spread and paprika?'

She covered her ears with her hands and squeezed her eyes shut. Why had this happened?

It was all her fault. She had convinced Timea to come with her to London. To leave Laszlo for a couple of years so that she could afford to give him a future for the rest of his life. She could hear herself saying it – the headstrong Lena of two years ago, full of plans to see the world. They would never get anywhere stuck in the village or in Debrecen. They would end up marrying one of the Lisdtok brothers and raising a brood of grubby boys who'd labour on the farm all their lives. There was more life to be had. More world to explore.

Timea hadn't been sure, but Lena had cajoled her into it. There had to be more, she had told her friend. I'll make all the arrangements. My mother will take Laszlo, you know how she dotes on him. And maybe taking care of him will stop her going on about grandchildren! They had laughed, and Lena had known her friend was coming round to the idea. And look what happened to Istvan when he left, she had said. We'll clean for a bit, work on our English, and then who knows what we might do? Things we cannot even dream of. So Timea had agreed.

But now it was all over.

There was a soft knocking on the door. 'I've made hot chocolate,' said Tomek. 'Please come out. I don't like you sitting there, alone in that cold room.'

Lena realised she was freezing. Her jeans were damp and her muscles were sore from sitting crumpled up against the shower. She looked down to the lino and saw a small silverfish bug investigating the edge of her boot. She fought the urge to stamp on it and extinguish its small life. Instead she struggled to her feet.

Lena unlocked the door and immediately found herself in a strong bear hug from Tomek. 'I'm sorry,' he said. 'I thought she'd be OK. I would not have said what I said . . .'

Lena let herself enjoy the warmth from his body for a moment before she wriggled free. 'I have to call my mother,' she said. 'Laszlo needs to know.'

78

CHAPTER 8

Lena sat in the police interview room waiting for the detective. It was a different room to before, with a small window that looked out to the Sainsbury's car park. The windows were reinforced with a steel mesh, reminding Lena of the chicken coops back home. An off-season fly repeatedly threw itself at the window with a panicked buzz, unable to comprehend how the air could have become solid. Its comrade had given up on life and lay on its back on the windowsill, its legs neatly folded across its body as if in prayer.

Lena folded her own hands in her lap, gripping her sweaty palms together. In her bag was a list of Timea's clients and their addresses, neatly written in her best handwriting. She'd put a helpful note next to each, but at Tomek's advice had kept it conservative. She wanted the detective to take her seriously.

To Lena, it seemed the police were much more interested in Timea now she was dead than when there was a chance she could still have been alive and they could have helped. The flat had become a hive of activity over the weekend, with uniformed officers and plain-clothes detectives searching meticulously through Timea's belongings. They clustered around the notebook, gleaning meaning from Timea's scribbled phrases with satisfied grunts. An earnest policeman in an ill-fitting uniform was excited when Lena confirmed the handwriting was Timea's. He'd popped the book into what looked like a plastic sandwich bag, sealed it and labelled it carefully.

'Sorry to keep you waiting, Miss Szarka. I'm Detective Sergeant Wilson,' said the policeman, breaking her reverie. He closed the door behind him and held out his hand to shake. Lena took it, looking at him. He was tall with slightly greying hair, and he looked sensible. She smiled at him. He would be able to help her.

He outlined what he knew so far. Lena listened to his account of where Timea had been found, how long she had been in the water. Lena stayed calm, not letting it sink in, wanting to keep her wits about her so she could help the investigation. When he had finished, Lena gave what she felt was a measured account of Timea's last days. He took copious notes and listened with an interested expression. He had a reassuring habit of repeating her last sentence back to her whenever she paused for thought.

'So Timea was worried?' he prompted her.

'Yes,' said Lena. It felt good to unburden her suspicions with a professional. She produced the list of clients from her bag and handed it to him, explaining how Timea had been worried about something and that she had told her a client was involved.

'And you say that she received a text message before she left?'

'That is right,' said Lena. 'But she lied about who sent it to her.'

'We've pulled her phone records,' he said. 'There was nothing out of the ordinary. Messages about cleaning, hanging out washing, sweeping steps.'

'That is wrong,' said Lena. 'She was excited when she received the message. She changed.'

'Did you see the message?'

'No,' admitted Lena. 'She snatched the phone from me, angry that I had touched it. She was sweet-tempered, but she could be private too.'

'OK,' said Wilson, writing something down. 'Her emotions were up and down.'

'She was scared,' agreed Lena. 'There was something wrong.'

'Not in her usual frame of mind,' said Wilson. He produced Timea's notebook, still in the evidence bag, and handed it to her. It was open on the page where Timea had written her note. '*I cannot live without him,*' Lena read.

'It seemed Timea was very upset about a man as well,' he said. 'Do you know who this man might be?'

'Her ex-boyfriend, Faisal, perhaps,' she told him. 'But I am not sure.' She gave him Faisal's full name, and where he could find him. 'I have not told him about Timea yet,' she said. 'We did not get on so well.' Wilson made a note.

'We'll arrange to make him aware,' he said. 'Timea also mentions a woman, "*I cannot do this to her.*" Do you know who she might mean?'

'Maybe Tracy, Faisal's new girlfriend,' said Lena. 'But it is odd that she should worry about her. They did not like each other.'

'Is there anyone else Timea could have meant, other than Faisal?'

'I do not think so,' said Lena.

'And where were you on Monday evening?'

'I was cleaning all day on Liberia Road, then I came home and spent the evening with my boyfriend.'

Wilson looked back at his notes. 'Tomek Nowak. He is your partner?'

'That is correct.'

'And he lives with yourself and Timea?'

'Yes,' Lena said. 'Timea was like my little sister.' Lena looked back to the fly, still flinging itself at the glass. It truly believed that there would be a way through, a route to freedom.

'We will need to talk to Tomek as well,' said Wilson. 'He can reaffirm your alibi, and he may have been the last person to see Timea alive. Now, we need to build up as much information about Timea as we can, so that we can work out what happened to her.' He looked up at her and gave a half-smile. 'You have already been very helpful,' he said. 'Not many people come prepared with a list of suspects. We appreciate your support.' He passed her back the list she had made of Timea's clients.

'You can keep that,' she said. 'You will need it.'

'Don't worry. I've taken down notes of everything relevant,' said Wilson.

Lena sat back. The fly had given up on the window and was circulating the room. It felt good to have unburdened herself, as if she had abdicated some of the responsibility for finding out what had happened to Timea. These men would take over now.

Wilson stood up and Lena realised the interview was over. 'Will Cartwright be working with you?' she asked, as he shook her hand.

'Who? Oh yes. No. It is with CID now. I shouldn't think we'll need him again on this investigation.'

'Oh,' said Lena, looking at the dead fly. Its live companion was noisily exploring the fluorescent light bulb.

'We'll be in touch again on Thursday, after we get the post-mortem results through,' he told her. 'We'll know more about what could have happened at that point.'

Lena left the police station. She pushed through the doors, wanting a long walk to clear her head. She started towards Upper Street. Angel was quiet; rush hour had passed and lunch hour hadn't started. Even Faisal had packed up his papers and gone. A few were abandoned, blowing in the wind like paper birds. Lena thought back to when she and Timea had last been here, of the thief who got away. All the awful people in the world, and Timea was the one who was gone. Timea, who wouldn't harm a spider.

Lena wondered how little Laszlo was coping. She would know soon enough. Her mother had immediately declared they would come to London. Lena wished she knew who the boy's father was: he shouldn't be an orphan like Timea. It wasn't fair.

She walked through a small gaggle of pigeons arguing over a piece of abandoned croissant. Two flew upwards, flapping in her face, but a third waddled away from her, limping. It had one healthy foot, but the other mangled into a ball. She wondered if it was caused by stepping in chewing gum, spat out by someone when the minty flavour was gone. The pavement here was spotted by gum; sticky until the dirt covered it, so it was just an intense spot of grime on the already filthy pavement. Timea had laughed at her when she complained, said Lena had found her calling as a cleaner. It didn't seem real that she wouldn't see her again – Lena wouldn't have been surprised to turn around and see Timea right behind her. Pitying the pigeon. Teasing Lena about the gum.

Lena didn't like to think of all the time Timea had spent in the dirty canal water. Water she hated. The detective had told Lena that she wouldn't have suffered. But her body had been there, likely floating next to Coke cans, used condoms, the abandoned shopping trolleys that always seemed to gravitate to the water.

She had been found in a quiet part of the canal. They thought that the body had quickly drifted after she'd died, carried by the currents from the locks, until it became lodged under a canal boat, staying there until the owner tried to move it. That was why she hadn't been found for several days. When the narrowboat moved, Timea had been freed a final time, floating to the surface. A ghoulish apparition for the frightened boater.

The case was with the police now. They would discover what had happened to Timea. For a moment Lena felt a weight had been lifted, but then a much heavier one fell. She'd never see her friend again.

For Lena the ensuing days passed in a chocolate-coated haze. Feeling like a spoiled child, she refused Tomek's offers of sandwiches and pancakes, accepting only Dairy Milk, and asking that he call the agency for her and tell them that she would not be working. She ate in bed, leaving the purple wrappers scattered over the blankets like messy little popes. When she did clamber out of bed for the toilet, she felt her head spin with the exertion. Whenever she could sleep she did, looking anxiously at the clock when she woke up, keen for as much time to have passed as possible.

The chocolates reminded her of Istvan. Just before they'd broken up the final time, he'd showered her with heart-shaped boxes of her favourite Stühmer brand. Lena had been suspicious.

'Why so many chocolates all of a sudden?' she had said to Timea, polishing another one off with relish, enjoying the crunch of the nut at the centre.

'He loves you,' Timea had replied, refusing a chocolate from the box Lena proffered. 'He loves you no matter what.'

'He wants me fat,' said Lena, popping another into her mouth. That one had more toffee than she'd expected. She paused to chew before continuing. 'If my father hadn't run off with our savings, I would have thought he'd offered my weight in dowry.'

'You will be such a beautiful couple at your wedding,' said Timea. 'When do you think he will ask you, officially?'

'I suppose it will have to be soon,' Lena joked. 'While we can still find a dress that fits.'

On Wednesday Tomek went to work and Lena drifted back to sleep. She woke with a start, but rolling over was pleased to see it was the afternoon already. The intercom rang again and Lena got up, thinking Tomek must have forgotten his key. She paused, leaning forwards. Everything was dark a moment, as the blood flowed back to her brain, then she made her way to the buzzer and pressed to let him in. She left the door on the latch and sat down on the sofa. Tomek had left a Cadbury's Fruit and Nut chocolate bar on the coffee table and Lena leaned forwards, grabbed it and tucked in. Perhaps he'd make her a cup of coffee when he came in, she thought. She wanted one so much she could almost taste it, but not enough to walk to the kitchen and turn on the kettle.

'Make me coffee,' she said when she heard his footsteps in the hallway. 'Did you bring more chocolate?'

'I'd be happy to make you a coffee, but I didn't bring any chocolate I'm afraid.' Lena turned around. To her horror, an embarrassed Cartwright was standing in the doorway. For a moment, Lena felt the urge to send him away while she cleaned up, showered, got dressed. She was in her oldest pyjamas, featuring a faded unicorn on the front of her top with a chocolate smear speared through its horn. She hadn't showered since she had got back from the police station, and she could smell her own sweat mixing with the sweet aroma of the chocolate. The flat had never been in this state before, with Tomek's dishes and her wrappers lining the tables and floors.

But then she leaned back into the sofa. This was her house and her friend was dead.

'I did not think I would see you again,' she said. 'I heard the murder detectives took over.'

'Well, I knew I was going to be in the neighbourhood, so I told DS Wilson I'd be happy to stop by and fill you in since my shift is over. I hope I'm not intruding,' he said, looking uncomfortably at her pyjamas.

'Has the detective caught him?' she said, gesturing for Cartwright to come in. 'Has he found out who murdered Timea?'

'Let me make you that coffee,' said Cartwright, picking his way carefully to the kitchen.

'That means no,' said Lena, more to herself than to him. She listened as he opened and closed cupboard doors, searching for the coffee granules.

After a few minutes, Cartwright returned with two mugs and a smile. He settled himself down on the chair opposite her and handed her a milky coffee. She took a sip of the insipid drink, far too weak for her taste, and waited for him to talk.

'So,' he said, then took a swig of his own tea. He put the mug down on the coffee table. Lena noticed he used a chocolate wrapper as a makeshift coaster. He took a breath. 'I'm so sorry about what has happened,' he said. 'I really didn't think . . . none of us did. You see, with her demographic, it really did seem like she would be OK. She should have been OK.'

'What progress have you made?' Lena asked.

'I'm sorry, of course,' said Cartwright. 'DS Wilson will give you a full update when the autopsy comes in, but I know you are keen to hear what we've learnt so far. I'm afraid that the manner of Timea's death, and the delay in recovering the body, does throw out some particular challenges. Normally, when a body is recovered, the police examine the crime scene for clues, evidence of what has happened. But in this case, there is no crime scene. We simply cannot tell exactly where Timea died.'

Lena held the mug a centimetre away from her lips, letting the steam condense on her face. 'She didn't die in the canal?' she said.

'Well yes, we think she did,' said Cartwright. 'But the problem is where she went in to the canal. The nearest lock is almost a kilometre upstream. She could have floated a fair distance, giving us a huge potential crime scene. Plus, it has been several days since it happened but we don't know exactly when. Of course not before Monday, but we don't know exactly how long after that. It is much harder to tell time of death when a body has been immersed in water. The officers are searching the canal banks. But the uncertainty is an issue. We'll keep looking, but with each day that passes our chances of finding something new diminish.'

Lena put the mug down and closed her eyes. An image of a drowned Timea came to her, floating at the side of a derelict barge. She opened her eyes with a start. Cartwright continued. 'So we don't know exactly where and when it happened. It's hard to even know where to start looking at the CCTV footage. We have, though, we've been trawling through hours of it.'

'And?' said Lena.

'Again, without knowing where and when, and even exactly what we're looking for, it's slow going. Cameras always seem to be pointing the wrong way, I'm afraid. All I've heard so far is that there are more ducks than you would expect at this time of year.' Cartwright managed a half-smile at Lena that she didn't return. 'Global warming, I expect,' he muttered. He picked up his mug and blew on his tea.

'So do you have any news?' asked Lena.

'The police have also been going door to door at the flats overlooking the canal,' he said. 'That's ongoing. But without knowing exactly where it happened, it is very difficult to find witnesses. As more time passes, people are unlikely to remember seeing anything.'

'But you are doing more?' said Lena.

'We've put up a sign, of course,' he said, lamely. 'A few signs, actually, along the canal where it could have happened. Signs appealing for witnesses.'

'A sign?' Lena said, spitting out the word. 'Did the detective talk to François, at least?'

'Well, as you know, he was out of the country. That's a pretty strong alibi.'

'Margery?'

'I'm afraid that wasn't a route that was felt to be particularly promising.'

'Faisal?'

'I know he has been informed and interviewed, but I don't think the police feel there's any evidence to suspect ...' Cartwright trailed off.

'Tracy? Faisal's girlfriend?' Lena could tell what he was going to say. She felt the blood rising in her again. 'So what evidence have you found?' she said. 'You must have some clue who did it?'

'I'm sorry, Lena, we are doing everything we can. But when there's no crime scene and no exact time of death and no obvious witnesses . . .' Cartwright picked up his mug of tea and then put it down. Then he coughed again and moved the cup a little further from him on the table. He caught Lena's eye and then looked back to the mug. 'There'll be more information when the results of the autopsy are in,' he offered. 'That will be soon. And Timea's body is the best clue we have. I can't make any promises, but I think there's a good chance we'll at least be able to rule some options out.'

Lena sat and stared at Cartwright. He took a sip of his tea and tried to smile at her. She stood up.

'Thank you for the update,' she said, moving towards the door. 'It was good of you to come. I know you must be very busy.'

Cartwright took the hint and a final sip of his tea, and stood up to leave. Lena opened the door and shepherded him out. As he left he turned to say something to her, but Tomek chose that moment to appear. The men nodded to each other in muted greeting as Cartwright left.

'I've got your biscuits,' said Tomek, throwing them to her. 'What did he want?'

'To tell me they had nothing,' said Lena, catching the packet and putting it on the table. Tomek sat down on the sofa and opened the pack, taking four and then offering the packet to Lena. She shook her head. 'No thank you,' she said. She looked around her. 'This flat is disgusting. I will clean it and then I will shower. Then I will visit DS Wilson. It sounds like he needs my help.'

CHAPTER 9

DS Wilson did not look thrilled to see Lena, but he greeted her politely and led her to the same interview room as before. 'I understand that PC Cartwright volunteered to give you an update on the case,' he said. 'Was there something he couldn't help you with?'

'Why do you not talk to the clients?' asked Lena. 'I showed you the list, and I told you that one of them could have been involved. But you have done nothing.'

'We have not done nothing,' said Wilson. He sat back in his chair, and spoke as if he had said the words many times before. 'We have been exploring all avenues and deployed a substantial amount of resources into finding witnesses to what happened to Timea. I'm sure that PC Cartwright explained that without a murder scene—'

'Yes yes,' said Lena. 'You have got nowhere.' They sat and looked at one another for a moment. Lena could feel Wilson hardening to her. She decided to change tack.

'My friend Timea, she had a little boy, just eight years old. I need to tell him what happened to his mother. We need to bring the murderer to justice.'

'I do understand that this is a difficult time for you,' said Wilson. 'But I can assure you—'

'I do not want assurances,' said Lena, leaning into him. 'I want the truth.' She banged her hand on the table. Immediately afterwards she felt a little ridiculous. That was the kind of behaviour she had seen on *Heroes of Law*.

Wilson waited for her to calm down. 'I do have some new information,' he said slowly. 'I was going to visit you tomorrow, but since you are here today, and clearly getting frustrated—'

'What is it?' asked Lena. 'What have you found?'

'It is the results of the autopsy,' said Wilson. 'They came in today.'

'What does it say?' said Lena, feeling hot and cold all at once.

'One moment. I'll go and fetch the file,' he said. 'I wasn't expecting this visit.' Wilson got up and walked to the door. 'Prepare yourself,' he said as he left. 'This may not be the news you were hoping for.'

Lena sat back in her chair and waited. She looked to the windowsill. The dead fly was still lying where it had been last time, its legs still neatly folded across its chest, still praying for a salvation that was slow in coming. She glanced at her watch. Wilson had only been gone a minute, but it felt much longer. She wondered what he had to tell her. How Timea had left the world. What had he meant – 'may not be the news you are hoping for'? Did it mean Timea had suffered? No, she wouldn't think about it. Lena looked to the ceiling and the long fluorescent bulb flickered back at her as though it was winking. The ceiling itself looked as if it was made of polystyrene.

Wilson came back into the room holding a brown folder. He placed it on the table in front of him and sat down. Both he and Lena looked at it in silence for a moment.

'It is very hard for forensics to give an accurate time of death when a body has been in the water,' he began. 'They have estimated an interval between one p.m. on Monday and five p.m. Tuesday. You yourself last saw Timea on Monday at eleven a.m., and she was seen by your partner later that day.' Lena nodded.

'Death was asphyxiation by drowning,' he continued. 'The microbes in the water found inside her lungs matched those of the canal. That confirmed that she drowned in the canal, rather than being moved there later. There is no bruising on her body or other signs of trauma.'

Lena breathed a sigh of relief. Timea had not suffered. She struggled to concentrate on what Wilson was telling her.

'That would suggest that it is unlikely that anyone else was involved in her death.'

'So you think she just fell?' Lena tried to make sense of it. 'She is a grown woman. She can swim. I taught her myself when we were children.'

'No, I'm not saying that she just fell.'

'Someone pushed her? This city—'

'No. Please let me finish. The toxicology reports came back. Timea had a large amount of diazepam and paracetamol in her system. Sedatives and painkillers.'

Lena sat back in her chair.

'You told us that your friend was unhappy,' he continued. 'And, as you know, Timea had written some disturbing things in her notebook.' He spoke gently now. 'I'm sorry, Lena, but the evidence strongly suggests that no one else was involved in your friend's death.'

Lena looked at him. It seemed impossible to her. 'She . . . she would not . . . her son . . .' she began.

'I'm not saying that it was necessarily suicide. We will never know what Timea's intentions were,' he said. 'But the evidence suggests that this was not a murder. We'll finish our line of inquiry and make sure all loose ends are tied. But I'd be very surprised if at this point we can find anything that suggests more than what we call "death by misadventure".' He looked at her and spoke more softly. 'We don't know if Timea meant to do this or if it was a tragic accident. A slip.'

'But she could not have slipped,' said Lena. 'She always stayed away from the water's edge.'

'I'm sorry,' said Wilson. 'Perhaps there is someone I can call for you?'

'No,' said Lena, getting to her feet.

'There is one more thing that I need to tell you,' said Wilson. 'I think you should sit back down.' Lena obeyed. 'The post mortem found that Timea was three months pregnant.'

The squirrel sat up on its haunches on the wall around Mrs Kingston's front garden. It watched Lena, cocking its head to one side. An autumn leaf, the colour of a sunset over Lake Balaton, floated down from the horse-chestnut tree above. The movement spooked the squirrel. Shooting Lena a look like it was her fault, it scrambled up into the depths of the tree, upsetting more leaves. They floated down to join their friends on the cold pavement.

Lena took a breath. A pair of beady eyes in the window of the house caught her eye. Jasper, Mrs Kingston's rabbit, had been watching the squirrel. Now it was gone, Jasper turned around and disappeared from sight. Lena approached the door and rang the bell. By the time Mrs Kingston opened it, Lena was crying.

Lena sat on the well-worn sofa. One hand was clutching a pink tissue, damp and salty from her tears. The other was gently resting on Jasper. He had hopped over to her as soon as she had sat down, peering up at her until she leaned down and lifted him to her lap. The warmth of his body was comforting, like a hot-water bottle on a cold day.

'Sorry,' said Lena to Mrs Kingston, who was sipping from her brandy glass. Lena's sat empty in front of her. 'I have never cried in front of a client before. It is not professional.'

'Professional scropessional,' said Mrs Kingston. 'Poor Timea. I can't believe it.'

'Death by adventure, they said.'

'Misadventure,' Mrs Kingston corrected kindly, leaning forwards to refill Lena's glass. Lena raised her hand to stop her. 'For your nerves,' she said, pouring a healthy two fingers. 'The investigation is ongoing, I presume?'

'I do not think so, no. They do not think it is suspicious. They have other work to do.'

'That's outrageous!' Mrs Kingston finished her brandy in a gulp. 'They have a duty to explore all avenues. What are you doing about it?'

Lena shrugged. 'I know it is not suicide. Timea, she would not do that. Laszlo, he means more to her than anything. And with the baby inside her too, she would have fought to the death to save that little life. And she would not have taken those drugs. Timea didn't even take paracetomol, let alone a sedative.' Lena could feel tears fighting with anger inside of her. Anger now had the upper hand. 'I will find the truth!' she declared.

'And you'll have help,' said Mrs Kingston, so loudly that an alarmed Jasper jumped from Lena's lap. 'Now, let me think.' She sat back. Jasper retreated to beneath the sofa, unused to such excitement in the house. 'It's been a while since I had much to do with the police. But I have written a good few exposés in my time at the *Gazette*. Always had them cowering.' Mrs Kingston chuckled. 'What's the name of that policeman leading the investigation?'

'DS Wilson.'

'Hmm. After my time, of course. No matter, they are all the same.' Mrs Kingston settled back in her chair. 'I shall put in a call,' she said finally. 'Let's see how much he'd like a story about a mother's murder being swept under the carpet. Perhaps a bit of speculation that if she were a British citizen, it would be a different kettle of fish altogether.' She licked her lips thoughtfully. 'Especially after the negative coverage that police sergeant got when he said those dreadful things about putting immigrants back on their boats. Just the threat of more of that kind of thing should do the trick. I would go down to the station – I love to look into the whites of their eyes when I've got them – but my hip means I'll have to do it by email.'

'You have done more than enough,' said Lena. 'I cannot repay you.'

'Find out what happened to Timea,' Mrs Kingston said, her eyes sparkling. 'And then tell me all about it.'

Tomek began to rub her shoulders again. 'I am so sorry,' he said to her, planting a gentle kiss on her neck. 'Can I help? With the funeral? Even your mother?'

'*Szar*. That is all I need.'

'She'll ask about when we're getting married. She always does.'

'Nosy old woman.'

'What shall we tell her?' Tomek kissed her neck again, then moved around to hold her face cupped in his hands, so that they were looking into each other's eyes.

The intercom buzzed. Lena jumped up and ran over to it. 'It is the police,' she said. 'Mrs Kingston told me it would not take long. They will help me now.'

Tomek pulled the blanket over himself and turned the TV on.

Lena left the door ajar behind her and tapped her foot as she waited for the lift to deliver the policemen. She smiled to herself, feeling more empowered than she had for a long time. With Mrs Kingston's help she would get the police force back on side. She would find out who had done this to her friend and she would enjoy the look on DS Wilson's face as he realised she was a force to be reckoned with. She wasn't just some girl from a Hungarian village he could fob off.

The lift arrived with a jolt. The doors opened. Cartwright was its sole occupant.

'Where is DS Wilson?' she asked, peering around, as if DS Wilson could be hiding in the tiny cubicle.

'I've been assigned to investigate.' Cartwright stepped out of the lift. 'They have entrusted the case to me,' he said, a smile breaking over his features. 'I am going to ensure that nothing is overlooked.'

'*Viccelsz velem*,' said Lena, staring at him. 'Is this a joke?'

'What do you mean?' said Cartwright. The smile was starting to fade like over-washed denim.

'They send me trainee?'

'I can assure you that I will do everything in my power . . .' The sentence died on his lips under Lena's harsh gaze. 'Can I at least come in?'

Lena could hear the *EastEnders* theme tune from the living room. 'No,' she said, reaching in to grab her handbag and coat and pulling the door closed behind her. 'We go out.' She thumped the lift button. It opened its doors for her obediently, as if aware of her impatience. She stepped inside and gestured for Cartwright to follow her. They stood together in uncomfortable silence as the lift trundled downwards. Lena looked at Cartwright. His eyes were pointed to the floor, studiously avoiding eye contact with Lena and the crudely drawn penis on the wall. By the time they arrived at the ground floor, Lena felt herself softening a little towards him. Perhaps she'd been too harsh.

'We have coffee,' she said, not unkindly. It was only 5 p.m. but the light had already faded. Lena led him to a small café that Tomek raved about. When they stepped inside she was hit by the greasy smell of a day's worth of fry-ups. A couple of kids for whom school was over for the day were sharing a plate of chips, but otherwise it was quiet. Lena ordered a double espresso and Cartwright an Earl Grey. Feeling calmer, Lena sat down opposite Cartwright and watched, a little amused, as he took a deep breath. She decided to take the lead.

'So is the case being reopened?' she asked.

'No,' said Cartwright. Lena opened her mouth but he continued quickly. 'That is, it was never closed. The homicide unit did not feel that there was enough evidence to merit further resource, but due to press interest,' he said with a cough, 'they have changed their minds and assigned me the task of continuing the investigation.' He paused and looked Lena straight in the eye. 'Which I fully intend to do. I may not be the most experienced police officer on the force, but I will not rest until we discover what happened to Timea Dubay. Her age group, sixteen to twenty-nine year olds, are the second most likely to be murdered. One in every fifteen million people. Did you know that?'

'Who is the most likely?' said Lena, taken aback by his enthusiasm.

'Children under one,' said Cartwright. They sat in silence for a moment as Lena absorbed the information.

'The best way to get to the bottom of this is for us to work together,' said Lena. 'I will help you.'

'That's very generous of you, but I'm not sure that procedure allows—'

'We will start with Faisal, his girlfriend Tracy, and then we'll work through the client list.'

'I really don't think that . . .'

Lena looked at his conflicted face. She released her mug to take his hand. It was soft and warm. 'She was my friend. I will help you.' Lena paused for a moment. 'I am fed up of being treated like I am invisible.'

'You're definitely not invisible, Lena.' Cartwright said the words softly.

Lena felt herself colour slightly and noticed that Cartwright was blushing too as he broke her gaze. But she could tell she had won.

'So where shall we meet tomorrow?' she asked with a smile. It felt so good to have someone on her side. Someone who would help her find the answers she wanted so badly.

Lena sat cross-legged on her bedroom floor and unfolded the large map of Islington she had bought in WHSmith. She carefully marked where Cartwright had told her Timea's body had been found. She added a Post-it note to that spot, detailing what she knew. *Likely death occurred between Monday afternoon and Tuesday morning. No struggle. Drowned. Diazepam and paracetamol.* She looked at it. No wonder the detective thought it was suicide. Could there be more to be learned from the boat owner who had found the body? Perhaps Cartwright could help in the morning when they went to see Faisal. Then she marked where she had last seen Timea, with the time and a note that said '*Text?*'. After that she marked each of Timea's clients' houses, and put a Post-it note next to each with the address and what she knew about them.

Margery. Barnsbury. Beaten by husband? Yasemin. City Road. Messy with hungry cat. Steven. Stoke Newington. Adulterer. François. Canonbury. Letch. She put a note at Angel Station for Faisal and she added Tracy too, for good measure. There wasn't much to go on but at least it was a start.

CHAPTER 10

Lena sat at a cold metal table outside Costa Coffee, watching the last of the Thursday morning commuters bustle around Angel. Cigarette butts filled the ashtrays – even in the cold, plenty of people couldn't enjoy their morning coffee without a smoke. She noticed a handsome man in the corner of her vision. He was walking towards her from the café. He was athletic, but his steps were tentative. He held two enormous paper cups. She looked at the empty space on the table. She supposed he did have more right to sit there than she did as she hadn't even bought a coffee yet, but there was no way she was giving up her spot. He placed one of the cups down, right in front of her. Lena opened her mouth to tell him where he could put his coffee. Only then did she realise it was Cartwright.

He looked so different out of uniform, grinning at her nervously. 'I got you a cappuccino with chocolate sprinkles,' he told her, sitting down opposite. 'And some of those little waffle things you balance on your cup to make the caramel melt. They have them on the Continent, I think, though I'm not sure if they have them in Hungary? I can get something else if you prefer?'

Lena took the coffee and sipped at it. Cartwright was wearing corduroy trousers with a padded jacket over a crumpled blue jumper that matched his eyes. Without his uniform bulking him up, she noticed his shoulders were naturally broad. His silky hair fell a little in his eyes. She hadn't noticed its colour before, but it was like sand, still damp from the caresses of the sea. She felt unnerved. 'Where is your uniform?' she barked. It came out more aggressively than she had intended.

'Sorry,' he said, opening the waffle packet and offering one to her. 'I thought it might be better to go inconspicuously at first so we can ask a few casual questions without arousing suspicion. It's amazing how much people clam up when you're in uniform.' Cartwright smiled. 'Plus it's my day off,' he confessed. 'I haven't really been given enough time to do this justice in my regular hours.'

Lena took a waffle, admiring his work ethic. Tomek never offered to drive her anywhere in his taxi on his frequent days off; he was always letting her get the bus. Even when it was raining.

'Faisal is over there,' she told him, pulling herself together. 'The sleazy man with a goatee who is dancing a little as he hands out the papers.' She took a bite of the waffle. It was chewier than she had expected and a crumb escaped on to her lip. She wiped at it quickly. 'Shall we go and talk to him?'

'In a moment. I've got something to show you.' Cartwright produced an expensive-looking laptop from his briefcase and opened it up, shifting his chair closer to Lena so that they could both see the screen. It sprang into action. 'I spent last night making a matrix,' he said. 'It's got all the suspects on it and I've put a column for motive, means and opportunity against each.' Lena peered at it curiously. 'Then I've percentage weighted it according to how likely they are based on statistical analysis, and sorted by value. See? I've colour-coded Faisal red, because he's our most likely suspect and therefore top priority.'

'This is how police do it?' said Lena. She couldn't quite imagine Gullins, or even DS Wilson, poring over such a spreadsheet.

'Not yet,' said Cartwright with a smile. 'One day, hopefully.'

Lena shrugged. 'So why Faisal?'

'I'm pleased you asked that,' replied Cartwright. 'I've been looking at the statistics and built it into this matrix of my own invention. Women are much more likely to be murdered by their lover, or their ex-lover – fifty-one per cent of the time, according to the last thorough survey a few years ago. Whereas with men, it's most likely that an acquaintance will be responsible. Thirty-nine per cent of men are murdered by a friend or acquaintance. Stranger murders are actually very rare.'

'And Tracy?'

'Faisal's girlfriend? You'll see she's in yellow – I won't bore you with the mathematics of how I arrived at that. She's not a particularly likely candidate, although I think her odds will increase if Faisal was the father of Timea's unborn baby and she was aware of that. It will be clearer soon – I'm building some software to help visualise the links between Timea and all the other suspects.'

Lena thought of the map she had made, a little embarrassed. It was lining the bedroom floor. Tomek had got a Post-it note stuck to his foot and almost eliminated Margery from the investigation. When he complained about the paper everywhere, Lena had threatened to add him to the map. Later today she'd treat herself to a corkboard and some pins to keep it all together. She'd enjoy sticking a pin through Faisal's grinning face.

'I do not know if he was the father or not,' she said. 'Faisal and Timea broke up, maybe six months ago.' Lena couldn't suppress a small smile at this. That had been a good day. 'But it is possible, I guess, that she went back to him. She might not have told me because I did not approve of him.' She thought for a moment. 'Timea and he saw each other that morning. They didn't speak though. And when I asked him, he said she had a new boyfriend.'

'We'll need to add that boyfriend to the list, if he exists. Did she really never mention him to you?'

'No. But she did not tell me about the baby either.' Lena looked at her shoe. Timea had told her less than she thought. 'Anyway,' she said, 'we must go and talk to Faisal.' She started to get up.

'Let's plan what we're going to say first,' said Cartwright. He produced a printed sheet from his bag and handed it to Lena. 'I've drafted some questions here.'

Lena looked at the paper. The questions covered both sides of the paper, single spaced, ten point.

'You are joking,' she said, hopefully. 'You said a few *casual* questions.'

'I need this to get all the inputs for my formulae. At the moment there are too many variable data points. And I'm sure you can make them sound casual when you ask. It's all in the tone of voice.'

'You want me to do it?' she said. 'Faisal is not my biggest fan.' She watched Faisal for a moment. He was far more interested in giving his papers to the women than to the men. No wonder Tracy was crazy jealous. She scanned the crowd for Tracy but couldn't see her. She must have let Faisal out alone for once.

She caught a glimpse of a figure she recognised and for a moment the familiarity made her think it was a friend. She scanned her memory and realised.

Lena pulled Cartwright close to her and whispered. 'It's him – the thief! Remember? He is the one that stole the handbag, on the day Timea disappeared.'

'Are you sure? Is that definitely him?' said Cartwright, his breath warm on her ear.

'Arrest him,' said Lena, getting up. 'Quick. I can catch him.'

Cartwright stood up too and looked at the man for a moment. 'Let's sit down again,' he said, getting his phone from his pocket. 'I'll take a photo of him and we'll observe his behaviour.'

'You are not going to arrest him?' said Lena, incredulous. 'He is a thief.'

'He's most likely part of the new criminal gang in town, but if he's working the streets like this he'll be very low down in the pecking order. It isn't worth derailing our investigations for,' he said. 'If we arrest him they'll put someone else in his spot tomorrow and he'll be in an even worse state than he is now, poor man. And I'll end up spending all day filling in forms instead of being able to investigate with you.' He smiled at Lena. 'But if we could get higher up the food chain, that would be a completely different thing. They are the ones exploiting immigrants like our man over there.' He snapped a few shots of the man discreetly before putting his phone back in his pocket and turning to Lena. 'Besides, today we're investigating a possible murder.'

Lena sat down, not sure whether to feel pleased or disappointed. She sipped the hot coffee. The cappuccino just tasted like hot milk, much weaker than the espressos she was used to. Coffee for adults in the UK was like what her mother fed her when she was a toddler.

They both stared over the road. Faisal continued to hand out papers; the thief leaned against the station wall.

'So how long have you been here?' said Cartwright, without changing his gaze. 'In this country, I mean?'

'Two years,' said Lena. 'Timea and I came together. I left the village and moved to Debrecen as soon as I could. Timea joined me a few years later when she finished school. But even with both of us in office jobs, after we paid the bills each month there was never any money left. When we came here we started cleaning to earn some money while we improved our English, and then we planned to get better jobs. Timea wanted to work with children. A teaching assistant in a primary school.' Lena paused, thinking about the wasted dreams. She wished she had left Timea back in Hungary now. It seemed strange to think, but she would have been better off in Debrecen than in London. Alive, at least.

'And you?' said Cartwright. 'What do you want to do?'

'I have not decided yet,' said Lena. 'I like cleaning. Perhaps my own agency, one day. Perhaps I try something different.' She looked back at Cartwright. 'How long have you been a policeman?'

'It's been a year and a half now since I joined the force,' he said. 'I still feel like I'm everybody's dogsbody.' He smiled again. 'It's what I wanted, though, something practical after I'd finished all those degrees, otherwise I would have disappeared into a world of numbers and professors and being no use to anyone. Joining the police, coming to London. That was my way, I suppose, of getting away from my village. Of course my village was only in Oxfordshire, so I haven't travelled as far as you.'

Lena smiled at him, then her attention wandered. 'The thief, he is talking to Faisal.'

It was a glance between the two men; a couple of words exchanged. The man reached into the depths of his oversized black jacket and pulled out a package. He handed it to Faisal and sauntered away. Faisal looked around and then put it in his bag. He looked around some more and put the papers he was holding in a pile on top of the *Metro* dispenser. With one more look, he left, walking briskly towards the junction with City Road.

'So it looks as if Faisal's involved with this man. And this man is a thief and probably part of the new criminal gang,' said Cartwright. 'I wonder what they're up to.'

'He is paid to be there for another hour,' said Lena.

'It's a good thing we got those drinks to go,' said Cartwright. 'Let's follow him.'

They crossed the road at the lights to Angel Station. It was crowded as always this time of day, with commuters switching between tubes and buses on their daily pilgrimage to the office. They followed the men down City Road towards central London. Lena felt a bit uncomfortable. Although they were following Faisal, she got the feeling again that they were being followed too. She blinked it away as they passed a tiny park the size of a roundabout and an Italian deli before Faisal ducked down a side road. Cartwright and Lena hid behind a phone booth that – from the smell – seemed to have reinvented itself as a urinal.

Lena peered around. Faisal was putting something through the letterbox of one of the houses. 'Paper round?' she said to Cartwright, doubtfully.

'I don't think that was a paper,' he replied. 'Let's see where he goes next. I'll go first in case he spots you.' Faisal continued along the road and they followed, keeping a little distance behind.

'Oi!' Lena spun round to see Tracy hissing at her. 'Why are you following my man?' Lena looked round, but Cartwright had vanished.

'I have a client here,' said Lena innocently. 'Is Faisal here too?'

'You were following him. I saw you.'

Lena looked at the small angry woman in front of her and decided to see what she could find out.

'You know Timea was pregnant when she died?' said Lena.

'What?' Tracy took a step back. Lena tried to work out if it was genuine surprise. She thought so.

'Do you think it could be Faisal's?' she asked gently.

Tracy stepped forwards again, full of aggression. Lena could see the dandruff in the dark roots of Tracy's tightly ponytailed hair. She could smell her hairspray and for a second she thought she felt Tracy's eyelashes stroke her chin as she blinked.

'Faisal is with me,' said Tracy, tilting her head upwards, right into Lena's face. 'And I give him plenty. What would he want with your friend?' Tracy spat on the pavement to emphasise her point. 'That cheap slut.'

Lena's hand made contact with Tracy's cheekbone before she even realised how angry she was. Tracy paused in shock for a moment, processing what had happened. Then she charged towards Lena, grabbing her around the stomach in what seemed to be an attempt to wrestle her to the pavement. Lena jabbed her elbow at Tracy's ear and pulled her head back by her ponytail.

'Look at you two,' said Faisal, attracted by the commotion. He prised them apart. 'Fighting like a couple of cats with no fur.' Lena looked at him, releasing Tracy's ponytail. Cats with no fur.

'I'm sorry, ladies, but there's only one of me,' he said. 'You'll have to share.'

'Do not flatter yourself,' said Lena, regaining her composure and stepping back. She tried to think for a moment of Cartwright's list of questions, but couldn't remember a single one. It wasn't as if now was a time for a cosy chat, anyway, at least not with Tracy standing there, looking like she was ready for round two. 'I have better things to do,' she said, turning away.

Behind her, she could hear Tracy berating Faisal. 'Months ago you promised me it was over with Timea.' Lena left them to it. Glancing at her watch, she realised she was exhausted already and the day had barely begun. She had to fit in the cleaning she had missed yesterday, then start today's jobs. If she didn't hurry up, she would still be working when clients arrived home. The clients who were at work all day didn't like to see her. She knew too much about the mess they left behind.

CHAPTER 11

'I thought this country was meant to be rich,' said Greta. Lena's mother's loud Hungarian voice was attracting the attention of fellow passengers. 'Where's the Mercedes?'

'Everyone takes the tube here,' said Lena. 'We're on the Piccadilly line.' Lena looked around the tube carriage, thankfully not too full on a Friday lunchtime. A woman had been steadily glaring at them, but dropped her eyes when she caught Lena's. Lena was glad the commuters couldn't understand what her mother was saying. She dreaded the moment her mother burst into the broken English she was so proud of.

'You could have picked me up by car at least. Doesn't that boyfriend of yours drive a taxi?'

'This is quicker. And Laszlo likes it.' Laszlo had his hands and face pressed to the window, a trail of condensation, or perhaps spit, running down the pane. Lena had her suspicions that he'd been licking the glass. He had barely said a word.

Greta wrapped her short arms around Laszlo's neck, prising him away from the window. He resisted, like a mussel reluctant to leave its rock. 'Poor little soldier,' she said, covering his face with kisses. 'We are all poor soldiers without Timea.' She looked at Lena, serious for a moment. 'She was like a daughter to me, a sister to you,' Lena could see the beginnings of tears in her mother's eyes. 'But we will pull through this for the boy,' she said, wiping her eyes. 'We will be brave.' She turned her attentions back to Lazslo. 'Would you like a sandwich, my brave hero?'

Laszlo shrugged off her hug and his face went back to the window.

Greta took this as a yes and began rummaging through her bag. Lena's lap was soon filled with squashed cheese spread and paprika sandwiches wrapped in cellophane, a sad-looking orange that had seen better days and a well-travelled carton of juice she must have smuggled through customs. It was threatening to spring a leak at its next touch. Lena saw a glimpse of what she took for amusement in the eye of the lady next to her.

'The price of sandwiches here,' said Greta, trying unsuccessfully to prise one into Laszlo's glass-pressed hand. 'No wonder you can't afford a nice car. I went in a shop in the airport while I was waiting for you. A small fortune for a tiny sandwich. And not even any paprika! It's a good thing I made these at home.'

'He's not hungry,' said Lena.

'Of course he is,' said Greta, unwrapping the sandwich and taking a large bite herself. 'He's a growing boy,' she said, spraying Lena with crumbs of half-chewed sandwich. 'You don't lose your appetite when your mother dies. You'll find that out one day. I'm not immortal, you know.' She devoured the rest of the sandwich. 'Want some juice?'

'I'm fine,' said Lena, watching her mother spurt a drop of the purple juice on to her neighbour's knee. 'Be careful with that. You're making a mess.'

'Uncle Attila wanted to come too, you know. But he's got that infection back. Hurts when he pees. It's swollen right from the tip to the base. The size of a marrow now, he tells me.'

'How's Istvan's mum?' said Lena, keen to change the subject.

'Dora is devastated. Almost as devastated as me. She always loved Timea. Istvan's upset too, she told me. They were pretty friendly, you remember. Not like you and him, but close.'

'I know.'

'I can't believe it. You two both in London and never meeting. Crazy.'

'It's a big city.'

'I thought you'd marry him, you know. Then you would have had a Mercedes. He makes a fortune – his mother told me he was paid six figures this year. Six!' Greta held up six fingers, dropping the juice on the floor as she did so. 'Why didn't you?'

Lena bent to pick up the carton. 'So the size of a marrow?' she said. 'That must hurt.'

'You can't go out,' hissed Tomek. 'You can't leave me with her.' They were standing in the hallway as Lena tried to put on her coat. Tomek snatched it from her.

'She likes you,' Lena said. 'And I have to go to work. I will lose the job if I don't go.'

'You'll lose me if you do,' he said, dramatically. He dangled the coat above her head.

Lena gave him a little pinch on the arm. He yelped and released the coat. She leaned forwards and planted a kiss on his cheek. 'Thank you for this.'

He kissed her back on the lips. 'At least she cooks,' he said.

'She cooks when she is upset. When my dad left she baked enough *kifli* for everyone in the village. This time it is sandwiches.'

'I love sandwiches,' said Tomek.

'Look after Laszlo,' said Lena, putting on her coat.

'Of course.'

Cartwright was waiting in his car. It was his own, not the police vehicle she was expecting. And definitely not a Mercedes. 'Sorry,' she said, clambering in. 'Family.'

'It's a difficult time.'

'It is always a difficult time with my mother.'

108

'And mine.' He smiled at her.

'Are you sure you want to come with me to my work?' Lena looked at Cartwright doubtfully.

'Of course,' he said with a smile. 'We need to understand more about all of Timea's clients so that we can populate them in the matrix. What I have at the moment is terribly rudimentary. Once we have more information, we'll know where to focus next. It's important to know as much about Timea as we can. Victimology.'

She shifted in her seat. Cartwright's car was old and had an intensely enginey smell to it, of oil and exhaust. She wondered vaguely what car Istvan drove. It had been years since she'd seen him in the flesh. Just his image on the television, looking as smug as always. But perhaps he would come to the funeral – her mother certainly thought so.

'Would you mind if I came in with you?' Cartwright asked.

'Only if she is not at home.'

'I could pretend to be your assistant. I'm pretty handy in Marigolds.'

Lena laughed. 'You look too British,' she said. 'You would not pass for an immigrant.'

'I have an Estonian grandmother,' Cartwright offered.

'Really?' said Lena, looking at him doubtfully.

'She fled Estonia to escape the Soviets in the Second World War.'

'So I am not the only one with immigrant blood in this car,' Lena smiled at him. 'I would not guess.'

'An advantageous marriage and a couple of generations of public school gets rid of an ethnic heritage surprisingly quickly,' said Cartwright. 'We're here.'

'I will see if she is home.'

Cartwright's face became more serious. 'You are concerned that this client may be a victim of domestic violence?'

'Her name is Margery. I think so. Her face was all bruised and she would not tell me why.'

'Surely there could be another explanation for the bruises?' said Cartwright.

'You have not seen them like I have,' insisted Lena. 'It is clear to me what has happened.'

'Fifty percent of injuries due to domestic abuse are on the face,' admitted Cartwright. 'But that is not enough to jump to conclusions. Could you see any defensive marks on her arms?'

'They are probably there,' said Lena. 'But I could only see her face.'

'Did she seem depressed or scared?'

'She was in a terrible mood.' Lena thought for a moment. 'She is in hiding because she does not want anyone to know what happened,' she said. 'Perhaps Timea was the only person who did know. And now she is gone.'

'If that is what happened, is there any chance . . . Timea could have used what she knew? To get money. For her son back home, of course?'

'No. Not Timea.'

'It would give the husband a motive, Margery too, for wanting Timea out of the picture. If domestic abuse is present, I think we should consider it. And blackmail is more common in this country than people think. Did you know the word has its origins in the English–Scottish borders, back when there were rampaging hordes?'

'Timea would not blackmail.'

'OK. In that case see what you can find out without making Margery suspicious. I'd suggest you don't tell Margery about what has happened to Timea; she could get frightened and close up, especially if she's on edge anyway. And we mustn't rule out that she could be involved in Timea's disappearance too. Just try to find out a bit more about what has happened. There might be another explanation we should explore.' He looked down for a moment, then back at Lena. 'Domestic violence is a lot more common than people think,' he said. 'One in four women and one in six men. Twenty-two per cent of all violent incidents are domestic. If this is the case with Margery, we need to help her, whether there is a connection to Timea or not.' His radio began making noises. 'Sorry Lena,' he said, fiddling with it. 'That's duty calling. I won't be able to come in with you after all.'

Lena clambered out of the car. She approached the house and rang the bell, looking back at Cartwright driving away. It was a pity he couldn't stay. She laughed out loud at the thought of him in Marigolds.

The door swung open to reveal Margery, wearing enormous movie-star sunglasses and foundation that looked as if it had been applied with a trowel.

'What's so funny?' said Margery, her hand going up to her face.

'Nothing,' said Lena. 'Timea is still sick. I clean today. Did the agency not call you?' She studied Margery's face for a reaction to Timea's name. With her eyes and skin covered, it was hard to tell what Margery was thinking.

'Still? I'd prefer her, of course, but you can come in. The living room is filthy,' Margery said, as if it was Lena, not her, who had stopped her from cleaning that room last time. Margery stood to one side allowing Lena to pass. 'Start in the kitchen. Do everywhere but the bedroom today. I need to rest later.'

Margery disappeared into the living room and Lena began her work in the kitchen. There were several bowls that seemed to contain glue. Lena poked at the sticky substance, wondering if it was some sort of clue. Then she realised that it was muesli and yogurt which, left for several days, had formed a sticky paste. She ran the bowls under the hot tap to desolidify the mixture before placing them in the dishwasher. Wiping the counter, she found a multitude of tiny black specks that looked suspiciously like cockroach droppings. No wonder, with the state the kitchen was in. Then she discovered the source – an open bag of tiny black pellets labelled 'chia seeds'.

Cleaning a kitchen was satisfying, especially one as dirty as this. But she was learning nothing from the plates, except what they'd eaten for breakfast over the past week. Chia seeds and muesli mainly, it seemed. Some toast. Eggs. They couldn't tell her what had happened to Timea. There was no sign of paracetamol or diazepam. Not that that would even be particularly incriminating. She needed Margery to tell her what had really been going on.

She finished the kitchen as quickly as she could. She gave the stove a quick wipe instead of a deep scrub, and left the oven door unopened. Whatever was there this week could fester, she thought. She felt a pang of guilt but pushed it aside.

Margery was watching television in the living room when Lena entered.

'Look at her,' Margery said to her, pointing at the television screen, where a pretty girl was predicting rain with a smile that revealed her perfect teeth. 'She's practically a child. I doubt she's even done a degree in meteorology.'

'She looks like she is Timea's age,' said Lena. 'Starting out.'

'Before life beats you down,' said Margery. 'She'll learn that soon.'

Lena began to dust as Margery changed the channel. The room was long but narrow, with sofas and a television near the bay window and a dining area overlooking the garden. It was painted a sky-blue colour, except for the wall where the fireplace had once been, which was covered in wallpaper, a painted tree stretching its branches up the chimney breast as if it wanted to escape the house. Lena had a few clients with variations on that decorating theme: sometimes trees with birds, sometimes butterflies, sometimes just foliage.

She looked back to Margery who was curled up on the beige velvet sofa, clutching a carton of coconut water and watching the television intently through her sunglasses. She looked like an over-grown child in dressing-up clothes. It was rare for clients to watch television while she worked. Often they would pretend to be busy if they were there while she was cleaning. She remembered when Mrs Ives worked from home. Tapping away at her laptop, looking important. But when Lena had caught a glimpse of the screen, she'd realised it was a game of Solitaire.

'Are you often in during the day?' Lena asked, wondering how to turn the conversation about cleaning and weathergirls into one about abusive husbands and murderers.

Margery looked at her. 'No, of course not. It's only temporary that I'm here at all. I can't let people see me like this – I've my reputation to think of.'

'Don't you think you should tell someone?' Lena looked at the woman. She couldn't fathom how this woman could tolerate what was happening to her. Why she wouldn't fight back.

'It's none of their business,' said Margery, putting her hand to her face to adjust her glasses. 'It's private.'

'Did you tell Timea?' asked Lena, continuing to dust and keep-ing her eyes away from Margery.

'I thought I could trust her. She's such a pretty girl.' Margery began inspecting her red polished fingernails. 'I always liked her.'

'Did Timea ever meet your husband?'

'Why would she?' Margery turned off the television, her atten-tion finally drawn from her nails. 'Do you know something? Did she say something about him?'

'Could I speak to your husband?' Lena put down the duster and turned to face Margery.

'Of course not. Don't be ridiculous.'

'You can get help.' Lena knelt down in front of Margery so they shared an eye level. She reached out and touched her hand.

'What?' said Margery, snapping her hand away.

'With the problems. I know someone who can help.'

'I don't have problems,' said Margery, her hand going to her face. 'It will settle down, it just needs time. And I don't like you pestering me about it, making these insinuations.' Margery was on her feet, and began to shoo Lena out like a dog. 'I don't want you here.'

'You need help,' persisted Lena.

'I don't know what you are talking about. Now get out. I don't need some little Polish girl insulting me in my own house.'

Lena barely had time to grab her coat as Margery pushed her through the door. 'I am Hungarian,' she muttered.

'Don't come back,' said Margery. 'I'll find a new cleaner. One who can mind her own business.'

CHAPTER 12

'How you get so fat?' Greta asked Tomek, in her best English. 'What she feed you?'

'I have big bones,' said Tomek, giving Lena a pat on her knee. 'Common in Poland.'

'You not buy sandwiches?' said Greta, suspiciously. 'Between meals?'

'At London prices? Of course not,' said Tomek. Lena squeezed his hand, impressed at how well he was coping with the matriarch ordeal.

'I never get Lena fat,' said Greta. 'Not even when her no-good-father run away. Hard for her to find husband so thin.'

'Tomek,' said Lena, taking pity on him. 'Maybe take Laszlo for a walk?'

'How about it, little man?' said Tomek, getting up. 'I can introduce you to the greatest English cuisine. The fry-up. Perfect man-fuel for a Saturday morning.'

Laszlo nodded in agreement.

'Get your coat on,' Tomek told him. 'It's cold out.'

Lena followed him into the hallway while her mother fussed over the location of Laszlo's gloves. 'Thank you,' she said, touching Tomek's arm. 'He has really taken to you.'

'Maybe if you were here more he'd take to you too.' Tomek wrapped a scarf around his neck.

'I have to work,' said Lena, straightening his scarf. 'I have Timea's clients and my own. You know that.'

'Give hers up,' said Tomek, struggling to do up his coat buttons around his ample belly. 'Two jobs is too much for you. I am working too. We can do without the extra money.'

'It is not just the money,' said Lena, picking some fluff from Tomek's jacket. 'I am finding things out.'

'You and Sherlock?' He stepped back. Lena left his jacket alone.

'Ready,' said Laszlo, emerging into the hallway.

'Wait,' said Greta, from the kitchen. 'I make sandwiches.'

'Do not be silly, Mama,' said Lena. 'They are going out to eat.'

'They might need,' said Greta. 'Growing boys.'

'Mama. Do not make sandwiches.' Lena opened the door for them. 'Tomek, just go,' she said.

'Ham please,' said Tomek, ignoring the open door.

Greta emerged from the kitchen in no time with a large cellophane-wrapped bundle. 'You boys enjoy. I make chicken soup with *csiga* noodles for dinner. Good for making grandchildren.'

Lena closed the door behind them and went back into the flat. She felt like giving it a therapeutic clean, but her mother had got up early and done it all. She could hear her now, muttering something to herself as she clacked plates around in the kitchen. The whole flat smelled of chicken. Everything was put back slightly in the wrong place, and the big brown sofa was at a jaunty angle in the room. She sat down on it and waited for her mother to start berating her about something. At least Lena could go out soon; Cartwright was meeting her later at Yasemin's flat to have a snoop around. She decided to sneak some ham from the fridge for the cat. Its skin looked quite a lot like ham, poor little thing. She wondered what Cartwright would make of it.

Her thoughts were interrupted by the sound of the intercom. Her mother reached it before she had even managed to get up. 'Hello, hello,' she said, jabbing at the buttons. 'Why you call?'

'Find out who it is, don't just let them in,' said Lena, reverting to Hungarian.

'What?' said her mother, pressing the button that opened the door. 'Crazy phones in this country. Modern but no good.'

'I've told you. It's not a phone. It's the intercom. Probably someone delivering junk mail,' said Lena. Was that what Faisal had been up to?

'Perhaps it was Istvan's mama,' said Greta. 'Calling to see what car you drive.'

The doorbell rang. Lena jumped up and hurried over to it first. She didn't want her mother inviting in a baffled postman for sandwiches. She opened the door and gasped.

The man in front of her was extremely attractive. He smiled perfect teeth at her and ran his fingers through his shiny black hair.

'Hello Lena,' he said, leaning forward to kiss her cheek, as though it was the most natural thing in the world. His stubble lightly grazed her face. 'You haven't forgotten me?'

'Istvan!' she said. That was all she could manage. She stepped backwards and felt heat rising in her cheeks, as though she'd leaned into an oven.

Her mother pushed past her, shoving her unceremoniously into the coats that hung on hooks on the wall. 'About time!' she said, launching into Hungarian and giving Istvan a wet kiss on each cheek before pushing him away from her to get a proper look at him. 'Handsome but bad,' she declared. 'You haven't been back to the village, your poor mother misses you. Where's your wife and why no children? We watch your show, you know, but we are two seasons behind back in Hungary. Who murdered Melinda? Was it Derek? I think it is Derek. You must have heard about my poor darling Timea.'

'Yes.'

'It's dangerous here in London. You're better-looking than you

117

used to be. Lost that puppy fat. Oh, if only Timea were here to see you. Why are you just standing there? Come in.'

'What are you doing here?' asked Lena, stepping in front of him to block his path into the flat. She'd regained her composure while her mother blathered.

'You haven't changed,' he said, with a smile. Lena looked at his teeth again. They definitely hadn't been that straight, or that white, when he lived in the village. 'You're still so cynical. It is lovely to see you again.'

'Get out of the way, Lena, and let Istvan in!' said Greta, giving her another shove. Istvan took the opportunity to step past her into the hallway.

'It wasn't Derek,' said Istvan, with relish. 'It was his evil twin. Sebastian.' He strode into the living room and stopped dead. 'Oh,' he said. 'It's cosier than I thought, very . . . retro decor.'

'Sit down,' said Lena. 'Mama, I'm sure Istvan would like a sandwich and a cup of coffee.' Greta disappeared into the kitchen. 'Evil twin!' said Greta, chuckling as she left. 'Whatever next?'

Istvan perched on the edge of the sofa, as if he was worried it would dirty his trousers. 'I knew you were in London,' he said. 'But I didn't know you lived like this. You should have got in touch.'

'We aren't all movie stars,' said Lena. 'But I'm fine.'

'I'm not exactly a movie star,' said Istvan, his fingers on his hair again. 'I've only starred in one film, an independent, arty production. Plus some minor parts, of course, in the States. That was before I got my television show.' He leaned in. She could smell his aftershave. Hugo Boss, like her client on Liverpool Road wore. 'I was so sorry to hear about Timea. You two were close, weren't you? She was always such a sweet girl.'

Lena couldn't believe the dismissive tone he used. They had all been like one family. Did he think she had forgotten?

He carried on. 'We had fun, the three of us, back when we were kids.'

'Before you left,' she reminded him.

'I heard that they think it might be suicide. I can hardly believe she would do such a thing.' He paused. 'You haven't found a note? A reason?'

'No,' said Lena. 'She drowned.' She looked into Istvan's eyes and could tell he understood. He broke eye contact and looked at his shoes.

Greta came back into the room with a plate piled high with sandwiches. Lena wondered how she made so many so fast. Or did she keep a constant stock in reserve?

'I can't get the ingredients like back in the village,' said Greta. 'Or I'd make you all a goulash. Lena barely has a frying pan. I don't know how Tomek got so fat living with her. Does your wife cook? Your mother is desperate to meet her. When will you bring her home?'

'The village isn't really Catherine's type of place,' he said. 'We holiday in the Caribbean, mainly. Mustique is our favourite island. And of course Catherine needs to be at Cannes every year; she needs to be seen whether or not she's got a movie showing. Connections, you know. Networking.'

The women looked at him blankly.

'I was sorry to hear about Timea,' he began again. 'I had no idea things were so tough for her here.' He looked around the room. 'For you both.'

'We are fine,' said Lena defensively, before she realised that Timea wasn't. Not at all. 'We were fine. We were happy, living here.'

'And where is Laszlo?' Istvan's voice was casual. 'My mother told me he is a very good boy. And handsome.'

'He's out,' said Lena. 'Getting a break from the poverty.'

'He is being a brave hero,' said Greta. 'But it is so sad for him. An orphan.'

'Listen, I want to help you,' said Istvan. 'Help the poor boy.'

Lena looked at him suspiciously. He was wearing expensively pointed shoes and white trousers, with his cream linen shirt unbuttoned so she could see the hairs on his muscular chest. He was tanned, with his black hair voluminous and his green eyes looking earnestly into her own.

'How?' she said.

'You clearly need money. Let me give you some. Television work doesn't pay so badly, you know.'

'Thank you!' said Greta. 'Always such a good boy.'

'No,' said Lena. 'We need nothing from you.'

'I want to see Laszlo,' he persisted. 'You must let me help. We're from the same place, after all. And I've done pretty well.'

'We're fine,' said Lena.

'If he wants to help, let him,' said Greta. 'Of course he does. I remember when you two used to run around naked in the village park when you were just five years old.'

'I told you we don't need his help. I will provide for Laszlo. Goodbye Istvan.'

He stood up, brushing the backs of his trousers. 'I want to come to the funeral,' he said. 'To pay my respects.'

Lena looked at him. He was smiling, but she could see pleading in his eyes. He desperately wanted to be there. 'OK,' she said.

'You'll bring your wife?' said Greta.

'It's a busy time for her. A new project with Film Four. They are partnering with the Icelandic Film Council. Very exciting.'

'The funeral is on Monday,' said Lena.

Istvan got up to leave.

'Thank you,' he said. 'I'll bring daisies.'

'Your old friend Istvan just turned up, out of the blue?' Cartwright said, as he picked up an empty pizza box and shoved it into a black bin bag. They were cleaning Yasemin's modern flat, which would have been so lovely were it not for the food remains. It was as disgusting as last time.

'He must have found out where we live from my mother,' said Lena. 'She tells everyone everything.' She added a half-eaten plastic tub of something glutinous that had once been sweet and sour to the bag. 'He was friends with us back home, before he left to make his fortune. He always thought his looks were wasted in the village.'

'Was he ever in a relationship with Timea?'

Lena looked up sharply. 'No. We were friends only. The three of us.'

'He's very dashing-looking,' said Cartwright. 'In his show.'

'I have not seen it,' lied Lena, wiping up the dregs of some soy sauce that had leaked out of a little packet with a rogue serviette.

'I think we should add him into our suspect matrix,' said Cartwright decisively. 'I'm not sure how to calculate his probability, but it does seem strange he would want to give Laszlo money. Even if he is rich, it is very rare to just offer money to an old friend's son. Is generosity a Hungarian trait?'

Lena laughed at him. 'You have not met many Hungarians.'

'You are the first,' admitted Cartwright. 'Was it a lot of money?'

'He did not say. He was always generous, for a Hungarian.' She thought back to the time he had bought her that bracelet. A cheap plastic thing, but he had saved for it. She still had it, hidden at the back of her closet. 'But we do not want his charity money.'

'Did you part on bad terms?'

'He just left. Wanted a better life. Not with us.' Lena felt the hurt of it welling back up from all those years ago. Cartwright was watching her.

'This flat is a proper pigsty,' he said with a sniff. 'Have you met the occupant?'

'No, but I know what she is like,' said Lena. 'I can tell from her flat.'

'Oh you can, can you?' teased Cartwright. 'Please go on. What conclusions do you draw from the evidence before you?' Cartwright poked a used napkin disdainfully with his foot.

'You first. You are the policeman.'

Cartwright looked around, getting into the game. 'I'm officially off-duty today, but OK. He is obviously a bit of a slob. That hardly requires any deduction.'

'He?' said Lena.

'Clearly. And he must be overweight. Just take a look at what he eats.'

'Go on,' said Lena.

'He's likely divorced,' said Cartwright, gesturing to the pizza box. He seemed to enjoy the freedom to conjecture. 'His wife used to take care of him, then he got comfortable and maybe something happened with a female colleague and his wife got fed up. She took the kids and the pile in Kent, and he rented this little apartment and eats takeaway.' Cartwright paused, looking pleased with himself. 'What do you think?'

'It is a woman,' said Lena. 'Yasemin Avci. It says that on her mailbox downstairs, so we won't count that. She is thin and short. With long dark hair. That is easy.'

'You've seen a photograph,' objected Cartwright. 'That's cheating.'

'There are no photographs. That is strange. But I have seen her hairbrush, full of long dark hairs. Her clothes are size eight. The trousers have been shortened. She always wears high heels.'

'I'm impressed,' said Cartwright. 'Please continue.'

'She does not have a normal job, in an office.'

'How can you tell that?'

'People who work in offices want you to come during the week. We are here on a Saturday. She must be working today. And she has lived all over the world,' continued Lena. 'She probably has a father who is an entrepreneur. Powerful. She is an only child and she is single. Secretive. Unsentimental. And money-driven. I think she will do a lot for money. Anything.'

Cartwright laughed. 'And how do you work that out?'

'You can tell a lot about people from what they keep in their houses,' said Lena. 'I will teach you one day. You can impress your police friends.'

'You've met Gullins. I wouldn't call him a friend, exactly.'

'You can impress your enemies then,' said Lena. 'Look, it is the cat I told you about. Bald as a monk!' The cat emerged from the bedroom and sidled up to Lena, jumping up to rub his head as high on her leg as he could manage. She bent down to scoop him into her arms and turned to Cartwright. 'Stroke him. His skin feels nice. Like a bald man's head.'

'I'm not really a cat person,' replied Cartwright, recoiling. 'I have a goldfish instead. He's called Pythagoras. He's remarkably intelligent, for a fish. I'm quite convinced he recognises me when I feed him.'

'It is odd that, when I argued with Tracy a few days ago, Faisal should say we were fighting like cats with no fur,' said Lena, thoughtfully. 'They are not common creatures.' Lena bent to give the cat a small kiss on its bald skin. It began to purr. 'I think there is something suspicious with this lady too. Perhaps she deserves a special place on your list. No photos. No pictures, ornaments, nothing. Just perfectly ironed suits. Nothing in the medicine cabinet, not even paracetamol. And she does not feed her cat enough.'

'Is that your definition of a murderer?' said Cartwright with a laugh, still keeping his distance from Lena and the animal.

'I do not think she is a good person.' Lena set the cat down and went to fetch the ham from her bag. 'And I think she hides things.' The door swung open.

A thin short woman with long dark hair stood in front of her.

'What are you doing in my flat?' she said, reaching in her hand-bag for something. Probably pepper spray.

Lena had been mistaken for a burglar many times. How did these people think she cleaned their houses? By telepathy?

'I am your cleaner,' she said, with a deferential nod. 'You must be Yasemin.'

'OK,' said Yasemin pushing past her. 'Finish up.'

'I bring some ham for your cat,' said Lena. 'Can I feed?'

Yasemin turned to look at Lena. 'Kaplan doesn't eat ham,' she said. 'I'm home now. If you can't finish in the next ten minutes, come back tomorrow.' She spotted Cartwright, who was busy pretending to dust the mantelpiece. 'Who is that?'

Cartwright opened his mouth but Lena jumped in. 'He is my brother,' she said. 'No English. Helps me move furniture. To clean behind.'

'Really?' said Yasemin, looking at him. 'He doesn't look like you.'

'Your cat is very unusual,' said Lena. 'But everyone is talking about cats with no fur now. My friend Faisal mentioned them just yesterday, as he made his deliveries.'

'Faisal?'

'Yes, he gives out the newspapers at Angel, just around the corner. I do not think he could afford a cat like that, though. Expensive.'

'I recognise you,' said the woman to Cartwright. 'Why?'

Cartwright did his best impression of looking blank. 'He is just over from Hungary,' Lena said, wishing for a moment Cartwright didn't look quite so quintessentially British. 'You will not know him.'

CHAPTER 13

When Lena returned home, Greta was jigging around the apartment. 'We are rich,' Greta said, waving the cheque in Lena's face. 'I always knew Istvan was a good boy.'

'It's Laszlo's money,' said Lena sternly. 'And I told you not to take it.'

'Of course it is for Laszlo,' said Greta, full of indignation. 'I want nothing for myself. Timea would have been so happy. I am just excited to tell him when he gets back from Lidl with Tomek. I only think of the boy!'

'I'm sorry, Mama,' said Lena, relenting. 'I know you do.'

'I live for him,' said Greta. 'Like I would live for your children.'

'Don't you think it's odd that Istvan would give all that money to a boy he doesn't even know?' said Lena, changing the subject.

Greta tutted. 'That is why he had to come back when you were not here. So suspicious. He is from the village. He is rich. Laszlo is from the village. Laszlo is an orphan. He is poor.'

'But it doesn't make sense.'

'You have been in the city too long,' said Greta. 'Back home, we look after each other. You forget that we used to be a communist country.'

'He didn't give anyone else money.'

'You don't think Laszlo is special? He deserves it.'

125

'But what does Istvan want? It's not like they are related . . .' Lena stopped herself. Her mother continued talking but she couldn't hear a word.

Was it possible?

'You make all good things bad,' said Greta. Lena snapped back to the present as her mother used the cheque to gently slap her arm. 'You don't get that from me. Your father, that rogue. He was the pessimist.'

'Did Istvan leave his address at least?'

'No,' admitted Greta. 'But that is a good idea. I will ring his mother and find out where he lives. We must visit – I will make a *dobos torte*. I bet Istvan hasn't had a proper seven-layer *dobos torte* in years. How many cake pans do you have? None I expect. God knows how my only daughter survives without a cake pan.'

Lena looked thoughtfully at the cheque, which her mother was still waving in the air like the Hungarian flag. Money had always been important to Istvan, as it so often was with people who were poor. And Istvan had been poor, even for the village.

But that was a long time ago. She didn't know Istvan today. She went into Timea's room, so different now, with her mother and Laszlo staying. Most traces of Timea had disappeared, replaced by her mother's industrial-strength bras and greying underwear. She rummaged a little and found that the magazine with Istvan's picture was still there. Also grabbing the framed photo of Timea and Laszlo, she went back to her room.

Taking a pair of scissors, she cut out Istvan's picture from the magazine. His handsome face looked so smug she was tempted to cut his luscious black curls off the top. Instead she retrieved her suspect map, now neatly pinned to the corkboard and hidden in her closet. She pinned Istvan's picture on the middle of the board. Then she lifted the photograph of Laszlo, entwined in Timea's arms, and held it up to Istvan's picture to compare. She sat back and looked. Then she took another pin and stuck it firmly into Istvan's head.

Lena walked up to the door, painted a dark green reminiscent of the leaves of the horse-chestnut trees in the churchyard back home. She knocked and assessed the place while she waited. The house was a large Georgian end-of-terrace overlooking Highbury Fields. Double-fronted, with three floors plus a basement. Windowboxes rested on the sills, in flower even at this unseasonable time of year. Maintained by an overpriced agency, Lena thought. This house was grander than she had expected.

Istvan opened the door. Lena looked down before glancing up at him. She saw his feet: bare, tanned and perfect. The welcoming smile on his face turned to agitation when he saw her.

'You can't come here,' he barked at her in Hungarian. 'Catherine could have been in. The neighbours might see.'

'So what?' said Lena. She pushed past him. He closed the door and followed her to the sitting room. Lena ran her finger along the dado rail as she went. She examined her fingertip. No dust. Lena felt a pang of anger that Istvan had a cleaner.

'I know the truth,' she said, as soon as they arrived in the living room.

'What are you talking about?' Istvan looked at her, puzzled. But she could tell there was guilt in his eyes. She could almost smell it emanating from the shiny dark curls that adorned his beautiful head.

'You and Timea,' she said, pausing to watch the effect these words had on him.

'I don't know what you mean,' he said, his eyes widening in mock innocence.

'For an actor you are a terrible liar,' said Lena. 'I know about the two of you.'

127

'What about us?' said Istvan, looking around the room as if to find his escape route. 'I haven't seen Timea for years.'

'To be more exact, nine years ago you were very close. You saw a lot of her then, didn't you Istvan?'

'What?' said Istvan. 'Maybe, I don't remember.' He scratched his eyebrow and she knew he remembered very well.

'You are Laszlo's father,' she said. The words hurt as they came out, as though they were coated in shards of glass. What he and Timea had done. Had hidden from her. 'Don't lie to me, Istvan. You forget that I know you.'

'I'll never forget that,' he said, sinking down on to the sofa and inviting Lena to do the same. 'I'm sorry. But I don't know that it's true. Not for sure.'

Lena ran her hand over the sofa. The plush velvet material felt like the belly of a mole under her fingers. She sat down and looked around. The room was large, divided into two by an empty gateway, like so many of the houses around here. It was painted a colour that another of her clients had called 'duck egg'. The ducks back home laid eggs that were white, but apparently the fancy ones in London laid bluey-green eggs. It had likely been years since Istvan had seen a duck egg, she thought. Unless it was poached over asparagus.

She tried to focus, figuring out what to ask Istvan. He was looking at her with a mournful stare. What did she want to know? When had it started? Were they in love? Had the two of them laughed at her? She forced herself to swallow these questions. What mattered now was Laszlo.

'What do you mean you're not sure?'

Istvan visibly squirmed, like a schoolboy who needed the loo. 'I don't know that I was the father.'

'But you had sex with her?' Lena couldn't look Istvan in the eye when she said this. His betrayal was too much.

'Yes.' Istvan looked down, suddenly fascinated by the swirling patterns in the silk rug.

'And nine months later a baby was born. It doesn't take a genius to work it out.' Lena found her voice was rising.

'She never said. She didn't tell me.' He sounded like a sulky child. 'There's no paternity test.'

'But you know he is yours,' Lena told him, more softly now. 'You must do.'

'Yes,' Istvan admitted. He looked up at her.

'You owe that boy more than five thousand pounds,' she told him. 'You owe him much more than that. He needs a father.'

'I can't do that,' he said. 'My wife can't know. I will give him more money. That will be better for him.'

'More money?' Lena felt her voice rising again.

'I'm doing well,' said Istvan. 'Look at this house. It's a long way from how we used to live.'

'You've got plenty of money, I can see. That's always what you wanted.'

'It is what everyone wants,' said Istvan.

'Laszlo wants parents.' Lena leaned back in the sofa and plucked at a small white feather that was poking through one of the cushions. Hungarian goose down, she thought. Trust Istvan to bring only the most luxurious of his country's exports into this new home of his.

'I would like to meet him,' said Istvan, standing up and walking to the fireplace. It had a wood-burning stove, Lena noticed, even though the house was centrally heated. Cast iron with elaborate Victorian-style carvings. Totally impractical to clean and totally unnecessary. She'd spent hours on Mrs Ives's one, scrubbing the burnt-on ash off the glass window with wet newspapers. 'But I don't see how I can. There's no way I can acknowledge him. It would be a scandal. That would destroy my wife.'

'Don't be ridiculous. No one would care.' Lena scrunched the feather between her fingers, rolling it into a small ball before flicking it to the otherwise spotless floor.

'My wife would.'

'But it all happened before you met her. You have to tell your wife about Laszlo.'

Istvan looked agitated. 'I can't do it. It will be in the papers. What will my wife's friends think?'

'They'll have to get over it. Laszlo is an orphan. He needs you.'

'He has your mother and I'll help. Financially. I have my own money too. He'll be just fine.'

'No.' Lena wasn't prepared to negotiate on this. 'His mother just died. He's not going to be an orphan, not if he doesn't have to be.'

'Lena please. You don't understand.' Istvan put his head in his hands. Shiny strands of jet-black hair stuck out from between his fingers, as though it was trying to make a getaway. 'All of this. I need her.'

'You have to tell your wife,' said Lena. 'I owe it to Timea to give her son a father. If you don't tell Catherine, then I will have to.'

Istvan was silent. 'You have until Monday,' said Lena. 'By the funeral, Laszlo needs his father.'

Lena got up to leave. She paused by Istvan's hunched figure, then reached out to put her hand on his own, still clutching his head. She felt his silky hair, poking out between his fingers, tickling her palm. 'You can meet your son,' she said, more gently. 'He's a good boy. You'll be proud of him.' Istvan looked up, the motion of his head pushing Lena's hand back to his warm nape, coated in soft, downy hair. She left it there for a moment, remembering how much she had loved this neck. She wanted to ask how he could live with himself. Betraying her. Abandoning Timea and the unborn baby all those years ago. Was he afraid of what Lena would do? She pushed those thoughts to the back of her mind.

'The boy needs you,' she said, leaving the room and walking along the corridor. The carpet was soft as moss under her feet, a series of modern abstract paintings were expensive little splashes of colour against the otherwise beige walls.

'Lena,' Istvan called, 'I'm sorry.'

She exited the front door, closing it behind her with a bang. She crossed the road and walked into the park, breathing deeply. She started to walk faster and faster until she was running. She left the path, and felt the mud squish under her feet. The cold air filled her lungs.

When had it happened, Lena wondered. She thought back. Laszlo was eight now, so it must have been almost nine years ago. That would make Istvan twenty-four. He had long since left the village. How had they even been near each other? Then she remembered.

Natasa's wedding.

Lena had been living in Debrecen, working during the day and studying at night. She had been tired and stressed and hadn't wanted to go back for the wedding. Her mother had insisted.

'Your father's sister is going to be there,' Greta had said. 'You know how much I hate Boglarka. She is bringing her daughter Sarika. I need you to be there too or I will murder them both. Remember how she insulted me last Christmas? Saying my *bejgli* were dry? I'll give her dry. Even Istvan is going to come back. His mother has barely heard from him since he went to Budapest, but he will be at the wedding.'

So Lena had agreed to go. She'd felt odd at the prospect of seeing Istvan again. It had been nearly six years, and they had not parted on good terms. She had looked down at herself and sucked in her stomach, wishing she'd not given up running.

Lena had travelled back after work on Friday and gone to her mother's house. She had been going to skip dinner, but ended up eating chicken paprikash with pickled cabbage, mashed potatoes and a chestnut cake for dessert. Timea had come around after dinner and quizzed her about life in Debrecen.

'Come when you finish school,' said Lena. 'You can live with me.'

'I want to come now,' pleaded Timea, then sixteen and impatient.

'It is not long,' replied Lena.

'Have you seen Istvan yet?'

'No,' replied Lena. 'I am not looking forward to it.'

Although it was springtime, there was a chill in the air and pregnant rain clouds threatened the horizon. Lena didn't catch sight of Istvan until after the civil ceremony. They were in the traditional procession to the second ceremony at the church. Timea tugged at her arm. 'There he is,' she hissed. Lena looked. A collection of village girls surrounded Istvan like petals on a daisy. 'Doesn't he look handsome?' said Timea.

Lena had to admit he did. He'd grown into his previously lanky frame, and a sprinkling of stubble gave him a rugged, grown-up air she hadn't seen before. She sucked her stomach in again and went to greet him, Timea close behind.

'How's the acting going, Istvan?' she said, by way of greeting. It came out more sarcastically than she intended.

'Good actually,' said Istvan, leaning forwards to give Lena an awkward kiss on each cheek. 'I've mainly been doing theatre work, which is why you haven't seen me on television yet. But I have a big audition lined up next week. I'll be rich and famous before you know it.'

Timea dived in and hugged him. Istvan looked winded. 'Timea!' he said. 'I didn't even recognise you. You've turned out beautiful.'

He was right. Lena looked enviously at Timea's hourglass figure and delicate features. The girl smiled at the compliment and blushed. 'I've missed you, Istvan,' she said.

Istvan smiled back at her, then looked at Lena. 'Have you missed me too?' he asked.

'I've been too busy,' replied Lena. She instantly regretted saying it. The three stood in silence for a moment.

'There's Natasa,' said Istvan. 'I'll give her my congratulations.' He disappeared into the procession.

Lena felt guilty throughout the church service, and tried to find a moment to apologise to Istvan at the dinner, but he always seemed to be deep in conversation with someone. She consoled herself with goulash, stuffed cabbage, several pieces of wedding cake and plenty of *Tokaji* wine. She ignored Natasa's squeals as people tried to steal her shoes in the traditional wedding games, and tried to tune out her mother complaining about Boglarka's most recent slight.

After the wedding dance, feeling a little sick and more than a little unsteady on her feet, she had made her way into the moon-lit night to go home. She had recognised the sound of Istvan's laughter and turned to look to the storage barn. Sure enough, there he had been, with a girl. Lena had stumbled home, trying unsuccessfully to hold the tears back.

Lena sat down on one of the park benches. The wood was slightly damp beneath her, and the area under her shoes had turned to mud where people's feet had trampled the grass and the rain had drowned it. She did some quick calculations. That must have been the night.

For a moment Lena felt anger at what they had done. That was replaced by sadness that Timea had never told her what had happened. Was she so terrifying? Or did her friend not want to hurt her? She wanted to talk to Timea, confront her, probably forgive and comfort her. But she'd never get the chance.

She got up from the park bench, her bum cold. She turned around and looked back at Istvan's house before heading to the bus stop to take her back to Haringey. Istvan had everything he used to want; he'd achieved what he had always said he would. But it didn't seem as though he was happy.

'So he slept with Timea all those years ago, got her pregnant with Laszlo, and then off he scarpered back to Budapest for an audition, leaving her to bring up the kid alone?' Mrs Kingston said, scooping up an unwilling Jasper from where he was nibbling a piece of lettuce on the floor and popping him on to Lena's lap. 'What a rat!'

Lena pulled Jasper further towards her, but he was wriggling to escape. 'And then back he comes now, wanting to help Laszlo.'

Mrs Kingston stooped with a small groan and picked up the half-eaten lettuce leaf, placing it on Lena's lap. Jasper tucked in again with relish. 'And Timea never tapped him up for cash before? I've seen him in that show of his. He must be worth a fair bit.'

'Timea never told me that he was the father. Never even told Istvan, apparently. Though he must have done the numbers. He is not totally stupid.'

'What does your policeman friend think of all this?'

'I meet him tomorrow before the funeral.'

'I still can't believe they just gave you some trainee. I must have lost my touch.'

'He is OK,' replied Lena. She caressed Jasper's ears, soft as silk. He ignored her, focused on the lettuce leaf.

'Because I can contact David at the *Gazette*. He'll help me with the article. That will light a fire under them!'

'I am happy with PC Cartwright,' said Lena, still fiddling with Jasper's ear. 'I think he is good. And he is clever. And I have never met someone before who is so much a gentleman.'

Mrs Kingston looked at Lena and smiled. 'Perhaps I'll hold off on that article then,' she said. 'Let's see how things pan out first.'

CHAPTER 14

Even on a Monday morning, there were plenty of people in the park with children or dogs, and the sounds of laughing and barking filled the air. Lena and Cartwright cut through the rose garden as they strolled through Clissold Park, enjoying the heat of the rare November sunshine on their skin. Cartwright had rolled up his sleeves to the elbow and Lena found herself surprised by how well formed and perfect his arms were. The rose stems sticking out of the earth, by contrast, looked decidedly unimpressive. Lena found it hard to believe that flowers would cover them again in spring. Timea had loved the roses, had made Lena stop to smell them all, back when they were in bloom. But Timea had always preferred the daisies, poking up through the grass. They weren't meant to be there, she had said. No one looked after them. But they had made it anyway. Full of hope.

Lena blinked the memories away.

'I am glad to get out,' said Lena to Cartwright. 'The funeral is at four. Mama is fussing. Making beef *paprikás* and a lot of noise. I needed a break.'

'Your mother sounds absolutely formidable.'

'What?'

'Sorry, it means she must be quite something.'

'Yes,' said Lena. They shared a moment's awkward silence. It had

136

been a while since Lena had not understood an English word. Why couldn't it have happened with a client instead?

'You said that the funeral is at St Mary's?' said Cartwright. 'It will be a Catholic service, presumably?'

'Yes,' replied Lena. 'I do not think it will be Catholic enough for my mother, though. She was not happy with the regular service in the village until enough incense is burnt to choke us all.'

'Has anyone else travelled from home – Timea's parents, perhaps? If so we should take the opportunity to interview them.'

'Timea was an orphan,' Lena said, looking away from him. 'We see if there are turtles on the rocks,' she said. She led him towards the lake.

'So Timea's client Yasemin,' said Lena, changing the subject. 'She is thin and pretty for a divorced man, do you not think?'

'I thought you might feel the need to gloat,' said Cartwright. 'You were right of course.' He bent his head to her in a small bow.

'Did you see Yasemin's face when I mentioned Faisal?' said Lena. 'She knows him.'

'Yes. I think you're right, as usual.' he said. 'There is something going on with her – she knows Faisal, and Faisal knows the man in the gang. It's a tenuous link, but I'm going to pull her records from the system and see what her history is.'

'You should,' replied Lena. 'I have cleaned many houses. I know when my clients have something to hide.'

They reached the lake and stood together, watching the sunlight dancing in the ripples. A duck glided towards them, his feathered head opalescent like a bluebottle. He quacked in their direction, informing them that it was time to throw him some food. Lena glanced at the self-righteous sign next to her, telling her that bread was bad for ducks. Apparently she should have brought grapes or oats.

Timea would have wanted to bring Laszlo here, she thought. Lena would bring him the next time she came. And she'd rebel and bring bread. The ducks back home loved it.

'I am no closer,' she said to Cartwright, her eyes still following the duck as it glided away. 'It is the funeral this afternoon and I have no clue what happened to Timea. I have no comfort to offer Laszlo.'

'It takes time,' said Cartwright, also watching the duck. 'Murder cases are slow and painstaking. You have to investigate every lead, every suspect, every clue, and that's what we're doing. My spreadsheet is getting fuller all the time. We'll work out everyone's timeline, their alibi, their motive. Don't worry, Lena. Twenty-first-century police work will have its day.'

Lena looked at him. 'You like being in the police?'

'Of course,' he replied.

'How did you know,' she asked, 'that was what you wanted to do?'

Cartwright smiled at her. 'My father wanted me to be a lawyer like him, finding loopholes to get rich, guilty people off scot-free. But when I studied Maths, he started hoping I'd be a banker. He hit the roof when I joined the police force.'

'You joined to make him angry?'

'No, but his disappointment reassured me I was making the right decision.'

Lena smiled at him, thinking of her own mother's horror when she gave up her office job to clean in London.

'If you guessed now who murdered my friend,' she said, 'who would you say?'

'Now we know that Istvan was in a relationship with Timea, I suspect him. Like I said, lovers or ex-lovers are responsible for over half of all women's murders. Although I haven't calculated the effect of time on those statistics. I wonder if it has some kind of half-life, like in nuclear physics . . .'

Lena turned away from the lake. The duck quacked reproach-fully at her failure to provide food. She knew all there was to know about Istvan. All those years, together in the village.

'You two most have been close,' said Cartwright, reading her thoughts. 'So I know this is hard for you. But Timea had been lying to you about him.'

'She was not lying. She just did not tell me everything.'

'We don't know what Istvan has been up to for the last decade. I'll have a look in the system. Perhaps fill in some of the blanks.'

'He would not hurt Timea,' said Lena.

'I will look into him anyway. We need to be methodical, and he is, statistically, a viable suspect.'

A viable suspect. Lena thought back to all the times they'd walked hand in hand through the village. She could still feel the grip of his hand on her own. She could almost taste his lips. But that was a long time ago, she told herself. They'd both changed from those love-smitten teenagers.

Cartwright began to emit a beeping sound. He rummaged through his pockets and found his phone.

'It's a new case,' he said. 'I need to go.' He put his hand on her arm. 'I hope that the funeral goes well. Call me if you need me and I'll come straight there.'

'Thank you,' said Lena. 'I should get back too. Mama will be making beef *paprikás* for an army.'

'Lena where have you been? Disaster after disaster here. And on the day of his mother's funeral!' Her mother was running around the flat, opening and closing cupboards. Even Tomek was off the sofa, pacing the room.

'What's going on?' Lena asked.

'It's Laszlo,' said Tomek. 'We can't find him.'

'What?' said Lena. 'What happened?'

'Your mother was on the phone, talking to Dora,' explained Tomek. 'I didn't understand what they were saying, but Laszlo must have done. He locked himself in his room at first. We were in the kitchen, making him a snack to cheer him up. When we went to take it to him, he was gone. He must have crept out.'

'*Eltűnt*. Gone,' proclaimed Greta. 'It is my fault,' she said. 'I was talking to Dora, saying how unhappy Timea must have been to take those evil drugs and abandon a fine boy like Laszlo. When I went to Laszlo's room he was gone. And his mother's funeral this afternoon!'

Lena took a deep breath. If Timea had asked one thing from Lena before she died, she would not have wanted justice for herself or revenge for her murderer. She wouldn't even have cared who it was who had killed her. She would have asked Lena to keep Laszlo safe. But it was happening again. People were disappearing. She wouldn't let it. Not this time.

'Mama, you head north. Search the cafés . . .' Where could he be? Lena realised she knew nothing about what this boy liked. '. . . the cafés, the library, the park. Tomek, you go south. Look . . . everywhere. I will call the police. And Istvan.'

'Why Istvan?' said Greta, scrabbling around for her handbag.

'We'll talk about that later,' she said. 'We need to find Laszlo.' Her mother nodded.

Tomek put his hand on Lena's arm. 'Where have you been?' he said. 'We needed you here.'

'I am here now,' she said, brushing his hand off. 'We need to find him and make sure he is safe.'

'You are right,' said Tomek, wrapping his scarf around his neck. 'But we need to talk later.'

CHAPTER 15

Tomek was right. She should have been there for the boy. She noticed a number written on the message pad and recognised Istvan's scrawl – it had barely changed since he'd used it to copy her homework. It took her expert eye to distinguish his fumbling fives from his spindly threes. Istvan should be enlisted to help find Laszlo. She dialled.

A woman answered with a cultured-sounding 'Hello', reminding Lena of a client's voice. It must be Istvan's wife. She wondered for a moment if she already knew about Laszlo, but most likely Istvan had put off telling her. Perhaps she should disguise what she needed, make up some cover story to explain a strange woman calling her husband. The woman said 'Hello' again, the voice growing impatient.

Lena decided she didn't have time to be sensitive. She demanded to speak to Istvan and the woman didn't argue back. Saying things in a commanding tone invoked people's natural urge to obey. Pack behaviour. She wished for a moment she was a general, not a cleaner.

When a worried Istvan declared himself on his way, Lena called Cartwright, leaving him an urgent message. Then she took the lift downstairs. She'd search.

When she got on to the street, she saw nothing but danger for an eight-year-old boy from the village. Everywhere. The cars

141

careered down the road like they were on steroids. Shady-looking men lined up like kidnappers in waiting. In the village, Laszlo would know who to trust and who he should give a wide berth to. He would know never to get into a car with Mr Jozsef, no matter how many sweets he was offered. Here, he was helpless.

Lena racked her brains. What did Laszlo like? Would he have tried to find a park, a café, a train? She'd barely spoken to the boy since he'd arrived, leaving him to her mother and Tomek. And now she had no clue where he would have gone. She leaned on a lamp post, feeling nausea wash over her.

Thirteen days since his mother's death. The morning of his mother's funeral. What if the same person who had taken Timea had come for her son? What would they want with Laszlo?

It felt as though an evil force was following Timea and her family. Like a curse. With surprise, Lena noticed a pang of superstition in herself that she hadn't felt since she was a child, listening to her mother's stories about young men picking lilies and turning into silvery fish.

The memory of it brought Lena to her senses. This was not a fairy tale. This was life. In life, bad things happened but they made sense. People did not turn into fish or snakes or ducklings: they went where they needed to go.

Gradually it dawned on her: she knew where Laszlo was. Lena reproached herself for not figuring it out sooner.

A car beeped its horn. Lena ignored it, deaf to the sound of the traffic while she scanned the road for a taxi. It would have to be lost, coming up here, she thought. She should try Cartwright again. She rummaged for her phone in her bag.

'Lena,' shouted a voice. She looked towards the car. Istvan rolled his window down. 'Have you found him?'

'Does it look like it?' she replied, as she darted into the traffic to clamber into the passenger side. 'Drive. Towards Angel.' Istvan followed her instructions. Her phone rang and Lena heard Cartwright's breathless voice when she put the device to her ear.

'Lena, I got your message and I've put an alert out. He's high risk because of his age, so every policeman on the beat is looking for the boy. I've issued a description from what you've told me but a photo would help. And his last known position. We won't let you down, I promise. We'll find him.'

'I know where he is,' she told him. 'I think I do. Send someone to Regent's Canal. To where Timea was found.' The car stalled. Lena looked over to Istvan. He was pale. Traffic blasted their horns around them.

'How do you know?' said Istvan.

'Just go there,' said Lena, and hung up the phone. She turned to Istvan, who was clutching the wheel and not moving.

'We need to go too,' said Lena. 'Now.'

'I don't want to go there,' said Istvan. 'I don't want to be where she died.'

'Don't be a baby,' said Lena, as though they were thirteen again and Istvan didn't want to go to be de-loused by the school nurse. 'Laszlo needs us.'

'I don't even know where to go on the canal,' said Istvan. 'How would I?'

'I do,' said Lena. She looked at her watch. They only had an hour till the funeral was due to start. She hoped she was right.

Laszlo was sitting on the concrete edge of the canal with his legs dangling down over the water. There was a barge in front of him, dusty and old, with huge logs for firewood piled on top. Laszlo hadn't seen her yet. He was staring down into the water. Sitting there, he reminded Lena of Istvan as a boy. Innocent, confused, forlorn. She looked at the man standing next to her now, also watching the child, and she wondered if he saw himself in the eight-year-old as well. He turned towards her to say something, but she put her fingers to her lips. 'Go call Greta,' she whispered. 'I will talk to him.' Istvan obeyed.

Lena walked up to Laszlo, padding quietly. She sat next to him, her own feet also hanging down. The murky water reflected the grey of the overcast sky. Laszlo began to swing his legs, the back of his trainer hitting the wall with a rhythmic thud.

'I'm glad I found you,' said Lena to Laszlo in soft Hungarian. 'I didn't know where to look at first. We don't really know each other very well, even though I've been there since before you were born.'

Laszlo made no reply. He didn't even move his eyes. Lena followed his gaze to the canal's depths. The water was opaque and unappealing, but at least there wasn't too much litter. Just a couple of rusty Coke cans floating around an old leather jacket.

'But then I thought about what had happened and I knew where you'd be,' said Lena, trying again. 'You must have found my board, with the map. That was clever.'

Laszlo ignored her. She could tell she was right. The map poked out of his pocket.

'You must be pretty good at reading maps, to get all this way on your own. But it is not safe. This is a dangerous city.'

'I'm not an idiot,' said Laszlo. 'I can look after myself.'

'We were all so worried about you,' said Lena, ignoring the hostility in his voice. 'Greta and Tomek and me. London is not like the village.'

'You don't care about me,' said Laszlo. 'I want my mother back. I want Timea.'

'I suppose we do have something in common after all,' she said. 'We both loved Timea.'

'You stole her,' said Laszlo, giving the wall an extra-hard kick. 'She's my mum and you stole her.'

144

'She came to London for you,' said Lena, taking the boy's hand. It felt cold and unresponsive under her own. 'She wanted to provide for you.'

'You made her leave me,' said Laszlo. 'I heard you, telling her to come to London.'

Lena didn't know what to say. He was right. It was her fault. 'I'm sorry,' she said. She watched the jacket, the Coke cans bumping up against it, drawn by the water's ripples. It wasn't soft like an empty jacket, but substantial. Substantial like someone was still wearing it.

'And now she has left me, for good this time. She didn't love me.' Lena turned her gaze from the water to the small boy sitting in front of her.

'She didn't want to leave,' she said. 'She loved you more than anything.'

'Why did she do it then? They said she killed herself.'

'She didn't,' said Lena, taking the boy's hand. 'I know she didn't.' She looked at him, but he continued to stare into the canal. 'You have to believe me,' she said. 'She wouldn't have left you alone. Everything she did, it was all for you.'

'I heard them talking about it,' said Laszlo. 'Greta said, on the phone, that was what my mother did. You are lying'

Laszlo snatched his hand away and picked up a small stone. He threw it into the water. They both watched it hit the surface, then disappear for ever.

'You know she loved you, more than anything. She would not have done this. Never.'

'If she didn't do it,' said Laszlo. 'Who did?'

'That's what I am going to find out,' said Lena. 'I promise.'

Lena swung her legs up and pulled Laszlo with her. 'Come,' she said. 'We need to say goodbye to your mother.' She turned him away from the canal and forced him into a hug. He allowed her arms around him but didn't reciprocate.

They walked together along the bank. Greta, Cartwright and Istvan were all standing around the corner. Greta ran to Laszlo.

'My angel,' she said to him, giving him a hug that lifted him off the ground. 'Where have you been? The day of the funeral. And you are in your jeans. Hurry, we'll go home.' She turned to Cartwright and spoke in English. 'You policeman take us home in flashing light car. Quick quick now.'

'Istvan can take you,' said Lena, 'in his Mercedes.'

'Maserati,' said Istvan, automatically. He glanced at Lena and then down at the ground. 'I'm glad you're OK,' he whispered to Laszlo. 'So glad.' Laszlo looked up at him curiously.

'I'll follow in a minute,' said Lena. 'Wait for me.'

Lena watched them go off to the car, then grabbed Cartwright's arm.

'There's something in the water,' she told him, leading him around the corner. She pointed at the jacket. 'There.'

'That's just some rubbish,' said Cartwright, looking at her in surprise. 'Leave it. You need to get to the funeral.'

'Look again,' she said to him. 'It is not right.'

Greta called to her. 'I have to go,' she told Cartwright. 'But promise me you'll check. It is not floating like an empty jacket. It floats like there is a man inside it.'

CHAPTER 16

'When we get there you must touch nothing in the house,' Greta told Laszlo, glancing at the same time at Tomek's bulky form. 'You must not break anything. Play your cards right and it could all be yours one day.'

'Mother!' said Lena. After the funeral, Istvan had told Greta the truth about Laszlo. She had listened quietly for once, and allowed him to talk to Laszlo. Now, the following day, they were paying a visit to see Istvan's house and meet his wife. Finally Istvan was facing up to his responsibilities.

'It's true. He needs to get the wife on side, then they will adopt him.' Greta swooped upon Laszlo and began covering his face with kisses, leaving little lip-shaped prints on his skin from her special-occasion lipstick. 'I will miss him so much,' she said. 'But I am happy for him. And he will remember his Greta, when he is a millionaire.'

'I don't want to go,' said Laszlo, for once returning Greta's embrace, clinging to her like a koala bear.

'It's just tea,' said Lena. 'We're not going to leave you there.' She gave her mother a warning glance, but Greta just smiled back, her teeth smeared a bright fuchsia.

'Go get ready Laszlo,' said Greta. 'I've cleaned the ketchup off your black suit. Lena, what are you wearing?'

'Don't make him wear the funeral suit,' said Lena.

'It's the only suit he has and it cost me a fortune. Soon he will have one for every colour of the rainbow.'

'No,' said Lena. 'We go as we are.'

'Even Tomek?' The women turned to look at him, in his grey tracksuit bottoms and red sweatshirt. He looked back at them blankly, unable to understand when they gabbled together in Hungarian. He must have picked up something critical in their gaze, as he sucked in his stomach under their scrutiny.

Lena laughed. 'We were not talking about your tummy,' she told him, back in English. 'You are fine as you are.'

Istvan's wife opened the door. Lena studied her face, trying to discern what she thought of the surprise addition to her husband's history. Her face was handsome but her expression hard to fathom. Too much money and not enough skin, decided Lena. The tell-tale signs of Botox.

'I'm Catherine. Such a pleasure to meet you,' said the woman, leaning in to kiss Lena's cheek. Catherine's perfumed face felt dry against Lena's skin. 'This handsome boy must be Laszlo,' said Catherine. 'He's a big boy for an eight year old.' She knelt down. Laszlo retreated to behind Tomek's legs. Catherine stood up again with a forced ripple of laughter.

Greta grabbed Catherine in a bear hug, then pushed her away again and kissed her twice on each cheek. Tomek and Laszlo both giggled at the lipstick marks she left behind on Catherine's taut skin. 'This house good,' said Greta, with her arms still tightly wrapped around Catherine. 'Like castle palace.'

'Thank you,' said Catherine, using a bit of force to disentangle herself. 'It's just a townhouse, but we have always been very happy here.'

'And now a child,' said Greta. 'A boy. A blessing.'

Istvan emerged into the hallway. 'Come through,' he said. 'We'll have tea in the salon.' Lena listened to his voice with envy. His English was almost fluent, better than hers. He expressed himself perfectly, retaining just enough of his accent to hint at an exotic past.

'You are like my son now,' Greta told him, reverting to Hungarian. 'I didn't think it would happen like this, but I always knew it would happen.' Istvan took Greta's hugs with good grace, letting her fuss over him.

It took a while for the seating to work itself out. Lena watched in dismay as Greta tried to get a stubborn Laszlo to sit between Catherine and Istvan. He clung instead to Tomek's leg, who made space for him on his oversized armchair. Eventually Greta settled for the next best thing, inserting herself into the small space between the couple. Catherine and Istvan shuffled uncomfortably, drawn towards the centre of the sofa by a landslide as the cushions sank to accommodate Greta's ample behind.

Catherine stood up. 'I'll be mother,' she said, reaching for the teapot. Lena saw glimpses of delight in her own mother's eyes and jumped up to avoid a catastrophe of misunderstanding.

'Let me help,' she said.

'I'm quite capable,' replied Catherine sharply, then laughed off her own rudeness. 'Perhaps you'd like a cake?'

Lena looked for the first time at the elaborate tiered structure on the table. There was an array of tiny cakes piled on to plates at different levels, like a multi-storey car park. At the bottom were scones, already spread with jam and cream. One level up were elaborate cakes topped with abstract folds of chocolate. They looked like sculptures. Pride of place on the top level were little pastries covered in jellied fruit, shining in their glory. Lena recognised them as from the Euphorium bakeries that were multiplying like amoeba on Upper Street. She totted it up in her head. It would take a full day of cleaning for her to earn the money to buy those cakes.

Lena glanced at Tomek. She caught his eye a second too late to prevent him stuffing a small chocolate cake into his mouth whole. He wiped his hands shamefully on his trousers when he saw he'd been caught. Catherine handed him a napkin. At least the cakes wouldn't go to waste.

Greta began again. 'Laszlo speak English,' she said. 'Like king.'

'He is a good boy,' said Istvan. Catherine smiled back at him.

'You have no children?' Greta asked Catherine.

'I've got my career,' said Catherine. 'I've never felt the need.'

Greta began to gabble about Istvan's show. Lena, realising that fictional territory was safe, let her mind wander. She took a fruit tart, inspecting the shiny glazed kiwi fruit on top before taking a custardy bite. There weren't many cakes left on the tray now, but there was a pile of crumbs on Tomek's lap.

'Istvan and my Lena. Lovers as kids,' said Greta. Her mother's voice brought Lena to attention with a jolt. 'I think Lena find husband early.'

'Not lovers,' said Istvan, with an awkward laugh, his eyes on Catherine. 'Only friends.'

Greta's indignation spilled into Hungarian. 'Don't you lie, Istvan Nemeth. You were practically engaged to my Lena. And to get her best friend pregnant, god rest Timea's darling soul.'

'You are upsetting Laszlo,' said Lena, feeling a bit upset herself. 'That is enough. It was years ago. We were not together then.'

Istvan emitted another laugh, this one hearty. Lena and Greta looked at him with surprise.

'Hungarian humour,' he said to Catherine in English. 'So ingenious. Cannot be translated though.'

'You're a terrible actor,' said Catherine coolly. 'But I'm not exactly threatened.'

Lena tried to ignore the slight, and hoped her mother had missed it. Unfortunately Greta's ear was highly tuned to insults, in any language. She began to struggle to get up, using Catherine's lap as a push-off point.

'My daughter skinny but you more skinny,' said Greta, failing to rise.

'Quite,' said Catherine, crossing her legs and knocking off Greta's hand in the process. 'But what's done cannot be undone. We'll need a paternity test, of course. Then we'll need to work out how to manage the story before the press get hold of it. Journalists do love a juicy secret. As charming as Laszlo is, a little illegitimate boy turning up like this needs the right spin. We wouldn't want to put the sponsors off.'

'We will leave that to you,' said Lena, deciding this reunion had gone on long enough. 'It is time to go.'

'Wait,' said Istvan, the urgency in his voice surprising her. 'We need to talk about Laszlo's future.' He reached across Greta to take Catherine's hand. 'We have agreed that we will take him in. Here with us.' He gave them all a generous smile.

Lena looked to her mother. This was what she had said she wanted.

'If he really is Istvan's son,' added Catherine.

Greta was looking at Istvan and Catherine's hands, held over her lap. 'No,' she said. 'He is like grandson to me.'

Istvan let go of Catherine's hand. 'You could come and visit,' he said, pleading. 'I would pay for your flights. You could stay with us.'

Catherine coughed.

'We will think about it,' said Lena.

'It will not be your decision,' said Catherine. 'There are courts for that kind of thing.'

'And what about what Laszlo wants?' said Tomek. The others turned to him, having forgotten he was in the room. Laszlo was clutching his hand.

'Of course,' said Istvan hurriedly. 'What Laszlo wants and what is best for him. We will talk together, Laszlo and I, about what it would be like living here. I can show him his room . . .'

'That is enough for today,' said Lena. 'We leave now!'

In the general kerfuffle of getting up, getting Greta to the loo and picking the chocolate crumbs from Tomek's lap off the Persian rug, Lena's phone rang.

'Tell Greta I have to go,' she told Tomek, once she had hung up. 'It's urgent.'

'Police business?' asked Tomek in a tone Lena didn't like.

'Yes,' she said. 'Take Greta and Laszlo home. I don't know when I'll be back.'

CHAPTER 17

'So tell me,' said Lena. 'Who was the body?'

'I can't believe you spotted him, just from what was above the water. My colleagues thought I was mad until they dragged it up.'

'Who was it?'

They were in the small café across the road from the police station. Lena had hurried there straight from Istvan's house.

'Sorry,' said Cartwright. 'It took forensics a while to identify him, I'm almost surprised they had a positive ID the next day. When a body is in water, its decomposition is very interesting. It is much slower in a way, due to the cold, but it is more dramatic. When they told me who it was, I couldn't believe it. I didn't recognise him, but then I'd only seen him from a distance, and the face was pretty bad – swollen and black.'

'I know.' Her imagined image of Timea's bloated face seemed tattooed to the insides of her eyelids.

'Of course you do,' said Cartwright. 'Sorry.'

She blinked, trying to ignore her eyelids.

Cartwright paused, looking at Lena's impatient expression. 'I'm sorry, I'm afraid I'm jabbering,' he said. 'The body was Faisal Javaid.'

Lena leaned back in her chair. Faisal. Thoughts darted through her mind like swallows catching flies.

'Was it the same?' asked Lena. 'The same as Timea?'

'You found him in the same stretch of water, as you know,' Cartwright said. 'Almost exactly the same place. But otherwise the case is totally different. Because the body was found so much more quickly, thanks to you, it's much more likely that they'll find some evidence. The place is crawling with SOCOs and there's a lot of uniforms there too. They are looking for blood splatter, to see where the murder took place.'

'Blood? But Timea drowned?'

'I know,' said Cartwright. 'However, Faisal was shot.'

'Does this mean that they have more hope of finding who killed Timea?' said Lena, thinking. 'If they find fresh evidence, it could take them to her killer too? It must be the same.'

'CID are treating them as separate cases,' said Cartwright. 'For the time being.'

'Why?' said Lena. 'That is crazy. They used to be lovers and now they are found dead in the same place.'

'Poirot says there are no coincidences,' said Cartwright. 'But the police don't. They are pretty different cases. Just because the bodies were found in the same place doesn't mean that's where they were both murdered; the currents would have pulled them there. Faisal was shot in the back, so it's definitely not suicide. It is anatomically impossible to shoot yourself in the back at that angle, even if you wanted to. This is definitely a murder. It's very different to Timea. I haven't worked out the statistical likelihood of it happening in the same place yet just by coincidence. But I can tell you it will not be high. Forty-five bodies are found, on average, in the Thames each year, but Regent's Canal is nothing like that number.'

'It does not seem likely that it is chance.'

'I've been thinking about it, more and more,' said Cartwright. 'Faisal was involved with that gang. We saw him talk to that thief. Then you mentioned Faisal to Yasemin and one day later he is murdered.'

'You think it is my fault?' Lena hadn't liked Faisal, and she had mentioned him out of suspicion. But she hadn't expected this.

'No no,' said Cartwright, putting his hand on Lena's arm. It was meant to be a gesture of reassurance, but his fingers quivered on her skin. 'You couldn't have known what would happen, but you were suspicious of Yasemin. You could tell just from what she had in her flat and how much she fed her cat. I've found out more from the database. You were right. Lena, I think you are a genius.'

Lena barely managed a smile, feeling far from it.

'Her past is just like her apartment: there's not enough there. The apartment is rented in her name, and one bank account is in her name too. But that's it. No birth certificate, no dental records, no school, no parents. She doesn't exist. It's a fake identity. She isn't Yasemin.'

'Who is she?'

'I don't know. But she certainly has something to hide. As soon as we gather more evidence, I'm going to take this to DS Wilson. It's time to get this case on the books.'

'That doesn't mean she killed Timea. Or Faisal. Why would she?' Lena could feel Cartwright getting distracted.

'She's up to something. And you're right. We need a motive.' Cartwright paused, popping another sugar cube into his tea. 'Normal people with nothing to hide don't just make up identities. We saw Faisal up to no good taking that package from your thief. We need to interview the people at the delivery address. We should interview the thief too and see what he's got to say. Of course, thieves aren't usually that keen to talk to the police, so that will be tricky. If we can even find him.'

Lena thought about it. She had suspected something, hence the deadly name-drop. But that was just a feeling, a guess.

'I will talk to her,' said Lena. 'To Yasemin. Question her when I clean there next.'

'No,' said Cartwright, putting his mug of sweet tea down. 'It's too dangerous to do that. If we're right she's already murdered Faisal. If you start sniffing around her, so to speak, then . . .'

'She might have killed my friend,' said Lena. 'I will find out the truth.'

'This could be something big,' said Cartwright. 'If she is connected to Faisal, who is connected to your thief, then who knows where it could lead? We could expose this new gang that is in town, terrorising Upper Street with muggings and phone thefts. Most likely they want to get further into the drugs market and are looking for a steady supplier. I know it is all connected – I just need some proof on how. We need that first link.' He took a final sip of tea. 'I need to get back to the station.'

Lena moved her arm from under his hand. 'I can talk to Faisal's girlfriend.'

'The police will do that.'

'I will do it. I know Tracy. She may not like me much, but she will like the police even less.'

When Tracy opened the door with no makeup, Lena barely recognised her. She even glanced down at the piece of paper Cartwright had given her to check she had the right address. They were seven storeys up in an enormous block of flats, worse maintained even than Lena's block. Unlike hers, the corridor was open to the elements. Lena tried not to look down.

'What do you want?' said Tracy. Her voice was small and dry, as though it had been worn out by sobs. Her face was pale and her eyes were pink and puffy but, even so, Lena thought she looked better than she had ever seen her. Without her makeup, her face looked naked and vulnerable. And so much more beautiful.

'I am so sorry,' said Lena, pulling Tracy to her in an instinctive hug. 'I know what it is like to lose someone.' She could feel Tracy's body tense as she held her.

'Come in,' said Tracy, stepping out of the hug and leaning out of the doorway to look the open corridors up and down. 'Did you see anyone outside?'

'No,' said Lena, following Tracy into the dark apartment. She blinked a few times and looked around. The walls were a dirty cream colour and textured with woodchip, as though many tiny little beetles had been crawling over the walls when it was painted and were now entombed there forever. The narrow hall took them into a small living room, where an oversized flat-screen television dominated. It was clearly new, and it threw into relief the shabbiness of the well-worn green sofa and chipped MDF coffee table. A series of school photos of a pale but smiley blonde girl adorned the mantelpiece. As they went to the right, in each one she looked a little older. At the far end, she was proudly sporting gold hoop earrings. But what struck Lena was the surprising number of Barbie dolls scattered around, dressed in a variety of outfits for every occasion, from a seventeenth-century ball to a motorbike ride.

'My daughter loves those dolls,' said Tracy, following Lena's eyes. She struggled to light a cigarette with her wobbling hands, and then offered one to Lena. Lena shook her head. 'She loved Faisal too,' said Tracy, taking a deep puff. 'My sister's taken her out. God knows how I'll tell her.'

Lena picked up a one-legged Barbie from the sofa and sat down in its place. The doll was dressed in jodhpurs, a smart brown blazer and a riding hat.

'How old is she?' asked Lena, sitting the doll on the coffee table in front of her. She turned it around so it looked out at the room.

'Seven,' replied Tracy, fiddling with one of the photos that wasn't sitting straight in its frame. 'Eight in December.'

'Timea's son is eight,' said Lena, trying to find common ground. Something was uncomfortable on the sofa. Lena reached behind her and found a small tanned plastic leg. She twiddled it between her fingers.

Tracy just shrugged at her. 'Good for him,' she replied, taking another long drag from her cigarette and glancing at her watch. 'What do you want?'

Small talk wasn't working. Lena decided to get to her point.

'Timea is dead, and now Faisal. Found in the same place. I think there is a connection.' Lena punctuated her sentence by placing the doll's leg on the table.

Tracy gave a half-laugh. 'God, you're always at it. They are both dead and you still think there's something going on between them. And I thought I was paranoid.'

'Why?' said Lena, leaning forwards. 'Why do you think you are paranoid?'

For a second anger clouded Tracy's face, but then weariness took over. 'I've wasted enough energy worrying about what those two were up to,' she said. 'Jealousy makes you do crazy things.'

Lena sat upright. 'What things?'

Tracy laughed again, a sharp, bitter sound. 'Well I didn't kill them, if that's what you're thinking,' she said. She picked up a doll dressed for a day at the office and began arranging its hair. 'There were times I wanted to, though. Sneaking around like they were. But I knew Faisal was a player. Didn't stop me loving him.'

'So it was still going on, him and Timea?'

'No. Only at first. It ended maybe six months ago. He thought he was so careful, but I knew when he saw her. He smelled different.' Tracy took a deep breath, as though she could smell it in the air now. It turned into a cough, and it shook the ash at the end of her cigarette to the floor. Lena looked at the cinders, which formed a neat grey pile on Tracy's worn brown carpet.

'But you still accused him, followed him around . . .'

158

'You can't switch off jealousy,' said Tracy. 'Once it's there, it's staying. Eating you up from the inside out like those wasp larva off the telly. I just didn't want to lose him.' Tracy laughed again, a harsh sound that was far from amused. 'Look how that worked out for me.'

'You must have some idea what happened to him?' said Lena, taking her eyes from the cinders to Tracy's face.

'No,' said Tracy, quickly. 'He got himself shot. Mugging gone wrong, the police reckon. Bunch of mugs themselves, those lot.'

'Then you do not believe them? Who wanted to hurt Faisal?' Lena leaned forwards again. The sofa was soft and she was sinking in to it. It made it harder to concentrate.

'You, perhaps? You've been sniffing around him. Thought he got your friend up the duff so you did him in.'

Lena ignored her. 'Why would someone want him dead?'

'It's dangerous in London these days,' said Tracy, looking straight into Lena's eyes. 'All these immigrants.'

'Very funny,' said Lena, deciding to take a chance. 'But I know about the drugs.' Tracy was silent. Lena knew she'd guessed right. She seized her advantage. 'Handing out copies of newspapers doesn't make much money. He was delivering more than the papers. Did dealing drugs pay for that television?'

'None of your business,' snapped Tracy. Lena ignored her.

'That kind of delivery brings you into contact with rough people. Violent people, happy to shoot you in the back if they need to.'

'Get out,' said Tracy, putting her head in her hands.

'I know you're frightened,' said Lena, reaching out to touch Tracy's arm. 'But I can help. The police can protect you. They already have leads. I have a friend there—'

'Didn't you hear me?' said Tracy, standing up. 'Get out now. And don't come back.'

Lena stood up and was pushed to the door. 'I have a daughter to think about,' hissed Tracy in her ear. 'I'm keeping my mouth shut. Like Faisal should have done.'

Lena heard the door slam shut behind her. As she walked along the windy corridor she dialled Cartwright. She had found out much more than she'd expected.

CHAPTER 18

Lena watched the pig lie happily in the cool November sunshine, its only movement the occasional flick of its ears. She breathed in deeply, filling her lungs with the earthy farmyard smells. She could hear chickens clucking, and an out-of-time rooster *cockadoodledoo*. This Wednesday was like being back in the village. It was what she had worked so hard to leave, but she loved the familiar smells and sounds of her childhood. For the first time, she considered going back. She quickly dismissed the idea. An hour or two at this farm would be plenty to satisfy her appetite for home.

'It's been a long time since I've seen a pig,' said Istvan, as they strolled through the small city farm behind Holloway Road. 'I've had plenty of prosciutto, pancetta and Parma ham, but I haven't seen a pig, live and in the flesh, so to speak, in years. This one is bigger than I remember the pigs being, back home.' Lena listened to how he articulated his *p*s. Over the top, with a large burst of air, as though he was on stage. Not that she could criticise his English.

Laszlo was climbing up on the fence to peer in at the enormous black sow that had plonked herself down in the cold mud. 'Timea was going to bring Laszlo here,' she said, reverting back to Hungarian. With Timea they'd had a pact to always speak English. With Istvan she felt it gave him an uncomfortable advantage over her. 'I remember her saying. She had a client locally, and she was so pleased when she found a city farm here. I told her Laszlo would see plenty of animals back in the village. The whole place is a farm. But she knew he'd love it. Strange obsession with animals that he has.' Lena thought back to the mountain goats, the chickens, the piglets. Laszlo would stare at all of them for hours if he could, imitating the noises they made. Timea thought he'd be a musician one day. She was saving to buy him a violin.

'I bet she was a great mother,' said Istvan, trying to avoid looking at the mud on his brown leather shoes. 'I wish I could have seen her in action.'

'Laszlo was the most loved child in the village,' said Lena. 'At first it was tough, with everyone judging Timea. Speculating on who the father was. But it got better. Once they saw how she loved that boy, it all got better.'

'Who did you think the father was?' asked Istvan.

'I never imagined it was you.' Lena looked at the farm garden, where brightly labelled beetroots poked their leaves out of the dirt. She could smell the healthy but unpleasant scent of miscellaneous animal poo. She supposed she should have guessed. 'But really, I think she loved you for years before. She worshipped you.' They stood in silence together, watching Laszlo try to tempt the pig into eating a bundle of dandelions he'd collected.

Lena thought back to the night she and Istvan had tried to run away to see The Moog in concert. She had padded softly into the kitchen with her knapsack. She hadn't turned on the light, making her way instead by memory and feel. She had successfully grabbed a spongy loaf of bread and had been reaching into the larder for some hard cheese when the light had switched on. She had spun around, trying to think of an excuse for her mother. Midnight hunger? Timea had peered back at her, blinking in the light. 'What are you doing?' she'd said, sleepily.

'Turn that off,' Lena hissed. 'It's none of your business.'

'I'm telling Greta,' Timea said. 'Unless you tell me.'

'OK fine. Istvan and I are just going on a little trip. Don't tell.'

'To that gig in Debrecen, the one Greta said you weren't allowed to go to?'

'Yes. Switch the light off.'

Timea looked at her, her finger on the switch. 'Take me with you or I'm telling Greta.'

'You're too little,' said Lena. 'You wouldn't enjoy it.'

'You do everything without me. It's not fair. I'm almost ten.'

'Istvan doesn't want to hang around with a baby,' said Lena. 'Go to bed. Maybe next year.'

'Greta,' Timea called. Lena rushed over and put her hand over the girl's mouth. Timea squirmed in her grasp. She couldn't hold her.

'OK, OK. You can come,' she said, releasing her. 'But you have to be quiet and do what we tell you.'

Timea spun around and enclosed Lena in a massive hug. 'Thank you thank you thank you,' she gasped. 'I'll be so good.' Lena smiled in spite of herself.

'Go pack,' she said. 'Enough warm clothes for two days. No dolls. Meet me out the back in five minutes. Not a sound. If you get caught, we'll go without you.' Timea tiptoed up the stairs.

Istvan groaned when he saw them both. 'What's she doing here?' he said.

'She was going to tell, I had no choice,' said Lena.

'OK, I suppose she can come too.'

Timea had thrown her arms around Istvan. 'You're the greatest,' she'd said. 'I'll love you always.'

'I suppose you can carry the bags,' he had said to her, disentangling himself and rolling his eyes at Lena. 'Let's get going.'

'I wish she'd told me,' said Istvan, bringing Lena back to the present. 'I would have done things differently.'

'Would you?' Lena doubted it. She ran her fingers along the wire of an empty cage, then rubbed the dirt that had accumulated between her fingers.

'Maybe not,' admitted Istvan. 'Maybe not at first. But I would have come back sooner. I'd have come back for both of them. And for you.'

Lena laughed. 'That would have been an odd little family group,' she said. 'No thank you. Let's go see the chickens.'

Laszlo led the way, pausing by a fluffy Persian cat to give it a stroke. He leaned his whole face into the animal's body, absorbing its warmth. The cat tolerated him with patience, familiar with the affections of children.

'I feel like she robbed me,' said Istvan, quietly to Lena while Laszlo was distracted. 'We could have been a family, at least of sorts. God knows that's what she needed, after what happened to her parents. But she kept Laszlo a secret, kept him from me. And then she went and committed suicide and I never had the chance to be a family with her and my son.'

'Don't you blame Timea,' said Lena. 'She must have had a reason for the secrets she kept.' Laszlo lifted his head away from the cat's body as she spoke, alerted by the tone of her voice.

'Don't fight,' said Laszlo.

'We weren't,' replied Lena. 'Look at that fat red chicken.' They all looked. The chicken was kicking the dirt around at the bottom of its cage, searching for bugs. It felt their eyes on it, and looked back at them, sounding an inquisitive cluck. Laszlo clucked back at it.

Lena spoke softly. 'I will never believe that Timea took her own life,' she said. 'She lived for Laszlo. And she wouldn't have done it that way. Never in the water. Not after what happened . . .' Lena paused for a moment, wondering whether to tell him. What harm could it do now? 'And she was pregnant.'

'What? Do you know who the father was?' Istvan looked to the ground again, but seemed to have forgotten the mud on his shoe.

'She kept that a secret from me too,' said Lena, watching one chicken peck the back of another. 'It's like she didn't trust me. But I would have helped her.'

'You always did look after her. You looked after all of us.'

Lena thought back again, to how it had been, the three of them as children. Timea, trailing around after her and Istvan. She remembered the time they had gone swimming in the public baths, the water from one of Hungary's many natural springs. That had been before the accident, of course, before Timea came to live with Lena's family. She and Istvan had leapt in the pool while Timea stood at the side, tugging at her swimming costume and starting to cry. Istvan had called her a baby, laughing at her as he dunked Lena's head under the water. But Lena swam up to the side, coaxing Timea in. Eventually Timea had stepped into her arms, and Lena had swum around with Timea on her back, Timea's arms almost strangling her, she had held her so tight.

'I couldn't help her this time,' said Lena. 'Not when it mattered.' She took a deep breath in. The smell reminded her of home. Muddy pig swill.

'But what was it, if it wasn't suicide?' asked Istvan. 'She fell and drowned?'

'I taught her to swim, remember? Before it happened,' said Lena, thinking back to the pool again. When Timea had finally let go of her neck, and taken her first tentative splashes alone.

'On *Heroes of Law* something like that happened,' said Istvan. 'A girl, very pretty with lovely big, um, eyes, fell in the water. It didn't help that she could swim because she hit her head on the way down. She was unconscious when she entered the water, so by the time my character dived in and rescued her, she'd already stopped breathing. Gave her mouth-to-mouth and that saved her. Did you see that episode?'

Lena ignored his prattle. 'I believe Timea was murdered,' she told him, her voice low and her eyes on Laszlo.

'That's crazy,' replied Istvan, stopping in his tracks. 'No one would want to kill Timea. She must have fallen.'

'I've been looking into her life,' said Lena. 'She was involved with some bad people. She may have kept her secrets when she was alive, but I'm starting to reveal them now. You and her. That's just one of the secrets.' She looked at Istvan. His eyes were still on his feet, squelching in the mud. He raised his eyes to meet her own. They were full of trepidation.

'Don't worry,' she said. 'That was years ago. I just wish you two had told me.'

Istvan let out a long exhale. 'I wish we had all told each other a lot of things. It would have worked out better.'

Lena smiled at him, and Istvan managed a nervous one in reply. 'Timea loved her secrets,' she said. 'Do you remember when she told us she had a new friend, Agnes, but wouldn't tell us where she lived or what she was like?'

'You had to follow her to the pond to find out who she was. I think you were getting jealous!' said Istvan, remembering.

'Maybe I was,' said Lena. 'Timea was like my own little doll.'

'And then do you remember?' said Istvan. 'When we found out who Agnes was?'

Lena laughed. 'That duck!' she said. 'Timea's new best friend was a duck.'

'They have some here,' said Istvan. 'Perhaps one of them is Agnes.'

'We did tease her after that,' said Lena. 'Every time a duck flew by we told Timea her friend was coming.'

'No wonder she didn't like to tell us stuff,' said Istvan. They shared a silence, watching Laszlo. He had reached his finger through the wire mesh, and was wiggling it like a worm at the chicken. The chicken was not fooled, and continued to peck at the earth.

'He's the same,' said Lena. 'I never know what he's thinking.'

'I want to,' said Istvan. 'Let me spend more time with him.'

'They need to go home,' said Lena. 'Laszlo has school. And my mother is driving me crazy. Visit them in the village.'

Istvan shuddered. 'I don't think I can face it back there. Can't he stay here?'

'He needs Greta with him. He's had such a hard time already. He needs the stability. But she has to go. Would you want your mother living in your flat?'

'Your place is tiny,' said Istvan. 'You must be under each other's feet all the time. And no,' he said with a laugh, 'I wouldn't even want my mother in that big townhouse I live in.' Istvan paused, thinking. 'But there's another option. How about if your mother and Laszlo moved out of your flat?'

'I can't afford a hotel. Neither can they.'

'But then they could stay another few weeks, couldn't they, so Laszlo could get to know me and I him?'

'You want them to stay with you?'

'Good god no!' said Istvan, looking horrified. 'Catherine would never agree. Actually, I don't think I could handle your mother at that proximity either. But I've got a place, nothing fancy, a little flat nearby.'

'Why?'

'It's an investment, for rental,' said Istvan. 'But I'm in between tenants at the moment. It's small but it's comfortable. I'll have to get some nice new furniture in and make sure it's cleaned up, but Laszlo and Greta could stay there. Please? You said yourself that Laszlo needs his father.'

Istvan turned his deep green eyes to Lena. They reminded Lena of algae-filled pools lit by the sunshine. Strangely beautiful.

'I'll put it to my mother,' she said. 'See what she says. Perhaps it would be good for Laszlo to have the chance to get to know you better.'

'Thank you, Lena,' said Istvan. 'For everything. Always.'

Lena smiled at him. 'Why don't you take Laszlo to see the goats?' she said. 'Goats are his favourite.'

CHAPTER 19

'Do you have to go?' Tomek whined at Lena, reclining on the sofa like a Roman emperor the next morning. 'I've got stomach ache again.'

'Just because you are hungry does not mean that you have stomach ache. Make yourself some food. You are like the baby here, not Laszlo,' said Lena, doing her best to plump up the cushions and tidy around him. 'And I was hoping you would go out.'

'So you and Sherlock can look at that board together? Lena, that board gives me the creeps. Besides, it's been so long since it was just the two of us in the flat. On our own.' He reached out and tried to grab her hand, but missed. 'Can't you cancel? It's not often your mother takes Laszlo out.'

Lena stepped out of reach of Tomek's grasping arms and wiped the dust from the television set. 'I thought you said you were sick,' she said.

'It might help,' replied Tomek, looking for a moment as if he was going to heave himself up. 'Please.'

'No,' said Lena. 'Lie there quietly or go to the café.' Tomek rolled over on the sofa so his back faced Lena. It was a foolish gesture, she thought. He wouldn't be able to see the television.

The buzzer went. 'That's Cartwright,' she said. 'He is helping me again on his day off.'

'Hooray,' said Tomek. 'I will go get the red carpet.' He got up and disappeared into the bathroom.

Lena opened the door and smiled at Cartwright. 'Mama is out,' she said, feeling like a teenager. 'Come to the bedroom.'

'Lena, that is amazing,' he said, as she withdrew the board from the closet. She propped it up on the floor and they both sat on the bed to look. She was extremely pleased with it. She'd had to buy a new map to replace the one that Laszlo had taken when he had run away, and she had redone all her Post-it notes with the most up-to-date information. She had marked everywhere that she knew Timea had been in the twenty-four hours leading up to her disappearance, and had stuck a smiling photograph of her in the middle of the board, with what she'd found out about her recently scribbled on a note underneath. All her clients' houses were marked, with a note on what she had found out on each so far. Yasemin's flat was double circled, and she'd drawn a dotted line from her to Faisal. His note had a black cross on it. Deceased.

'What's this?' asked Cartwright, reaching out to take Timea's necklace. Lena had pinned it to the board. He turned it in his fingers. 'It's beautiful,' he said. 'It looks like it's from Tiffany's?'

'Yes,' said Lena, impressed he could identify it. 'I found it in Timea's drawer, in its box. It was new. I think it could be a gift, from the man Timea was seeing.'

Cartwright held it up to the light. 'I'm surprised you got it back so quickly from evidence,' he said. 'Did it not have any fingerprints?'

'I do not know,' said Lena. 'The detectives did not take it.'

'That's unusual,' said Cartwright. 'Why not?'

'I hid it,' admitted Lena. 'A client had one like it, and I knew Timea admired it, and I was worried.'

'You withheld evidence?'

'I did not realise,' she muttered. 'I thought that perhaps Timea had taken it from a client. By mistake.'

Cartwright pulled a handkerchief from his pocket and carefully lowered the necklace into it.

'This could be an important clue,' he said. 'Perhaps the baby's father gave it to her. Lena, I can't believe you kept this from the police. That is an offence.'

Lena put her head in her hands. 'I am sorry,' she said. 'I did not want Timea to get into trouble, in case it was not a gift.'

Cartwright put his hand on her shoulder. Lena looked up, into his eyes. 'Don't worry. I'll ask the lab to do a quick search on it,' he said, taking his hand away and folding the handkerchief. 'Just in case. I have a friend there, we don't need to make it official unless it shows something interesting.'

'I am sorry,' said Lena.

'Don't be,' said Cartwright softly. 'You're doing an amazing job for your friend. This board is more methodical and thorough than anything I've seen DS Wilson pull together.'

'You have helped me so much,' said Lena. 'I am grateful.' She looked into his eyes and he looked back. They both smiled.

'Don't mention it,' he said.

Tomek chose that moment to come into the bedroom. Lena and Cartwright both stood up. 'She's impressive, isn't she, my girl-friend,' he said, gesturing at the board. 'Like a young Jessica Fletcher in *Murder, She Wrote*.'

'Absolutely,' said Cartwright. He coughed. 'I should be going now. Thank you, Lena. Great work.'

Tomek shook his hand, squeezing it tightly. Lena watched as Cartwright winced slightly. 'Firm handshake,' said Tomek. 'That's what you Brits like, isn't it? Firm handshake, stiff upper lip.'

'Yes, you're quite right,' said Cartwright. 'Lena, did you want a lift?'

'I'll be down in a minute,' she said. Cartwright left.

'What do you think you're doing?' hissed Lena at Tomek.

'What do you mean?' he replied innocently. 'Just being friendly.'

Lena tutted at him. He made his way back to the sofa. 'You'd better get going,' he said. 'Can't keep Sherlock waiting. His tea and crumpets could catch cold.'

Cartwright was waiting for Lena outside in the car. 'Sorry about that,' she said as she climbed into the car. 'It is nice to have a taxi service.' He handed her an enormous takeaway hot chocolate. Lena took a sip and got a mouthful of rich cream. She smiled at him. 'This beats the bus.'

'First-class service,' said Cartwright, turning on the ignition. 'Taxi, drinks and crimes solved.'

'Not yet,' said Lena. 'But I finally feel like we are closer.' She could feel excitement in her throat, curdling with the cream.

'I can't believe you left your poor Tomek here, with no food, all sick,' said Greta that evening, bearing down on Lena as soon as she stepped back through the door. Lena was exhausted from cleaning Yasemin's flat. Yasemin had been at home, so she hadn't been able to have Cartwright help her. But she had found plane tickets to Istanbul on her coffee table, and planned to bring Cartwright back to investigate properly once Yasemin was safely abroad. 'You do not know how to keep a man happy,' Greta told Lena. 'You will end up on your own.'

Lena went into the living room, where Tomek was still on the sofa, polishing off the end of a *pörkölt*, wiping up the meaty juices and bacon bits with a thick hunk of bread. He looked up at her, his eyes reproachful for a moment, before he stuffed the crust into his mouth.

'He could have starved to death,' said Greta, tucking Tomek's blanket around him. 'Poor boy. I don't know where you get it from. Your poor father, God rest his soul, never went hungry. Did I teach you nothing?'

'Tomek can feed himself,' said Lena, wiping crumbs from the coffee table into her hand to put in the kitchen bin. 'I have to earn a living.' Lena had gone straight from the unsuccessful search at Yasemin's to one of the houses she used to clean with Timea. It had been hard, without her friend. The time had gone by so much quicker with Timea's cheerful chatter. Lena realised that – although she hadn't always listened to her friend – she had enjoyed the sound of her voice, letting the stories wash over her like birdsong. Cartwright had disappeared back to the station to research the criminal gangs of Turkey and see if there was some link to Yasemin. She didn't rate his chances. And she didn't feel like being berated by her mother.

'I'm having a shower,' she told her, going into the bathroom and closing the door. She turned the water on and shrugged off her jeans and jumper before she realised that the floor was wet beneath her feet. She picked up her clothes but it was too late: they'd already soaked up water from the puddle. She gave up, threw her clothes back down and stepped into the shower.

She let out a scream. The water was freezing. Cursing to herself, she turned off the tap again and wrapped herself in a towel. Even that was wet.

She leaned through the bathroom door. 'There is no hot water,' she shouted to her mother.

'I always have a nice hot bath while I wait for the *pörkölt* to cook,' said Greta. 'You know that.'

Lena dried hurriedly, put the damp towel round herself and took her wet clothes back with her to the bedroom. She sat on the bed and wrapped her blanket around her body, shivering. Grabbing her phone, she dialled Istvan's number.

'I can't take this anymore,' she told him. 'Where's that flat for Laszlo and my mother? I hope it's ready before she drives me completely insane.'

Istvan was delighted to oblige. He told her they could move in on Saturday – he would make all the arrangements. He went on and on about a bed he would order for Laszlo, shaped like a racing car. Lena listened without concentrating, finding his excitement charming. Like it had been back all those years ago. She grabbed a pen and waited till he was ready to tell her the address. She wrote it down, and then looked at the scrap of paper in astonishment. She'd been to that flat before. And so had Timea.

Lena thought back to the only other time she'd felt afraid of Istvan. It had been fifteen years ago.

They had been at the village party to celebrate midsummer, listening to the band playing and watching the villagers whirl around into the self-induced dizziness that was the aim of every traditional dancer. The sun had baked their skin, turning Istvan's nose a brilliant pink. Lena had laughed at him, kissing it gently when he got upset. 'The sun loves your nose more than the rest of you,' she had said. 'So do I.'

They'd watched the sun sink and the villagers drink. Suddenly Istvan grabbed an overlooked bottle of *pálinka*, their strong local liquor, with one hand, and Lena's in the other. 'Come on,' he said. 'Let's find somewhere to drink this. On our own.'

'What about Timea?' said Lena, looking over her shoulder.

'Just us,' said Istvan.

Lena allowed herself to be dragged through the village streets, and out to the fields. They took it in turns to take long swigs, enjoying the heat of the potent alcohol as it slipped down their throats.

By the time they reached the old rope swing, Lena's head was spinning. She used the rope for support, hanging off it and laughing. Istvan offered to push her, but she felt as if she was swinging already. She let go of the rope and sank to the ground. Istvan sat beside her.

'Let's still drink *pálinka* together when we're married,' he said.

'If I marry you, I'll need to drink *pálinka* all the time,' said Lena, with a hiccup that brought the memory of the fiery liquid back to her throat. Istvan took the bottle from her and put one hand around her arm. Lena looked at it, trying to focus. His hand had got bigger, stronger recently. His fingers, firmly gripping her skin, could wrap right around the circumference of her arm.

'Do not joke like that,' he said, serious all of a sudden. 'You always put me down. Like I am nothing.'

Lena leaned in and kissed him. On the lips this time. His lips tasted like her own. They were soft and warm and wet. Lena broke away. 'I was only teasing,' she told him. 'You know I love you.'

'And I love you,' he said, with a smile. 'When I am drunk.'

Lena pushed him back, laughing. 'So you pretended to be upset, did you?' she said. 'To get a kiss?'

'I'd get a kiss anyway,' said Istvan. 'You can't resist me. Who can blame you? I am irresistible, after all. You'll have to beat other women off me, once we're married.'

'You'll be beating them off too, I hope,' said Lena, reaching for the bottle. 'I've seen you eyeing up Natasa.'

'You're the only one for me,' said Istvan nobly, taking the bottle back and drinking deeply. 'Always have been.' Istvan hiccupped.

'I'm lucky,' said Lena, only half sarcastically.

'You will be,' said Istvan. 'Once I'm rich as well as good-looking. You'll be the envy of everyone.' He leaned towards her again, his arms engulfing her as his mouth found her lips.

'Pompous donkey,' said Lena, her words muffled by the kiss. She didn't know whether he heard her, but he pushed her down strongly, so they were lying together on the earth, Istvan on top. She could feel the weight of his body over her, digging into her and pushing her hard into the ground as they kissed. She could feel every detail of the twigs that lay beneath her, making their imprint on her back. Istvan's hand was working its way under her shirt; up her belly until she felt its coldness squeezing her breast. She could see the moon above Istvan's beautiful head, the light reflected in his perfect black hair.

Then his hand was gone, exploring further, reaching down to her pants. This was more than they had done before, and Lena felt surprise mingled with pleasure and confusion. She put her face to one side to escape his kiss, to tell him to stop.

'Let me,' pleaded Istvan. She realised he was struggling to undo his flies with his other hand. 'I love you. I want you so much.'

Lena squirmed under him. 'No,' she said.

'Come on,' said Istvan. 'You know we'll get married. I promise.'

For a moment, Lena felt panic flood her. She brought her elbow into her chest, then released it at Istvan's face. Her elbow hit him square in the nose with more force than she had intended. He fell off her with a yelp and she sprang up to sitting, pulling her knees up into her chest.

'What did you do that for?' said Istvan. He reached his hand up to his face, and looked in horror at the blood on his hands. 'I'm bleeding. You'd better not have broken my nose.'

'It's a scratch,' said Lena, not wanting to look at it.

'I can't go to auditions in Budapest with a broken nose.'

'You can't go to auditions in Budapest with a pregnant girl-friend,' said Lena.

'It fucking hurts,' said Istvan, getting up. 'I need a doctor.'

Lena got up to follow him. 'I'm sorry,' she said. 'Let me see it.' His nose was red and a steady flow of blood was running down his face, but his nose looked to her integrally sound. 'It is just a nose bleed,' she said. 'Hold the ridge of your nose, like this.' She reached up, but he batted her off.

'Fuck off,' said Istvan. He stumbled off into the darkness.

Lena had sat back down. She had felt as if she was going to be sick, and for a moment she hadn't been able to tell which way was the earth and which the sky.

After a while, she had heard an owl hoot. She'd shivered, realising that it was late and she was cold. She had got to her feet and begun to stumble back to the town.

The love nest was Istvan's. No wonder there had been dust bunnies under the bed. Cleaning was not what Timea went there to do. What had happened at Natasa's wedding was not a one-off. Istvan hadn't told Lena the truth. What else was he hiding from her?

Lena went into her mother's room. 'Pack your things,' she told her. 'Take Laszlo and go back to Hungary. You must not stay in this country.'

'That was not a fun journey,' said Tomek as he came back into the flat. 'And what are you doing here? I thought you said you had to work late.'

'Thank you for driving them to the airport,' said Lena, not moving from her position on the sofa. There was a box of Milk Tray on her lap. She pretended to read the selection card.

'She was very upset,' said Tomek, standing in front of her. 'Told me a lot of stories about going without baths when you were a child so that she could wash your clothes. Three hundred and forty-seven cold showers she took on your behalf, she tells me. And I pretty much got a description of each one.' Tomek shuddered. 'Apparently it shrivelled parts of her body that I'd rather not know she had.'

'I am sorry,' said Lena. 'Thank you, Tomek, for taking them.' She kissed him on the forehead and reached for a caramel cream, drawing the blanket up to her chin again. 'But now I have more important problems than my mother. I owe it to Laszlo to solve his mother's murder.'

'Lena,' said Tomek, sitting down beside her. 'You need to let this go.' He pushed her hair back from her eyes and left his hand resting just above her ear. 'I know you loved Timea and you wanted to protect her, but she was unhappy. She took her own life and there was nothing you could have done.'

Lena jerked her head away from his hand. She could feel a little dribble of caramel sticking to her chin. 'She did not. She was murdered.'

'You might find that easier to deal with, and I know you're working through it your own way. But it is not helping anyone. Timea would have wanted you to be strong for Laszlo, not send him away in a tantrum over hot water.'

Lena wriggled to sit upright, upsetting the chocolate box. 'Look what you made me do,' she said, rescuing the chocolates that had escaped on to the blanket. 'You do not understand,' she said, her eyes scanning for errant chocolates.

'Then tell me,' Tomek said, more gently now.

'I did not send them back home because of the water,' said Lena, putting the box on to the table and turning to look at Tomek. 'I have new information. A new line of enquiry. They had to go home for their own safety.'

Tomek rolled his eyes. 'That policeman has a lot to answer for,' he said. 'Encouraging you. Can't you see it's just because he fancies you?'

'No,' said Lena, feeling heat creeping up her neck into her cheeks. 'He believes me; that's why he is helping me.'

'He knows it is suicide, just like the rest of us.' Tomek was speaking gently, but there was a hard edge to his voice. 'I think you know it too.' He took her hand again.

'No. I have evidence.' Lena paused, shook her hand free of his sweaty grip and then blurted it out. 'Istvan and Timea were having an affair.'

'I know that.'

'No, not just back then. They started again, just before Timea was murdered.'

Lena looked at Tomek. No surprise registered on his face. 'You knew?' she said.

'She told me.'

Lena felt as though he had slapped her. 'Why would she tell you and not me?' she gasped.

'Timea didn't want to hurt you. She knew she'd have to tell you eventually, of course, but she didn't want you to know that Istvan was the father until—'

'You knew that Timea was pregnant? And that the baby was Istvan's?' said Lena, scooting away from Tomek along the sofa. 'You knew all that and you kept it from me?'

'It wasn't my secret to tell,' said Tomek. 'Timea told me in confidence. I wanted to tell you and I thought I should, but I had promised. I couldn't break a promise to the dead.'

'That is withholding evidence,' said Lena, getting up. 'You should have told the police. I will call them.'

'The police won't care,' said Tomek. 'Except for Sherlock.'

'Shut up,' said Lena. 'Just because someone is on my side . . . the only one on my side . . .'

'I'm on your side,' said Tomek. 'I told Timea to tell you. But she was worried about how you'd react. She felt like she had betrayed you.'

'And when did you have all these cosy little chats?' said Lena. 'Was she crying in your arms while I was working?' Lena knew it wasn't true even as she said it. But he should have told her.

'Don't turn this on me.'

'I should go,' she said quietly, grabbing her backpack. 'I . . . I did not mean to say that. But Timea . . .'

'You should go,' agreed Tomek. He sank into her place on the sofa and pulled her blanket around himself.

CHAPTER 20

'I don't know who to trust anymore,' Lena told Cartwright, walking next to him as he did his Saturday beat. Now she was used to seeing him in his own clothes, he looked strange to her on duty. Like he was dressing up. 'Timea told me nothing about the affair with Istvan or about the baby. But she told Tomek. Even he kept that secret from me. I am glad I have sent my mother and Laszlo home. It is not safe in this city of liars.' Lena shivered and wrapped her hands around her polystyrene cup of coffee. It was a bitterly cold day. Not a day designed for being outside.

'We'll add all the secret-keepers to the suspect list,' said Cartwright, his eyes focused across the street on Holloway Road Station. 'But right now I'm most interested in the gang lead. That must be the top priority. And thanks to your work with Tracy, we know there is a drugs connection. I don't think the gang have much of a drugs supply as yet or they wouldn't bother with the thefts. But they will. And current statistics suggest that maybe half of all acquisitive crime is related to illegal drug use. If we crack this it could make a real difference.' Lena looked away. 'And we'd catch Timea's murderer,' he added quickly.

Lena moved to cross the road. 'I should leave you to it now. You are meant to be working.'

'Where are you going?' he said. 'Have I upset you?'

'I am glad that you are catching the bad guys,' said Lena. 'But I need to focus on Timea.'

'I'm sorry, I was distracted. Your investigation has led us to these criminals who killed Faisal, but most likely Timea too.'

'But how do we catch them?' said Lena. 'Faisal is dead. Yasemin has disappeared to Istanbul. I don't even know what we're doing here.'

'We're going to find your thief, the one we saw giving the drugs to Faisal,' said Cartwright. 'He'll lead us to Yasemin. He might even be the killer.'

'What? Because he chatted to Faisal one time? Perhaps they were friends,' said Lena, taking a sip of her air-chilled coffee. 'What makes you think he'd be here anyway?'

'We know he is a criminal and we saw him hand Faisal a package, and we know Faisal was dealing drugs. It's not a major leap to assume they had a business connection. Faisal knew Yasemin, so perhaps our man knows her too,' said Cartwright, continuing to look over Lena's shoulder. 'Someone matching his description was seen loitering here yesterday, but didn't make a grab. He's likely to have been scoping the place out as a new venue for a handbag snatch. We know he likes busy stations. It's his modus operandi. So I thought if I made sure my beat passed by here, I'd have a chance at catching him.'

'He wouldn't do anything with you here,' said Lena.

'You have more respect for the police than these thieves,' he said. 'My colleague witnessed a mugging practically in front of him just a few days ago. This gang don't seem fazed by the police at all. They are arrogant.'

'If you are sure, why are you here with me, not with Gullins?'

Cartwright shifted his gaze thirty degrees to look directly at Lena. 'You're better than Gullins,' he said. 'You're more observant, more perceptive, more determined. I've never met anyone like you before.' Cartwright glanced briefly down, then back at the station, colouring slightly.

Lena laughed, a little uncomfortable. 'I would be flattered,' she said, 'if I hadn't met Gullins.'

'I mean it,' said Cartwright. 'You are amazing.' There was a short silence between them. 'Plus I want to prove myself,' he admitted. 'I want to show my colleagues that I can make stuff happen. They think I'm all university degrees and theories and statistics, but I want to make arrests. Stop criminals.'

'You will,' said Lena. 'Starting with Timea's murderer.'

Lena paused outside the door to Istvan's 'rental' flat. She imagined it must have been conveniently vacant for some time. To welcome Laszlo, she saw that he had hung three balloons from the knocker, freshly blown up. Full of hope. Lena tapped the leftmost one with her finger, and watched as it in turn tapped its neighbour, then lightly drifted back. For a moment, Lena felt pity for Istvan, for the balloons his son would not see.

She heard Istvan approach the door and pause. Probably taking a deep breath, like before he'd go on camera. Preparing his face for the role of father, welcoming his son into his new home. Which was in fact a flat that he had used to seduce the boy's mother. A conflicted character role.

He opened the door with an impressive expression. First day of school: excitement mingled with trepidation. His welcoming smile faded as no Laszlo appeared to appreciate it.

'Where is he? Behind you on the stairs? I reported the lift problems, it will be fixed by tomorrow. Nothing for little legs to worry about.'

'He's gone,' said Lena. 'Back to the village.'

'I told you he didn't need to go back and pick up his things,' said Istvan. 'I've been shopping. He'll have all he needs here.'

'He's not coming here,' said Lena. 'Never.'

'What? Why?'

'You've been lying to me. All this time.'

'You can't do this,' said Istvan. 'We agreed. And I don't know what you mean.'

'You're lucky I haven't had you arrested,' bluffed Lena, pushing past him into the flat. 'Yet.'

It was different to how she remembered it. Istvan had turned it into a child's Aladdin's cave. Expensive-looking wooden toys filled the room. Everything was still in its box, cellophane-clad.

'Kids like boxes, don't they?' said Istvan in explanation. 'They like playing in the boxes.'

'That's cats,' said Lena.

A nervous laugh escaped Istvan, which he speedily turned into a cough. Lena almost smiled, remembering this trick they'd had when they had giggled together in class. You got in trouble for a laugh, but not for a cough. Then she saw Istvan smile back. Was he playing with her?

'He's here really, isn't he?' Istvan peered into the corridor.

'I've been to this flat before,' said Lena, lifting a boxed rocking horse from the sofa to the floor. 'I've swept behind the sofa, vacuumed under the bed. I've scrubbed the toilet.'

'What? Before I bought it?' said Istvan, still looking out of the door. 'I've had it about six months.'

'When Timea disappeared. It was on the cleaning rota. But she didn't come here to clean, did she?' Lena stood behind Istvan. He turned to her.

'I don't know what you mean . . .'

'Give it up, Istvan,' said Lena, feeling any sympathy she might have had drip away like bleach down a toilet bowl. 'Just tell me. Did you make her clean up afterwards? Wash your shame off the sheets in case your wife came to see your little investment?'

Istvan closed the door and turned to Lena. 'Catherine has never been here,' he said, as if that made it better. 'It was just for Timea and me.'

'How romantic,' said Lena.

'It was,' said Istvan, ignoring the sarcasm in her voice. 'Like heaven. I miss her so much.' Istvan sat down on the edge of the bed and gestured for Lena to join him. 'We were in love,' he explained. 'Not at first, all those years ago. I thought it had been a terrible mistake. But then, when we met again, it was different. It was like coming home. Nothing else mattered. I wanted her to tell you, but she was adamant it remained a secret.'

'What about your wife?'

'We couldn't help ourselves. It was like we were magnets, drawn to each other in a way it was impossible to resist. When she tracked me down, here in London, it was magical. We couldn't live apart another minute. It is a relief to finally tell you all this.'

Lena shrugged, wondering to herself how many more clichés Istvan could manage. 'So you knew about Laszlo, all along?'

'No. Only recently. She never told me back then. She wanted me to get my big break, to have the career I'd dreamed about. She didn't want to hold me back. Or hurt you,' said Istvan, accompanying his words with a few well-chosen dramatic gestures. Rehearsed, thought Lena.

'She hid the pregnancy from me,' he continued. 'By the time I heard about the boy from my mother, I thought she'd found someone else, that he was the father. But she never did.'

His story did sound like Timea, thought Lena, feeling a mixture of love and contempt for her selfless, secretive friend.

'Once I knew, I was going to help. I was going to start giving her money, to help Laszlo. I was going to finally meet him.'

'But you didn't give her any money,' Lena pointed out. 'You just carried on with your dirty little affair.'

'I think I've always loved her,' said Istvan, ignoring her. 'It all started that night after Natasa's wedding, you remember? She was upset and I comforted her.' Istvan paused, gently licking his lips. 'So warm and soft, not so little anymore. It felt so natural, so right . . . We didn't say anything because we didn't want to hurt you. Even though you and I weren't a couple, Timea was worried about what you would think. We both loved you.' He reached out to touch Lena's shoulder but she brushed it off.

'You must have given her that necklace,' said Lena, feeling it all coming together. 'And the baby, the unborn baby. That was yours.'

Istvan looked down. 'This time we were going to get it right,' he explained. 'Together. She didn't want to do it alone again, and I wouldn't have let her. She wanted me then, all of me. For herself, for Laszlo, for the baby. And I was going to stand by her and do it properly. This time. Poor Catherine. She was going to be devastated.'

He scratched at his eyebrow. What was he lying about? His wife? Lena reluctantly took his hand. She'd have to coax it out of him.

'That must have been a tough decision,' she said. 'But your wife must have known that something wasn't right?' Lena wondered how much of his story was authentic and how much from a dreadful screenplay.

'She had no clue. We were so careful, even having a special code for our text messages. "I need the carpets scrubbed" meant we met in the flat, and then she'd say "buy more detergent" which meant she would be there in an hour. "Sweep the front steps" meant let's meet by the canal. And "hang out the laundry" meant—'

'Meet by the canal?' said Lena sharply. 'You met her there?'

'We'd watch the swans swimming by, feeling like it was years ago, together, back in the village. Before it all went wrong.' He

185

broke down into tears. 'It's my fault,' he said. 'It's my fault she's dead.'

'What?' said Lena, snatching her hand away and standing up. 'What do you mean?'

'It was too much to give up.'

Lena reached into her backpack for her phone. 'Tell me what happened,' she said, starting to dial. 'What did you do to her?'

'Who are you calling?' said Istvan, looking up.

'No one,' said Lena. 'See?' She put the phone back in her bag and sat back down. She needed to know the truth and couldn't risk him closing back up. 'Tell me everything.'

'I had the chance to be with Timea and the baby and Laszlo, to have a proper family,' he said, looking straight at her. 'But my acting career and my lifestyle – all of that relies on Catherine. I signed a pre-nup, and she runs my career.'

'So what did you do?'

'I told Timea that I would have to think about it.'

'And then?'

'I, I hesitated,' he said, with a sniff. 'My job on the show, my beautiful house, I loved it too much. I hadn't done what I've done to end up with nothing.' He looked up at Lena. 'So I left it. I didn't get in touch with her. She was waiting for me and I just . . . did nothing.'

'That's it?' said Lena.

'The next thing I heard was from my mother, telling me that she was dead. Her body was found in the canal. That's where she chose to end her life. Because of my hesitation.'

Lena sat back down. 'Look at me, Istvan,' she said. He turned his face to her. The area around his eyebrows had gone red from the crying, like it had done when he was little. She'd known him so long, she would know if he was telling the truth. 'That's what you did? That is everything?'

'I should have chosen her, her and the children,' said Istvan. 'She took her own life because of me.'

Lena thought of everything they had gone through together. He had been there for Timea, for both of them, for all those years before he left. Lena's mind went to the night of the harvest festival, more than ten years ago now. Timea had been excited that night. 'I can't believe Bela's asked me to the dance. He's the most handsome boy in the village. Well, he will be once Istvan leaves for Budapest.'

Lena had looked at the thirteen-year-old Timea. She was quite short still but her beauty was budding. 'I can believe it,' she had said. 'You're getting quite pretty.' She gave her friend a little push. 'But Bela is too old for you. Isn't he fifteen?'

'I know,' said Timea. 'You should have seen Natasa's face when I told her. I'm lucky.'

'I've heard he drinks.'

'So does Istvan,' said Timea. 'You too.'

'That's different,' said Lena, not elaborating on why. 'Just be careful.'

'You can't be jealous,' laughed Timea. 'You've got Istvan.'

Lena coughed. Things hadn't been so easy with her and Istvan recently. There'd been rumours of what he'd been up to with one of the girls in the neighbouring village. She wasn't sure she even wanted to go to the dance, not with people sniggering behind her back. Timea wouldn't believe anything bad of Istvan. Ever since they'd been to that concert when Timea was nine, she'd believed Istvan to be perfect.

Lena had gone to the dance in the end. She wasn't going to let rumours, hotly denied by Istvan, stop her. The decorating committee had done themselves proud. The village hall was decked with carved pumpkins, filled with candles and bales of wheat made into the shape of fans. A fire hazard, thought Lena, putting the thought to one side and instead focusing on how beautiful it looked. The gypsies provided the music, the violins playing melodies that made you want to spin around and around. Everyone was drinking *pálinka*, the Hungarian schnapps that fuelled most parties. It was early in the evening and the mood was high, with people showing off the outfits they'd saved for all year. Later the evening would always descend into chaos. Couples would sneak out to embrace in the crunchy autumn leaves. Babies born in July were known as festival children. Fighting would start, too, and for subsequent weeks most self-respecting farmers would sport black eyes and broken noses. 'You should see the other one,' they would say, in chorus.

Lena danced with Istvan, losing herself in his arms. She noticed Natasa wink at him but she wouldn't start a fight. Not tonight. 'There's Timea,' she said, pulling out of Istvan's hold.

'Leave her be,' said Istvan, holding her by the waist again. 'I want to dance with you.' Lena ignored him, dragging him over to where Timea stood, grinning ear to ear next to Bela. The boys greeted each other stiffly and Lena hugged Timea.

Timea was dressed to make herself look more mature. She'd piled her hair on to the top of her head and plied her face with makeup. Her dress was a red halter-neck and she tugged it up uncomfortably. Lena noticed Bela's hand resting on Timea's back. He was swaying slightly, like an ear of wheat in the wind. Lena sent the boys to fetch her a *pálinka*, insisting that Timea stick to apple juice. Timea reddened.

'Don't embarrass me,' she said to Lena when they had left. Then she smiled. 'Isn't Bela gorgeous in that suit?'

'How much has he had to drink?' said Lena.

'He's so grown-up,' said Timea, her eyes following him. 'A proper man. Like Istvan.'

'We'll leave together at midnight,' said Lena.

'But the dance isn't over till two,' petitioned Timea. 'He'll think I'm just a kid if I leave early.'

'You are just a kid,' said Lena. The boys came back and the couples drifted apart. At midnight Lena got herself another *pálinka* and went in search of Timea.

It had reached the point of the night when people were either kissing, crying or fighting. A boy who'd lost his partner grabbed at Lena as she walked past, but a sharp glance convinced him it wasn't worth it. She ignored the desperate greeting of one friend, patting the back of another who was sobbing into a tissue. The music had become more haphazard now, the violinists having also partaken in the *pálinka*. Lena couldn't see Timea anywhere.

She stepped outside, into the cool, fresh air. For a moment she enjoyed the relative silence, the music still ringing in her ears. She took a deep breath, letting the air revive her. As her ears became accustomed, she realised it was far from silent. Someone was retching nearby. The smell of *pálinka* and semi-digested *szalonna* bacon assaulted her nostrils. The retching stopped, allowing Lena to hear giggles and moans and leaves crunching. Steeling herself and downing her *pálinka*, Lena went in search of Timea amongst the amorous couples.

She almost fell over one couple who blinked up at her in annoyance. As her eyes grew accustomed to the darkness, the woods revealed a multitude of previously invisible couples, dotted around like bales of hay. She investigated each one. Most ignored her. She recognised some couplings she'd expect, others that were a more surprising combination. But when she found that Timea was not among them, Lena didn't know whether to be relieved or worried. She gave up and stepped back into the village hall. The gypsies had stopped any pretence at playing music now and were gathered around the remnants of the *pálinka*. Someone had scattered the kernels from the wheat fan around the room like confetti. In the corner, Lena saw Istvan, his arms around a girl. She let out a small gasp, shocked that he would do that here, in front of everyone. She stormed over and yanked his arm away to reveal a tearful Timea, holding up her torn dress with one arm and clutching Istvan's hand with the other.

'Lena,' she said, letting go of Istvan's hand to take hers. Mascara had leaked down her face, leaving a grubby trail.

'Thank God you've turned up, Lena,' said Istvan. 'Don't worry, Bela won't try anything again.' He held up a bloody fist triumphantly.

'Are you OK?' said Lena to Timea. 'What happened?'

'Nothing, thanks to Istvan,' she said. 'If he hadn't been there . . .' She gave him a look of total adoration. Lena looked at him too, thanking him with her eyes.

'Let's get you both home,' Lena had said. 'I've got some bandages, we can clean up that hand of yours.'

'I'll do it,' Timea had said quickly. 'He saved me.' Lena had smiled and led them both out into the night.

Back in the present, Lena looked at Istvan. The devastation was real. He'd loved Timea too. He deserved to know that he had not driven Timea to suicide. He deserved the truth as much as she did.

'Istvan, I believe that Timea was murdered. I am going to find out who did it and I am going to bring them to justice. And if you want to, I will let you help me.'

CHAPTER 21

Claustrophobic clouds filled the sky, low and menacing. Lena looked out at City Road. The traffic was busy, as it always was on this wide London thoroughfare. Buses and lorries hurtled past, taking people and deliveries from North London into the City. A few intrepid cyclists took their chances, whizzing bravely along the edge of the road.

It was drizzling, and the tiny raindrops seemed to cling to the traffic fumes, making them linger in the air. Lena felt as if she could taste the exhaust in the back of her throat.

'I hope this is a case of keeping your friends close and your enemies closer,' said Cartwright, raising his voice to be heard over the din of traffic. They were on their way to Yasemin's flat. 'I don't trust Istvan,' he added.

Lena paused before replying, till the passing ambulance sirens were at a distance where they didn't deafen her. 'But you are convinced it is Yasemin's gang that are responsible for Timea's death,' she said finally. 'You said it all added up. Not everyone can be guilty.'

'The fewer people on a crime scene the better,' said Cartwright. 'He'll contaminate the evidence. I shouldn't even be there, let alone all three of us. Technically it is not breaking and entering because you've got a key, but snooping around people's houses without their permission isn't exactly model police behaviour.

And even if we did find something, without a warrant it won't stand up in court.'

Lena stopped. The rain was heavier now, and the wind blew it directly into her face. 'This is not about court,' she said. 'It is about the truth. And you do not have to come. Istvan and I can manage.'

Cartwright produced an umbrella from the large bag he was carrying and put it up, holding it to shelter Lena while he braved the rain. 'Of course I'm coming,' he said. 'I promised you I would help. I'm just saying that we should be careful. We don't know what Istvan could be involved in.'

Lena stepped closer to Cartwright and took his arm so they could both enjoy the shelter of his umbrella. 'I am sorry,' she said. 'I am not sure that I trust Istvan either. I want to keep him where I can see him for a while. And perhaps he will be able to help us.'

'What, with his vast experience in solving crimes on a TV show?' said Cartwright. 'I'm not sure how much value experience in flouncing around is going to be to us in this situation.'

Lena laughed. 'I want to give him a chance,' she said. 'See how he behaves,' she said.

'Badly, I expect,' said Cartwright. They turned on to the side street where the entrance to Yasemin's flat was. The rain had cleared up as suddenly as it had started, and Cartwright shook out the raindrops from his umbrella. 'At least he isn't late,' said Cartwright, gesturing to Istvan's Maserati. 'But is that car his idea of inconspicuous?'

Istvan emerged with a broad smile and shook Cartwright's hand in the condescending way only celebrities can pull off. He gave Lena a kiss on both cheeks. 'Give me a moment to pop some money in the meter and I'm all yours. It's been a while since I've searched a crime scene for clues, now my character has made detective chief inspector. Usually, these days, I delegate that kind of grunt work to the uniforms or one of my detective constables.'

Lena almost burst out laughing when she looked at the indignant expression on Cartwright's face. 'Delusional,' he muttered, while Istvan fished coins from his pockets and slotted them into the machine.

Lena took a deep breath. The air felt clean and damp now the rain had stopped, and sunlight was beginning to appear through the clouds. She gestured to the men to come closer to her and told them her plan. 'We will go up together, but do not talk to me once we reach Yasemin's floor. I will go in and check no one is there. But we should be safe. I saw tickets to Istanbul on the kitchen table last time I was here. They were for a flight yesterday. If something goes wrong and she does come back, the story is that I hurt my back so you are here to help me with the vacuuming. Cartwright you are my brother, Istvan my boyfriend.' Istvan smiled. 'Cartwright, you have been before so you know what it is like in there. Istvan, you will see the foulness people leave for their cleaners. You will probably want to give your own cleaner a pay rise.'

When they reached Yasemin's floor, Lena gestured to the men to wait in the lift and approached the door. Standing outside, she felt something was different. The temperature perhaps, or the smell. It wasn't right.

Taking a breath, she put the key in the lock and swung open the door. This time she wasn't greeted by a miscellany of takeaway remnants. She was greeted by nothing.

The black leather sofa was there still and the glass table, cleaned of all food remnants. Apart from the plant, continuing its slow death by dehydration, the flat looked like a rental show home. She stepped inside.

'I don't know what you were complaining about,' said Istvan. 'This place is even cleaner than my house.' He glanced round admiringly. 'But it doesn't look right for a gang overlord, or whatever you think. Far too plain and beige. It does have a funny smell though. Pungent.'

Cartwright began muttering about the lack of statistical evidence regarding criminals' preferences in terms of interior decoration. Lena ignored them both and went into the bedroom. The bed was neatly made, the duvet cover folded at the bottom. But the wardrobes were empty. The hairbrush was gone. Even the toothbrush was missing from the en-suite bathroom.

'We are too late,' said Lena, feeling despondency rising within her. 'She has left for good. Istanbul was no holiday. There is not a trace of her.' She sank down on to the bed, feeling the memory foam shape itself around her form.

'There's more than a trace,' said Cartwright. 'Come into the kitchen.' Lena joined him there and almost embraced him.

'I have never been so pleased to see a kitty litter tray,' she proclaimed.

'And freshly used by the looks of it,' said Cartwright.

'What a stink!' added Istvan, leaving the kitchen as quickly as he had entered it. 'Why are you two so excited about cat poo?'

'This means that Yasemin has not gone for good,' said Lena. 'She will come back for her cat Kaplan. Look, there is a food bowl. She would not leave him behind.'

'She already has,' said Istvan.

'She will come back,' said Lena. 'Where is Kaplan?'

'Found him,' said Cartwright. Lena followed his voice to the bedroom.

'Look.' He peeled back the edge of the duvet cover to reveal the cat, hiding underneath. Kaplan hissed at him.

Lena sighed with relief. 'She will be back,' she said, offering the cat her hand to sniff. It gave Cartwright an angry look, promptly licked Lena's hand, then rubbed its head against her. 'She would not leave for good without this one.'

'They are expensive, that breed,' said Istvan, standing back. 'Hypoallergenic. But so ugly.'

Lena picked the cat up, flooded with relief. Its warm body felt like a lifeline to finding out the truth. 'We should give him some fresh food and get out of here,' she said.

'Cartwright, let's get a surveillance team on this place,' said Istvan. 'We'll catch her when she comes back for the cat.'

'Surveillance? I'm not even supposed to be here,' said Cartwright. 'We've got no evidence, no reason to arrest her and only a hunch that she will come back at all. There's no chance we'd even get a surveillance team – I'd get laughed out of the station just for asking. Not to mention that we're trespassing.'

'I'll have a word,' said Istvan. 'Once they know who I am . . .'

'We'll call that plan B,' said Cartwright, putting his bag on the bed and opening it up. 'In the meantime, I've borrowed the fingerprint dusting kit. Don't ask how I got it out of the station, but if she's left a trace of herself, we'll find it. And if her fingerprints are on our system – and I bet they are if she's bothered to assume a fake identity – then we'll at least know who she really is.'

'That is brilliant,' said Lena, touching Cartwright's shoulder. 'I could kiss you.'

'It won't stand up in court, of course,' said Cartwright, blushing a little. 'But it could help us get closer to the truth.'

'I don't see any fingerprints,' said Istvan. 'That might be the fatal flaw in your plan.'

'You not actually being a policeman, just an actor, might be the flaw in yours,' muttered Cartwright.

'What was that?' said Istvan.

'I'll start in the kitchen,' said Cartwright, ignoring Istvan. 'Try not to touch anything.'

Lena followed Cartwright, carrying a purring Kaplan. 'I don't know who he thinks he is,' said Cartwright. 'Well, actually I do. He thinks he's Inspector Morse.'

'Do not be too hard on him,' said Lena. 'He is just trying to help.' Cartwright produced some powder and something that closely resembled a makeup brush and began sprinkling and dusting for fingerprints.

'Start on that cupboard,' said Lena. 'She never cooked so she would not have used the stove, but that is where she kept her cat food.'

'Brilliant deduction, Lena,' said Cartwright. 'Thank you.'

'That's not how they do it in *Heroes of Law*,' said Istvan, peering through the door. 'And will she be in your database, even if you do find a print like that? Isn't she Turkish?'

'Let me worry about that,' said Cartwright. 'I am the professional.'

'In my experience, cross-border operations are tricky. So much red tape. I remember when we went on location in Marrakesh, tracking that drugs gang. Almost impossible to get the local force to co-operate. That's why my character had to sleep with Fatima, to earn her trust so she'd spill the beans. You probably haven't experienced cross-border work before.' Istvan laughed. 'Doesn't come up much when you're directing traffic.'

'I am not traffic police,' said Cartwright. 'And you are insufferable.'

'Concentrate boys,' said Lena. 'We do not want to be here longer than we need to be.'

'I think your friend has lost his traffic cone,' said Istvan, laughing.

'I certainly had no trouble finding your record,' said Cartwright, putting the brush down, the colour rising up his neck. 'Does Lena know how you made your living before you got your big break?'

'Shut up,' said Istvan, stepping right up to Cartwright. 'You don't know anything. You're only a constable.'

'That's enough,' said Cartwright. 'I didn't want to say anything, it's not good form. But Lena deserves to know the truth about you.'

'Don't be ridiculous,' said Istvan, the colour draining from his face nonetheless.

'What truth?' asked Lena, looking up from the empty drawer she had been searching.

'She needs to know,' said Cartwright. 'But, because I'm a gentleman, I'll give you a chance to tell her first.'

'Just shut up,' said Istvan.

'Just tell me, Cartwright,' said Lena. 'Then we need to get out of here.'

'Final chance, Istvan. No? Well, Lena, I think you should know what your friend here was up to, once he left your little village and went to Budapest. He didn't make his money from acting. He was up to something much seedier.'

'That isn't true.'

'I have evidence. You were arrested.'

'There were no charges brought.'

'That doesn't mean it didn't happen.'

The men squared up to one another. 'You don't know what you are talking about,' said Istvan, his voicing rising to a shout. 'You should shut up.' Kaplan scrambled out of Lena's arms with a snarl and disappeared under the bed.

'I'm not having a gigolo tell me what I can and can't say,' said Cartwright, 'Tell him, Lena. Tell him he is not welcome here.'

Both men turned to Lena. She spoke softly. 'You don't know what it was like,' she said to Cartwright. 'Back then, back there. You never can. It's not easy to get out, to pull yourself up from the village.'

'That's it then,' said Cartwright, turning away from the pair of them. 'There are no fingerprints here.' He shoved the brushes back into his bag.

'Do not go like this,' said Lena. 'Stay and help us.'

'This was a waste of time,' he replied briskly. 'I'm going back to the station.' He zipped up his bag and hoisted it on to his shoulder.

'Be careful, Lena,' he said as he left. 'You don't know who you can trust.'

Istvan slammed the door behind Cartwright. 'He was lying,' he said. 'I never did anything to be ashamed of. Certainly nothing illegal. I swear it.' He looked beseechingly at Lena. She didn't reply. 'Tell me you trust me.'

'Shush,' said Lena. 'Did you hear that?'

'Hear what?'

'Someone is coming, I heard the lift. Quick, in here.'

'I thought we had our story worked out? You are her cleaner, and I'm your helpful boyfriend.' Istvan grinned at her. 'I like that scenario.'

'That was before we knew Yasemin was planning to leave for good,' replied Lena impatiently. 'If anyone comes in to this flat, I want to hear what they say. It might be our last chance to find out what happened to Timea.'

Lena clambered into the empty wardrobe. Istvan squeezed in too.

'Listen,' she said. 'See if you hear the keys in the door.'

They both waited in silence. There wasn't much room in the wardrobe and Lena could feel Istvan's breath on her ear. It tickled. She tried to wriggle away, but there was no room. Then she heard a jangling followed by voices.

'I've got the box, Erden,' said a male voice. 'That means you have to catch it.'

'I'm allergic to cat hair,' replied Erden. 'Brings me out in a rash.'

'It's hairless, you idiot. Just do it.'

'It still has whiskers.'

'Jesus. Fine. I'll do it. Little sod better not scratch. You seen it?'

'Try the bedroom. Yasemin lets it sleep in there with her.' Lena felt Istvan give a start next to her. She rested her hand gently on his shoulder to calm him. He reached his own hand to meet it and she felt the sweat on his palm. 'Rather the cat than me,' said Erden. 'Yasemin is fierce. You saw what happened to Faisal.'

Lena felt a rush of adrenalin. This was it. This was when she would find out what had happened.

'I'd still do her,' said the first man. 'Sort her out, a night with me would. Faisal just wasn't up to it.'

'She'd eat you for breakfast.'

'Hope so.' The man gave a dirty laugh and Lena could imagine what he was miming. Their voices were close now, just outside the wardrobe door. 'Where's this fucking animal?'

'Puss puss puss,' the other one said. 'Come on pussycat. I've got a nice piece of juicy kebab for you.'

'That was a good idea, to bring a kebab,' said Erden.

'I'm lying, you idiot. Hah, there it goes. Fuck, that is one freaky cat. Looks like a kebab itself.'

Their footsteps retreated into the living room. Lena heard a sigh of relief escape Istvan. 'Got it,' she heard. 'Let's get out of here.' Lena didn't share Istvan's relief. These men could have a clue to Timea's murder. Perhaps, if she was careful, she could follow them.

'Thank God,' said Istvan, extracting himself from the cupboard. 'That was close.'

'Shush,' said Lena, remaining in position. 'I haven't heard the door close. When we do, we need to be close behind them.'

Suddenly there was a hiss followed by an exclamation. 'Fucking animal,' she heard. Then a patter. Istvan threw himself back in the cupboard on top of her, but the door swung open behind him. Lena found herself staring into the cat's amber eyes for a moment before she grabbed the door. It was too late. She'd been seen.

CHAPTER 22

The plastic was digging into her wrists, and no matter how Lena squirmed she couldn't get the blood flowing through her arms. She couldn't see her hands, tied behind her back, but pictured them in her mind's eye. White and etiolated, like the plants that tried to grow under Mama's birdbath and only saw the light of day when the young Lena had tipped up the bath in search of slugs or toads to scare Istvan with. Now her hands, numbed and starved of blood, felt like they belonged to a stranger. Imposters.

Lena looked over to Istvan. She would have been able to escape the men if it hadn't been for him, but then they wouldn't be in this mess without her ridiculous idea of hiding in the cupboard. She found she couldn't feel angry at Istvan, not with his head slumped forwards. So vulnerable. If she had been able to move, she would have reached out and patted his shoulder, maybe even given him a hug. Suddenly she felt her heart swell with affection for him. When she had seen the men, she had charged out of the cupboard, kicking one and ramming past the other before he'd realised what had happened. She had expected Istvan to follow in her wake. But when she'd glanced back, she had seen he was in a choke hold. Then she'd seen the glare of the knife against his neck. She'd had no choice but to surrender.

She continued to chew the fabric gag they'd bound around her mouth. Soaked in her spit and cheap to begin with, the rag was steadily disintegrating under the patient pressure of her teeth. She paused to spit out some shreds and then explored the remainder with her tongue. Nearly through now. Not that being able to talk would do much good. She could hear Istvan behind her, whimpering gently. He would be just as powerless as she was, tied to a chair like a child strapped into a car seat. She'd been a little relieved when they had gagged him. Spouting about being an actor. That might help him get into a nightclub, but it was only making things worse here. And then there had been confusion when he had talked about his character, DCI Vlad, and the men had panicked that he was a policeman. Lena would have kicked him if the men hadn't.

The men had debated what to do for some time. Neither wanted to tell Yasemin. She couldn't work out if they were scared to speak to her, or worried about what the command would be. In the end they had agreed to go and see her. So they'd given Istvan another kick, checked they were both secured and headed out.

Lena ripped the final thread of her gag with her incisors and spat out the remaining material. She paused, enjoying the freedom this small victory gave her. 'Issy,' she whispered, 'Don't worry. I'll get us out of here.'

Istvan replied with a low moan. Still gagged and in pain, he wasn't going to be much use. Lena stretched her mouth wide open and closed it again. From the tiredness in her jaw and the numbness in her hands, she reckoned she'd been here for about two hours. And, despite what she had said to Istvan, she had no clue how they were going to escape. She looked around, but it was as hopeless as it had been while she was still gagged. 'Any ideas?' she whispered to Istvan. He just looked back, his eyes wide and wild. Lena took a deep breath and tried to assess the situation. Her hands were tied with plastic fasteners behind her chair. She experimented with wriggling them as she had before, but more methodically. Was there a weak spot? Any chance of slipping through with an act of contortion? No, she'd need something to cut through them. She moved her focus to her legs, bound at the ankles to the chair. No chance of freeing them without her hands and a knife. She tried to scoot the chair forwards, pulling up through her stomach to hop. No progress; without her feet to power her, she barely moved. She scooted again, but the chair only wobbled. Could that be useful? She could probably manage to throw herself on to the floor sideways. Lena thought for a moment. Would that help? She couldn't think how being on the floor could possibly be a good thing.

She heard a sound and froze.

A low hum. For a moment she thought it was a bee, trapped inside for winter. Then she realised it was a phone vibrating. Where? Not in this room, it was too far away. Istvan caught her eye, his attempts to speak thwarted by the gag in his mouth. Perhaps the men had left her phone in the other room.

This was more than she could have hoped for. But how could she get to it? All she had that she could move in any meaningful way was her mouth. Talking wouldn't get her out of this. She needed something sharp and a way to use it. It came to her. Of course. 'Keep still Istvan,' she said, as she began to rock her chair as much as she could. She leaned far to the right, but the chair stayed solid. Then she tried jerky movements, pulling to the right then letting herself fall back to the left. Eventually the momentum worked. She crashed to the floor. Hard.

It hurt more than she thought it would. Her shoulder had taken most of the force and was throbbing. She tried to ignore it, wishing the gag was still intact to bite into for the pain. 'Don't worry Istvan,' she said. 'That was my plan.' Istvan mumbled in response. Lena's head was a few inches from his feet. She scooted on the floor forwards, so that her mouth was right next to his shoes. They smelt of expensive calf leather, recently polished, and she could see the intricate pattern typical of brogues. Then, raising her head, she bit into the plastic around Istvan's right ankle.

It would take some gnawing, but Lena could tell it would work, as long as she had enough time. She glanced up at Istvan, who was looking back down at her, watching her spit drip on to his shoe. She had imagined her and Istvan doing many things together, but this was not one of them. She tried to think of something else to distract her. School came bizarrely into her head. It must be the taste of plastic, she thought. Like chewing a pen. Or the leg of her unfortunate Barbie doll.

Her mouth was sore by the time the plastic was worn through. With a final bite, it snapped. Lena rested her head back, exhausted. Istvan shook his leg in a small celebratory foot dance.

'Can you move now?' said Lena, feeling the pain sear through her shoulder again now the distraction of the task was removed. 'I don't know if there's time for me to do the other leg.'

Istvan experimented with his foot. Attempts to stand and hop almost sent him toppling over. But he could move pretty success-fully using his free foot like an oar to slide the chair along the parquet floor.

'Good,' said Lena. 'Remember the phone we heard earlier? We need to find it.'

Istvan made a noise of understanding and paddled off awk-wardly towards the living room. Lena lay on her side, waiting. The men had been idiots to leave a phone there. But then noth-ing they had done so far had made her think they were clever. That was good news.

After what seemed an age, Istvan dragged himself back. Lena thought he'd failed, until he gestured behind him. Scooting him-self around, Lena saw her backpack hanging from his bound hands. 'Drop it by my head,' she said to Istvan. 'I'll fish it out with my mouth.'

That was easier said than done, but eventually Lena had the phone in her teeth. She spat it to the floor, and with some sharp pokes with her tongue was able to call the last number she had dialled. She listened to the dial tone, cursing as the phone went to voicemail. She just had time to leave a garbled message before she heard the men coming back up the stairs. Istvan kicked the bag and the phone under the bed so the men would not see it. She just had to pray that he would pick up the message in time.

'I knew you were no cleaner,' said Yasemin. She had stooped and was kneeling on the floor with her head tilted so that her dark brown eyes, the colour of coffee beans, were in line with Lena's. Lena was still lying on her side, tied to the chair. 'So who are you?'

Lena blinked, looking into the woman's eyes. She felt her right side tingling underneath her, pins and needles setting in over the top of the pain. She could feel the numbness creeping into her mind as well. What could she say? What did she know about this woman that she could use?

'Lena Szarka. You may not know much about me,' said Lena, 'but I know about you. I know what you have done.' Lena tried to keep eye contact, but she was distracted by a flash of pink. Kaplan was sniffing around his owner's heels.

Yasemin grabbed the cat and pulled herself up. All that was in Lena's eyeline now were her shoes. Black patent leather, with the four-inch heel of a lady who wanted to be taller. Lena saw her own ghostly face reflected in them, looking back at her. Terrified.

'Impossible,' replied Yasemin. 'There's nothing here. I don't keep my secrets in my laundry basket. What can you know?'

'Put me upright,' Lena told Yasemin's shoe. 'We can talk properly. Woman to woman.' Yasemin paused, then shouted something to one of the men. He heaved her chair up. She looked at them. They were different from the men who had caught her. These men looked like soldiers, muscle-bound and silent. Lena attempted to wriggle her right hand, but it was still too numb to control.

Yasemin laughed as she stroked Kaplan's skin. 'You are not someone I have had dealings with before. Where are you from?'

Lena said nothing, concentrating on her toes. Feeling was eking in as she contracted and released them. It felt good to have the right side of her body back again.

'Let's ask your friend here instead,' said Yasemin. She spoke to one of the men. He went to Istvan and roughly yanked the gag from his mouth. Istvan spat on the floor. 'Romanian?' said Yasemin.

Lena almost laughed at the indignation on Istvan's face. 'Hungarian,' he said quickly.

'Interesting,' replied Yasemin. 'And you are from the police department?'

Istvan's earlier affront was forgotten. He beamed at her. 'People often say that,' he said. 'And it's easy to understand why, when I'm so convincing—'

'We are the opposite of the police,' interrupted Lena, a plan forming in her mind. 'We represent some powerful interests. And we like what we see here. Untie me, and we'll talk business.'

Yasemin laughed. 'You forget that I saw you with your friend. Janos, you called him. But I know who he really is. Who you all are. You are the police.'

Lena shifted in her chair. 'You are right. Janos is police. Luckily for you, he is in our pay.' She glared at Istvan's confused face, willing him to play along. Wasn't acting meant to be what he was good at? 'Many people are in our pay and they would not be pleased to see us being treated this way. Would they, Istvan?'

'What?' said Istvan.

'Our gang,' she prompted, wishing she didn't have to rely on Istvan. 'They would not be kind to people who hurt us.'

'Ah right. Yes. Well. You'd better untie us right now,' said Istvan menacingly. 'The Belatoks will not be pleased if you don't. They eat Turks for breakfast.'

Lena tried not to roll her eyes.

'You stay tied,' said Yasemin. 'It is easier to kill people who are tied to chairs.' She squeezed Kaplan more tightly and he hissed in objection.

'What?' said Istvan. 'Did you hear what I said? My people, they will spear you like a doner kebab . . .'

Yasemin said a word to the man. He promptly slammed his muscular fist into Istvan's face. Istvan gasped in shock, and then watched spellbound as a drop of his blood began to trickle from his nose, landing with a splatter on his white trousers. Kaplan took advantage of the confusion to wriggle free of Yasemin's grasp. He disappeared under the sofa.

'I do not care what your people want. Even if you are not police, you are here. In my flat. That is enough reason for me to kill you. You already know too much.'

Lena took a breath. 'You are a businesswoman,' she said. 'At least hear what we have to say. I think you might find it interesting. And extremely lucrative.' Lena paused. Yasemin was looking at her, listening. Now she had to think of something to say.

'We have been watching you for some time,' she said. 'You are careful. We like careful people. And you are clever. You need to be, to be so successful in a competitive market like London.' Lena saw a glimmer of satisfaction in Yasemin's eyes. But the power of flattery would only take her so far. She had to take a risk.

'But there's a problem. The thieves you have working for you will never make you rich. Really rich. Pickpocketing, stealing handbags, grabbing phones. It is barely worth the risk. And your people will soon be caught.'

'People are expendable,' said Yasemin, with a laugh. 'And these immigrants they are allowing into the UK. Romanians, Latvians, Bulgarians, even Turks. They can be very cheap.' She laughed. 'It doesn't matter if they get caught. The police think they work on their own. And they are too scared to say otherwise.'

'But drugs are the real money,' said Lena, remembering what Cartwright had told her. 'And your supply is limited.'

'It is growing,' said Yasemin, leaning back in her chair.

'But now it is a small operation. We could help you with supply. Stuff you cannot get from Turkey. But we will not help you with things as they stand.' Lena paused for a minute, wondering where this would get her.

'What?' Yasemin hissed something at her goon. He stepped up to Lena, his hands grasping her throat. 'Do not disrespect me,' said Yasemin. The man squeezed his muscular fingers.

'I apologise,' said Lena, coughing. Yasemin nodded and the man released his grip. Lena inhaled deeply, letting the air flood back into her lungs. 'You have built an impressive business here.'

'I know,' replied Yasemin. 'And it will grow bigger.'

'That is where we can work together,' replied Lena. 'We have sources. Sources that can take you into the big league.'

'And why are you telling me this?' asked Yasemin. Lena smiled. She could tell she had her interest.

'We need distribution. Someone who has a network of people who can deliver.'

'I have people,' replied Yasemin. 'If the price is right. But I need proof.'

'That will come,' replied Lena. She was starting to feel as though she was in the movies. She could see Istvan's eyes on her. Impressed. 'But first we have an issue,' said Lena.

'Issues can always be resolved,' said Yasemin. 'I need proof of what you can do.'

'You disposed of someone who matters to my bosses,' Lena replied, ignoring her. 'We must resolve that before we can do business.'

Yasemin laughed. 'Faisal was a nobody. Do you expect me to believe the Budapest mafia cared about a Pakistani paper boy?'

'I do not mean Faisal,' said Lena. She paused for a moment, then said the words. 'I am talking about Timea Dubay.'

Lena scanned Yasemin's face for recognition, a flicker of guilt. But she saw nothing in Yasemin's cold eyes. She looked at the men. They looked back at her blankly. Finally Yasemin broke the silence.

'What is "Timea Dubay"?'

Lena looked at her in confusion. She had been so sure. Yasemin had already admitted to killing Faisal. Why would she lie now?

'Tell us what you've done to her,' shouted Istvan, his voice filled with anguish. 'Tell us, *kurva!*'

Lena cursed under her breath and tried to keep a cool expression. Yasemin turned to her, ignoring Istvan, who was wildly kicking his freed leg at the air. 'He is not much of a gangster, your friend,' said Yasemin. 'Not even much of an actor.' Her expression had changed and she regarded Lena with less interest. 'I think perhaps you are not so powerful after all. You come to my flat uninvited, with a business proposition. But there are no samples, no money, and no proof.'

'That will happen in the next meeting,' said Lena, trying to sound as if that was the most natural thing in the world. 'We need to make some arrangements.'

'No,' said Yasemin. 'It was a pleasure to meet you, but no. This is over.'

'I understand,' said Lena. 'We will not bother you again.'

'You are correct.' said Yasemin. She barked something at the men and Lena found herself, chair and all, lifted up and thrown into the bedroom. She landed on her left side, less hard than before. Istvan was thrown in after her. His chair bounced and skidded until his face was inches from her own.

'You are making a mistake,' shouted Lena, as the door slammed shut behind them. 'You need to let us go.' She listened. Yasemin was talking at speed in Turkish to the men.

'What are they saying?' said Istvan. His face was so close she could smell the sourness of fear on his breath.

'How would I know?' she snapped back. 'Probably deciding how to kill us.'

Istvan emitted a sob. 'I'm sorry,' said Lena. 'Perhaps they will just leave us here and get out,' she lied. 'They won't kill us if they don't need to, it's too big a risk.' She remembered the cold look in Yasemin's eye. Like a lizard, devoid of emotion. She was someone who would give the command to kill in a heartbeat. Lena was surprised she had stayed alive this long.

'I thought you said she'd be in Istanbul?' said Istvan. Lena looked at him, so close it hurt her eyes to try to focus. 'Was he blaming her?'

'People miss flights,' she said. 'Plans change.'

'You said she would not be here,' said Istvan. 'And now we are going to die.'

'She believed my story,' hissed Lena. 'Till you lost your cool. I thought you were meant to be an actor?'

'That's right,' said Istvan. 'Insult me before you get us both killed. And she didn't believe your story. It was ridiculous.'

'Shut up,' said Lena, listening. She heard the front door open and close. Had they gone? The tinny sound of a football crowd cheering from the television answered her question.

'What's going on?' said Istvan. 'Have they left?'

'I think only Yasemin has gone,' replied Lena. 'At least one of the men is probably still guarding us.'

'So she is not going to kill us,' said Istvan. She felt a hot sigh of his relief on her cheek. But she didn't share his conclusions.

Most likely Yasemin had gone to double-check their story, make certain with her bosses that she did not make a mistake ordering their deaths. But, once that was confirmed, Lena could not see a scenario that did not involve the execution of herself and Istvan.

She looked up at him. 'I'm sorry, Istvan,' she said. 'It is not your fault. She didn't believe my story. It was a ridiculous thing to try, but I was desperate.'

'I thought it was rather good, actually,' said Istvan. 'I was impressed.'

'Thanks.' Something hot and wet hit her face. It was a tear from Istvan.

'I'm afraid,' he said. 'And I know it sounds selfish, but I'm glad I've got you here with me.'

'I feel the same,' she replied.

CHAPTER 23

Growing up, Istvan had always been there for her when she had needed him. She still remembered the day they discovered her father was gone for good. She had been sitting in the village coffee shop, stirring her Coke with a straw and building up a small maelstrom of bubbles. It had been empty in there. Just her and the owner, who was busy fiddling with his new coffee machine. Every so often he would punctuate her thoughts with a small 'a-ha' as another breakthrough was made in its complicated functionality. It was a relief for Lena to be out of the house. It had been three days since her father had gone out for more cigars and her mother had been praying constantly, clutching her bundles of rosary beads until Lena feared they would turn to dust. There were still rumours that wolves lived in the mountains. Hungry wolves.

Then they had discovered he had cleaned out their savings – and stolen the contents of the safe from the factory where he was foreman. Greta had baked *kifli* to feed her grief.

Istvan came into the café and sat down across from Lena. She handed him her Coke. He took a sip. Then he reached out and held her hand. They sat in silence, sharing the drink. Lena could feel a sob brewing inside her like coffee in the machine. She tried to force it back down, but in doing so made a noise that reminded her of a dog's bark. Istvan looked at her. She could see in his eyes that he was going to tell her something sweet. Her father still loved her, she hadn't been abandoned, he'd be back. She couldn't bear it. Istvan started speaking before she could stop him, and she braced herself to swallow more sobs. It would be like a kennel in the coffee shop.

'So guess how many dumplings I ate yesterday?' he said.

Lena choked in surprise and felt Coke bubbles squirting up her nose. 'Eleven at lunch and sixteen at dinner,' he continued. 'I think that must be some kind of world record. Perhaps acting isn't my calling after all – eating dumplings is my route to fame and fortune. Surely people would pay to see such a handsome lad attempt such a feat? And I wasn't even full, the dumplings ran out. At least that's what they told me.'

Lena burst out laughing. 'Where did you even get them all? Did your mama make them?'

'No, there was a special on at Jozsef's Place. All-you-can-eat dumplings. I did it instead of getting those new shoes, but it was worth it. I'd take you, but after me I think Jozsef has had second thoughts on the offer.'

'So you ruined it for the rest of us,' teased Lena.

'Yes,' he replied. 'I owe you as many dumplings as you can eat.'

Lena had leaned over the table and kissed him. It was a long and slow kiss, interrupted only by an embarrassed 'a-ha' from the café owner.

'You must be fond of dumplings,' Istvan had said, as they broke off the kiss. His face was bright red.

'Very,' Lena had replied, leaning in to kiss him again.

Lena wriggled, feeling her body, tied to the chair, beginning to go numb again. She could hear the cat meowing, perhaps in the next room. But all she could focus on were Istvan's eyes, filled with fear. He leaned forwards, closer to her. For a moment it felt like they might kiss. Lena turned her face away. His lips brushed against her cheek.

★ ★ ★

212

Lena opened her eyes with a start. The room was dark and she could barely feel her body; her limbs were like strangers to her. For a moment, she wondered if she was dead. No, there was too much noise. A commotion outside, someone barking out orders. Then a well-spoken reply. She tried to hear the words, straining her ears.

'What's happening?' said Istvan. Lena listened. Was it her imagination, or was that voice Cartwright's?

'In here,' she shouted. 'Help!'

The door swung open and she saw Cartwright, looking confused at the pile of chairs that imprisoned them. 'We're here,' said Lena.

'Thank God,' said Cartwright. He ran over to her and sliced through her bonds with a knife, releasing first her hands and then her feet. Lena barely had time to stretch before he had constricted her again in a massive hug. 'Thank God you're OK,' he said.

'Over here,' said Istvan. 'I'm here too.'

'Nice job saving the girl and ignoring the guy, Romeo,' said Gullins, stepping in to release Istvan. 'Smooth. Good thing we brought back-up to catch those two sleeping beauties.' He gestured to the other room. Lena could see the men, handcuffed and being led away by two uniformed policemen.

'Where's Yasemin?' she asked.

'Who?' said Gullins.

'She wasn't here,' said Cartwright. He coloured and let go of Lena. She shook herself, then rotated her hands and feet in circles, listening to the clicks of objections they emitted at the unexpected motion. 'But we'll get what we can from these two. Don't worry, we'll catch her.'

'She did not kill Timea.'

'That doesn't matter now,' said Cartwright. 'At least you are safe.'

'She had not even heard of her.'

'Don't worry, we've got plenty that we can charge her with now.'

Lena got to her feet gingerly and stumbled over to Istvan, putting her hands on his shoulders.

'We're not going to die today,' she said softly, in Hungarian. He put his hands on her own. Cartwright muttered something about a search and left the room.

'Right, you two,' said Gullins. 'We're going to need to get a statement from you down at the station. It's some mess you've got yourselves involved in here, and we need to get to the bottom of it.'

All Lena wanted was a hot bath, but the police seemed to conspire against that. Instead she was taken to a medical examiner to be poked and prodded and photographed. They got multiple shots of the red marks around her wrists and ankles, plus her shoulder, which was starting to get an ugly blue bruise on it. But nothing was broken. The medical examiner told her to get some rest and she'd be fine.

She didn't feel fine. Throughout the danger she had felt as though she was getting closer to the truth, to justice for Timea. She had put her life, and Istvan's, at risk. It was all for nothing. She closed her eyes and remembered Yasemin's blank expression when she had mentioned Timea. The woman didn't even know she had been her cleaner. Yasemin may have committed many crimes, but she was pretty certain Timea's death wasn't among them.

She was led from the medical room to an interview room by a plain-clothes detective. 'Can't I go home yet?' she said.

'I'm afraid not. I'm DC Clarke and I need to ask you a few questions.' She looked at the man. He was slight and tense, with greying hair. He put his hands on the desk and interlocked his fingers together. 'I'll be recording this interview.'

'Where is Cartwright?'

'PC Cartwright is at the flat, collecting evidence. I need you to tell me what happened. How did you get mixed up with those people?'

'I clean for Yasemin. She used to be Timea's client.'

'And Istvan Nemeth was with you?'

'Yes.'

'Why?'

'He was helping me,' lied Lena.

'An actor was helping you with your cleaning?' He released the grip on his hands and put them flat on the table. Lena watched as he lifted each finger up and put it down again in turn.

'That is right,' she said, as his fingers danced.

'OK,' said Clarke, strumming his hands on the table now, as though he was playing an invisible piano. 'How did it go from cleaning to being captured?'

'They tied us up,' said Lena.

'I gathered that,' said Clarke. 'But people do not normally tie their cleaners to chairs. What happened?'

Lena paused. She didn't want to get into this with the detective and was worried that she could implicate Cartwright. He had said that he shouldn't have been in that flat without a warrant.

'I do not know,' she said.

Clarke leaned back in his chair, putting his errant hands behind his head. 'When people are taken hostage there is always a motive. What did they want from you?'

'I do not know,' she repeated.

Clarke sighed. 'OK. You're not in trouble here. But those people have a record as long as your arm back in Turkey, and I'm willing to bet they're not in London sightseeing. What can you tell me about these two men? Which one is the boss?'

'Neither,' replied Lena. 'A lady called Yasemin.'

'Yasemin Avci?' asked Clarke, leaning forwards, his hands forming fists. 'Also known as Fatima Moustafa? Emine Adnan?'

'I think so,' replied Lena. 'Cartwright knows more about her.'

'Cartwright, eh?' said Clarke. He sat back and looked at the door. 'I heard he did mention something about it to Gullins,' he said, thoughtfully. 'But I didn't think—'

'He figured out that she was involved in the phone muggings. And some drug dealing.'

'That's her bag all right,' said Clarke. 'But where do you fit in?'

'Nowhere,' said Lena. 'I'm just her cleaner.'

Clarke looked at her, then interlinked his fingers again. 'Stopping Yasemin's gang in Islington before it's even properly started would be quite an achievement,' he said slowly. 'And Cartwright has something?'

'Talk to him,' said Lena. 'And perhaps take him seriously this time.'

'You've been very helpful,' he told her.

'There's one more thing,' she said. 'She confessed to me and Istvan. She is responsible for Faisal Javaid's death.'

'I never thought I'd be saying this,' said Gullins to Cartwright. They were standing outside the police station while Gullins smoked a cigarette. Lena stood with them, enjoying the fresh but smoky air. 'This is bloody good police work from you. Even Clarke said. We're close to putting Yasemin Avci − of all people − down for a good few years, and we've handed CID the chance of closing an open murder. I'll buy you a pint at the York later. For once, you've earned it.'

Lena watched as Cartwright relaxed his face into a reluctant smile. 'Thank you, sir,' he said. 'But Lena helped enormously.' Cartwright gave Lena a gentle tap on her back.

'Humph,' said Gullins. 'Almost got herself killed. Good thing she had the police force to rescue her.' He turned towards Lena. 'Leave the police work to the police, eh love. It's what we're good at.' Gullins winked at her. 'Even him.'

'I've just got something to fetch,' said Cartwright with a smile. 'I think you'll like it, Lena.' He disappeared into the police station.

'I am glad that we have helped,' said Lena. 'And I am glad to be alive. But if they did not kill Timea, we need to find who did.'

'Let's finish this job off first, shall we?' said Gullins. 'We're going to question the men who were holding you, see what information we can get them to give up. At the least we have them for assault, false imprisonment and illegal possession of a firearm. But I reckon they'll admit to much more, especially now we know someone in the gang committed a murder at Yasemin's command. Hopefully they'll identify more of these gang members too. And DS Wilson will want to talk to you again, about Faisal's murder this time.'

'And Yasemin?' said Lena.

'I'm not hopeful we'll catch her. That's the problem. The big guys always get away, leaving the small fry to take the heat. She won't be back here anytime soon, though; you've properly stitched her up. We've already got the authorities in Istanbul searching customs for the phones. And Clarke reckons one of those thugs in custody will confess to Faisal's murder if a plea bargain is on the table. In any case, with her out of the picture we should see the crime rate fall in this borough, which makes my life easier.'

Istvan joined them and took a cigarette from Gullins. His left eye had swollen up where the man had hit him, making his whole head oddly unsymmetrical. He limped, leaned against the wall and gave her a tragic stare. 'I look like a monster,' he said, grimacing at himself in the two-way glass. 'No one will want to see me on television looking like this.'

Gullins rolled his eyes, stamped out his cigarette and went back into the station. 'Poncey actors,' she heard him mutter as he went.

'You do not need to worry,' she told him. 'Even now you are a very handsome man.'

'Thank you,' said Istvan. 'But *Heroes of Law*. I'll be fired.'

'It is a police show,' said Lena. 'They can write in injuries. And think of the publicity. Their star solving real-life crimes. Perhaps I can get Mrs Kingston to write it up for you.'

'No one comforts me like you,' said Istvan, looking straight into her eyes. 'When we thought we were going to die, it meant so much to me, having you there.' He leaned forwards. For a moment Lena thought he would try to kiss her. She enveloped him in a hug instead, ignoring the pang of pain in her shoulder as she did so.

When she looked up, she saw Cartwright, standing in the doorway holding a box in both arms. Watching them. Lena gently disentangled herself from the embrace and smiled at him. Cartwright didn't move. The box meowed.

'You rescued Kaplan!' she exclaimed. 'Thank you.'

Cartwright looked down at the box he was holding in surprise, as if he had no idea where it came from.

'Yes,' he said hesitantly. 'I suppose I thought that you might . . . But I suppose that you . . . I can—'

He was interrupted by Gullins poking his head around the door. 'Your boyfriend just called,' he told Lena. 'He's on his way.'

Istvan sat down and Cartwright took a step back. The box meowed again. Lena looked at the two men who had risked their lives to help her find Timea's killer. She felt overwhelmingly grateful but she couldn't find the words to express it. She took a deep breath. She smelt of blood and antiseptic and sweat and relief.

'Does that box have holes for air?' was all she could think of to say.

'Yes,' replied Cartwright. 'I used my pen to make some.'

'Thank you,' she said, looking at them both. Then she turned and left.

CHAPTER 24

Lena gazed out at the Islington streets through the rain-streaked bus window. She watched as a woman battled the wind for her umbrella, regaining control for a second before another gust ripped it inside out, its metal skeleton crooked as a bird with a broken wing. She shifted her focus from the outside world to the window pane. The drops trickled down the glass like tears. Each raced to reach the bottom first, leaving a trail of water. Another droplet would assimilate into the trail, its way sped by its predecessor's left-behinds. Lena rang the bell on the bus and swung herself down the stairs, slippery with the moisture dripped from other people's umbrellas on this rain-soaked Monday. She wondered if it was a mistake coming back here. Margery, her face beaten and bruised, had told her not to come. But with Yasemin off her suspect list, Lena was running out of leads. And she needed to be here in case Istvan needed help.

She recognised his car, waiting across the road from Margery's house, though it was only a short distance from Istvan and Catherine's place. The windows were misted from the heat inside the car, and Lena took a minute to compose herself before leaning down to announce her arrival with a tap. A hand appeared on the glass, and wiped away the condensation until Istvan's anxious face appeared. She heard the central locking click open and he gestured for her to get in.

'Close the door,' said Istvan, pushing a button to activate the locks again after she had clambered in. 'That Yasemin lunatic is still on the loose and this area is not what I thought. It's a few minutes' walk from my place but I feel safer in the car with the doors locked.'

'You'll have seen worse in your Budapest days,' said Lena, instantly regretting it as she saw the hurt look on Istvan's face. They sat in silence for a moment. Lena looked at him and noticed that the swelling had gone down now. He'd be fine.

'So how well do you know Margery?' asked Lena.

'Well, you know she's a weathergirl. Quite a few people who work in TV live around here. We see each other at industry parties and local gatherings occasionally. I know her well enough to pop in for a coffee. Not well enough to confront her about the possibility that her abusive husband beat her up and then murdered my lover.' Istvan emitted a nervous laugh. 'But then I don't suppose I know anyone that well.'

'Start with the coffee.'

'I suppose we can talk about the weather. She's been off air for a long time, probably dying to tell someone if it will rain again tomorrow. I'll lead up to it gently.'

'Remember, if you have any trouble I am right here,' said Lena. 'And I can phone Cartwright if we need back-up.'

'Where is he? Busy getting the credit for the gang we cracked?'

'He cracked it too,' said Lena. 'He deserves this moment. You need to go in there, charm Margery, and see what you can find out without raising her suspicions. Try not to let her husband murder you.'

'Thanks for the encouragement,' said Istvan. 'Right, I'm going in.'

Lena watched him hurry to the front door through the rain, lifting his mac to cover his head and displaying the Burberry check lining.

220

Margery came to the door. She gave Istvan an enormous smile and a kiss on each cheek – a very different greeting from the one Lena had received. Istvan was more a part of Margery's world than her own, she reminded herself. Television and celebrities. They were welcome to it. Istvan stepped inside and closed the door behind him.

She thought back to how Istvan used to be, growing up. She remembered one time when they had been walking home together after school. They had stopped outside the bakery and looked in the windows at the *kürtőskalács* chimney cakes, long hollow pastries spiralled around spinning poles to bake. Istvan's stomach had growled.

'Let's go in,' Lena said.

'No, I'm not hungry,' said Istvan.

'You didn't have lunch today. Again.' Lena had seen him at lunchtime, searching his pockets for coins and slumping off when he retrieved only a small black button.

'I don't need to eat.' His stomach growled again, betraying him.

'It is my treat,' said Lena, pushing open the glass door.

Inside, the shop was simple, with apple crates serving as chairs, back when reclaimed wood was essential rather than trendy. Lena reached into her own pocket and found enough for one pastry. 'Cinnamon?' she said. 'We can share.'

Lena picked at the corner of the chimney while Istvan devoured the rest, leaving a dusting of cinnamon on his upper lip where a ghost of a moustache was attempting to emerge.

'I am the man,' said Istvan. 'I should buy.'

'Don't be ridiculous,' Lena laughed. 'I can look after myself.'

'One day I'll buy you all the chimney cakes you can eat,' said Istvan. 'When I'm a famous actor.'

'You have cinnamon on your face,' said Lena, with a smile. He wiped at his lips fiercely. 'I'll get it.' She'd reached out her hand

221

and brushed off the cinnamon with her fingers, licking them afterwards.

'You don't believe me but you'll see,' he had said. 'I just need to get out of this place.'

Lena had laughed at him.

Lena wondered what was going on now, inside the house. Had Margery found a new cleaner, or was she busy apologising for the state of her house? You just can't find the staff, she'd say. Istvan would agree, like he always did. He wanted people to like him. Then he'd forget what he himself thought, too used to pretending to remember his integrity. No wonder he'd made it as an actor. She considered what Istvan could discover and what that would mean. She started to wonder if she should have brought Cartwright here or told him what she was doing. But she hadn't wanted to, not after that hurt look he'd given her when he saw her embracing Istvan. Perhaps she'd been getting too close to him, to both of them. She was with Tomek.

Looking at Tomek when he had come to pick her up at the police station, she'd wondered if he'd lost weight. It seemed unlikely, but his cheeks had a certain sallowness to them, like a peach that is past its best. It was probably just that she hadn't seen him for a day or so and he'd always looked like that. She travelled back in her mind to when they'd first met. On a bus of all places. She'd sat down next to him and noticed the warmth of his body, his legs radiating heat into her own. When he had offered her a wine gum, breaking the entrenched London rule even she had learned of never talking to a fellow passenger, she'd heard something in his voice. Something gentle. Something that made her feel safe.

She could do with a wine gum now, she thought, feeling a dryness in her mouth. Idly she opened Istvan's glove compartment to reveal an expensive-looking pair of calfskin gloves, lined with cashmere. She flicked open the ashtray, which revealed a half-eaten packet of sugar-free extra-strong mints. That was better than nothing.

Popping one into her mouth, she wondered why she wasn't more nervous. Istvan could be discovering the truth about Timea's murder. Confronting the woman who had covered it up. Lena ran through the scenario. Margery, a successful weathergirl, was beaten by her husband. What had she done to anger him? Lena thought back to a magazine of Timea's she had read about battered wives. Most likely she had done nothing. Bought the wrong type of cereal. Forgot to iron a shirt. Perhaps even got the weather wrong. Her husband would have gone mad. Perhaps not for the first time. He'd hit her, hard and in the face. She would have screamed, but no one heard. The next day, she'd have called work. She would have to be signed off sick for a long time to recover. You can't read the weather with a face like that. Even the makeup hadn't really helped. She would have been at home. Alone. Scared.

Then Timea would have come.

They might not even have met until then. Margery could have been one of those faceless women you only know from their houses. You know what they eat, what they wear, what they throw away. But Timea would have been a stranger to her.

When you're alone and scared, even a stranger could be better than nothing. Timea would have seen the bruises, cooed and cosseted Margery in that motherly way she had. Made Margery feel safe. Then she would have coaxed the truth from her, so gently that Margery wouldn't even have realised she'd shared it. Margery would feel better. Relieved. Timea would be sharing the worry, wondering what to do, how she could help. Perhaps that was what she had been worried about, the day she went missing. She'd said it was a client. Timea was so sensitive, so attuned to the suffering of others. Even people she only knew from their dirty plates. She

223

would have fussed and worried and agonised, careful to do the right thing, to help without making things worse.

Had she confronted the husband? Lena knew Timea was no coward, but she wasn't a fighter either. It didn't seem her style. And the thought of blackmail? Lena dismissed it. Timea would not have done that. Her Timea was kind and loving. Too loving, it was true, but there was no malice. And if she had wanted to blackmail anyone, surely Istvan would have been the prime candidate.

No. It must have been Margery who told her husband that Timea knew about the abuse. Perhaps Margery had let it slip that someone else was in on their secret, then her husband would have pushed to know who, threatening her far-from-healed face with another blow. A blow she could not take. Margery wouldn't have been able to resist the urge to avoid the pain. She couldn't have known what he would do to the lady who'd cleaned her house and comforted her. But her husband couldn't risk anyone else finding out. His wife was high profile; weathergirls were well loved. He would have been pilloried, despised, lost his job. Probably gone to prison. He couldn't let that happen. He would have sent Timea a text, the one she'd received the day she died as she and Lena were cleaning. It would be from Margery's phone – Timea would of course have insisted that Margery contact her if she needed anything. It would say it had happened again, that Margery needed her help. Of course Timea would go to her aid. And he would be waiting for her.

The mint had disintegrated in Lena's mouth leaving a powdery sourness. She was nervous after all. Istvan wouldn't be able to cope with this alone. She felt sure he would find out nothing – or too much, and get himself into trouble. He needed her help.

Lena took Istvan's car keys from the ignition and opened the door. The rain had abated now, and as she stepped out she breathed in a cold blast of moist air. It felt clean in her lungs, like

224

the air itself had been washed by the rain. She pushed a button on the remote and the car gave her a reassuring beep as it locked itself. The car knew she was doing the right thing.

Outside the front door she paused for a moment. She still had the door key. But she would knock, save the key in case it was needed later. It was Istvan who came to the door.

'Go back to the car,' he said, trying to close the door in her face.

'Who is it, Istvan?' called Margery from the kitchen. 'If it's those gypsies selling pocket packs of tissues again, send them on their way.'

'I'm doing fine on my own,' hissed Istvan. 'You'll just make things awkward.'

'Have you found out where her husband is?' said Lena.

'No. We don't need to. I think we can clear this all up without making a fuss.'

Lena pushed past him. This absurd need to have everyone like him, to avoid confrontation. This was no job for a coward. She went through to the kitchen where Margery was sitting at the breakfast bar, sipping green tea. She looked up at Lena in surprise.

'What are you doing here? My, you are persistent!' She slowed her voice, speaking in the special way the English reserve for the foreign and the stupid. 'I have a new cleaner now. You go.' She turned to Istvan, standing impotently in the hallway. 'Thank goodness you're here. Get rid of her, will you? She's cleaned for me once or twice, but I think she might be demented. I fired her a week ago.'

Lena looked to Istvan. Indecision was written in his face. 'I don't . . .' he started to say.

'Where is your husband?' said Lena, casting a black look at Istvan first. 'What has he done?'

'What is this obsession you have with him?' said Margery.

'Honestly, Istvan, I wouldn't be surprised if this woman had been stealing his dirty underwear, she's that deranged.'

'You do not need to tell me then,' said Lena. 'We both know. And I want to help you. But what he has done to Timea . . . We need justice.'

'Lena—' began Istvan.

'Oh, so you know me now, do you?' said Lena, turning on him.

'Do you really know this woman, Istvan?' said Margery, doubtfully. 'You shouldn't let her clean your house. She's unhinged.'

'I know what your husband did to you,' said Lena, putting her hand on Margery's arm. 'To Timea.'

'What are you talking about?' said Margery, shaking off Lena's hand. 'Are you trying to tell me that something happened between my husband and the help?' She sat down on one of the kitchen bar stools and looked at Lena again. 'So she was pretending to be all friendly and secretly had her eyes on Rupert?' Margery stood up again. 'Where is she?'

'You do not know?' said Lena, incredulous.

'Funnily enough, I don't have a tracker on her. She'll have run back to wherever she is from already if she knows what's good for her.'

'Hungary,' said Istvan. Both women ignored him.

'You really do not know?' said Lena. 'Then you need to prepare yourself. I have something to tell you.'

'There's more? Really, this is too much. What else can she possibly have done? Added insult to injury by stealing my emerald earrings?'

'She's dead,' said Lena.

Margery sat back down and looked at her. 'What? When?'

'She disappeared three weeks ago. The funeral was a week ago today.'

'I'm . . . I'm sorry. She seemed like a sweet girl.' Margery absently picked up a salt grinder in front of her, filled with pink

Himalayan salt crystals, and gave it a shake. The three of them watched as tiny salt fragments fell on to the quartz worktop.

'That is why I am here,' said Lena. 'To find out what happened to her.' Margery was arranging the salt in neat lines in front of her.

'But what's that got to do with me?'

'What your husband did to you. To Timea. He is a dangerous man—'

Istvan interrupted. 'We should go, Lena. It's not what you think.'

'What do you mean?' said Margery.

'You've got it wrong, Lena.'

'I have got you wrong.' Lena glared at Istvan, then turned back to Margery.

'I know your husband beat you,' said Lena. 'I think Timea did too. You can't stay with him.'

'What are you talking about?' said Margery, finally leaving the salt alone and giving Lena her full attention.

'The bruises on your face. It's obvious he hit you. We can get you help but you need to leave here. He could kill you too, like he did Timea.'

Margery stared at her for a moment. Then she burst out laughing. 'Istvan, you could have told me. Is there a hidden camera somewhere? This must be a set-up.'

'What?' said Lena. 'Why are you laughing?'

'You don't understand,' said Istvan. 'I'm sorry, Margery, but I need to tell her.'

Margery nodded her consent, still looking around the room for a camera.

'There's nothing sinister going on around here,' said Istvan. 'Margery has had a facelift. Plastic surgery. That is all.'

Lena put her hands on the cold granite worktop for support. For a moment, there was silence.

'But Timea . . .' said Lena.

'We need to look elsewhere,' said Istvan. 'Margery, I'm sorry about this. But you look fantastic.'

'I know,' said Margery, with a nervous giggle.

'I might try it myself, in a couple of years. I've already got these unsightly lines on my forehead.'

'Get Botox early. It's preventative too, you know.'

Lena listened as they returned to normal chatter, but she could hardly hear them over the blood pumping through her brain. She started to feel sweaty and faint.

'I'm back on air next week. I can't wait. That girl filling in for me was dreadful, did you see her? She thought Chester was in Wales!'

Lena made for the door. Neither Margery nor Istvan tried to stop her. Like she didn't matter enough to either of them to register.

Outside, she took a deep gulp of air and fought the urge to vomit. Instead she started walking, breathing slowly in and out through her nose. She felt the cold acutely against her sweaty skin and pulled her coat closer to her chest. Even more powerful than the cold was the sensation of how wrong she had been. Her head was spinning, driven by the centrifugal force of her own stupidity. She had jumped to conclusions. Timea was gone, and she had failed to get her justice.

There had to be more suspects. She'd go back to the suspect board. She needed to make sense of it. She needed to find the truth.

For Laszlo.

She reached in her bag for her phone. There were four missed calls from Tomek, but she didn't have time to listen to him complain. She wanted to talk to someone who would understand. She wanted to talk to Cartwright.

★ ★ ★

'This is the last flat Timea and I cleaned together,' Lena said to Cartwright. 'Just before she got that text message and left.' Lena pushed a chair to the bookshelves, then clambered up to dust the picture rail. As she had thought it would be, it was filthy. That girl who'd been covering for her from the agency was awful.

'Careful,' said Cartwright, as Lena hung precariously to reach the furthest corner. He came and stood underneath her. 'I'll stand here and break your fall.'

'Timea hated it when I did this too,' said Lena. 'But I love it. Reminds me of climbing trees in the woods outside the village. At least I am good at cleaning. But not detective work. Still nothing, after all this time.'

'It's good that Margery's off the list,' said Cartwright. 'And the gang too. The shorter the list of suspects, the more we can focus and home in on who did do this.'

Lena jumped down, landing softly. 'But there is no one left,' she said.

'There's Istvan,' said Cartwright.

'Are you on that again? I thought you two had made up.'

Cartwright picked up a box of chocolates on the table and began to fiddle with it, picking away at the label. 'Think about it, Lena. All the lies he's been telling you about Timea, right from the start. And now, you yourself said that he treated you like you didn't matter, once Margery was there.'

'Put that down,' said Lena sharply. Cartwright looked at her, surprised, then down at his hands. He had absent-mindedly taken a chocolate from the box. 'Are you trying to get me fired?' she said.

'Sorry,' he said, replacing it. 'Surely they wouldn't notice.'

'These two lovebirds?' said Lena, gesturing around to sweep in the flowers, the chocolates, the empty champagne flutes. 'The chocolates are a trap. To see if I steal.'

'That sounds paranoid,' said Cartwright. 'People don't really do that. Do they?'

'Maybe not to you, a nice boy from Oxford,' said Lena. 'But you do not know these two like I do.' Lena began to dust a sorry-looking palm fern. 'He's a lawyer who often works late. Ended up closer to a colleague than he is to his wife. She knows what's going on but tries to pretend she does not, because she likes the lifestyle he gives her. And every time she gets flowers, or choc-olates, which is often, she knows it is because he is feeling guilty. It eats her up inside, sharing him. She hates anyone touching her stuff, but she is too lazy herself to clean. So she brings cleaners in and sets little traps. Crystal glasses balanced on the edge of tables, so the minute you close a door they fall to the floor and smash. An extra pound coin in the place she leaves your cleaning fee that you think is a tip but she thinks is stealing. Chocolates lying around, tempting you but carefully counted. You get fired for those kinds of things, if people complain. She had gone through four other cleaners in two years before Timea and I arrived.' Lena took a breath and stepped back to admire the fern. Its leaves shone back at her gratefully.

'That's awful.'

'It is understandable. Jealousy makes people do crazy things.'

She thought back to her own mother. When Lena's father had first gone missing, Greta had been terrified of what had hap-pened to him. She had embraced his shirts, putting her face in them to remember his smell. But when it turned out he had run off, taking their savings, she had taken her scissors to those same shirts, despite the fact that Greta had laboriously made them all herself.

'I have not fallen into her traps. So far. Put the chocolate box down and come help me in the kitchen.' Lena's phone chirped and she glanced at it, vaguely thinking it must be Tomek, still intent on tracking her down. It wasn't. It was a message from

Istvan that made her smile. The phone rang and Lena answered before even checking the caller. 'That was a lovely message,' she said.

There was a pause on the other end of the phone, before a hesitant voice spoke.

The colour drained from Lena's face. 'I am sorry, Cartwright,' she said. 'I have to go. Tomek is at the hospital.'

CHAPTER 25

Lena refused Cartwright's offer of a lift. It didn't seem right. But as she boarded the bus, waiting for a shaky old lady to dig her freedom pass out of her battered trolley, she began to wonder if she had made the right decision.

Cartwright was helping her. That was all. She had no reason to feel guilty. Istvan neither. Nothing had happened. She sat down and shifted uncomfortably, feeling the untruth of it in the lumps in the seat. She'd had more time for both of these men than she had had for her boyfriend. She had barely thought of Tomek, dismissing him and his illness like she would bat away a fly.

He was always complaining of some ailment or other, but after the first few times she had just started to tune it out. It became the background noise to their relationship. Her mother told her all Poles were like that. In Greta's opinion, too many pharmaceutical adverts on the television had created a nation of hypochondriacs. Her mother had thrown in a few other choice words about the Poles but Lena had ceased to listen. She paid about as much attention to her mother's prejudices as she did to Tomek's stomach aches. But when Tomek finally met her mother, he ignored her obvious dislike and treated her with the same gentle warmth as he did everyone. That gentleness was what had first attracted Lena to him. He didn't have the passion of Istvan, but then he would never hurt her either. Because he would never hurt anyone.

Lena thought back to what the nurse had told her. An emergency operation was all that she had understood. She found it much harder to understand what people said over the telephone, with bad lines and no body language to help her. Lena gripped her hands together, squeezing warmth into each finger. She wished she had listened when he had complained, made him go to the doctor instead of mocking him. It pained her to think that she had been sipping hot chocolate with Cartwright and driving around with Istvan when she should have been looking after Tomek.

And now it could be too late.

The bus seemed trapped in a time warp, but eventually Lena alighted at Homerton Hospital and navigated her way through the maze of signs indicating wards for disorders of every part of the body. Blood. ENT. Gynaecology.

A receptionist greeted her kindly and shepherded her to a waiting room. Its institutional nature reminded Lena of the police station where she had waited, three weeks ago, to report Timea missing. She picked up a magazine, glossy and well read. 'I buried my wife on our wedding day', she read. Lena put it down again, and focused her attention on the small TV screen affixed to the wall in a corner. It was the news.

She felt her attention wander again. There were four other people in the waiting room. A couple in the corner held hands and avoided each other's eyes. A suited man had formed an arch with his fingers and was tapping them together in a way that made Lena feel even more nervous. An old lady a couple of seats down was engrossed in the TV screen. The low murmur of the newsreader's voice was the only sound. Lena wondered if she would see Margery on the weather. Was this her channel? She rarely watched TV, just a little *Heroes of Law* now and again to indulge

Timea. Now she knew why Timea was so keen to watch – it had nothing to do with the terrible plotlines after all. But as her gaze honed into the small set, she realised something. The man on the screen was familiar to her. It was François, the client she had suspected when Timea had first gone missing.

Lena blinked, wondering if her eyes were playing tricks on her. But no. She looked again. There he was, plain as day, standing in front of an official-looking building, a handsome woman beside him. She leaned in, trying to hear why he was featured.

'Disgusting, isn't it?' said the lady next to her. 'You can't trust politicians. They like to spread it about.'

Lena looked to her. The woman's engrossed expression had morphed to one of contempt. 'What did he do?' said Lena.

'He's a dirty cheat who felt up one of his interns. Apparently he offered her money to keep quiet about it,' she said. 'But he picked the wrong girl. Her mother is a women's rights lawyer. She went berserk.'

'That woman next to him?'

'Don't be daft. That's his wife.' The woman laughed, a small bit of drool escaping her mouth and making a run for it down her chin. 'Standing by him for the cameras. Look at her face, though. She wants to kill him.'

Lena leaned in to look more closely at the set. It pixelated under her gaze, but she could make out the woman's expression. She was trying to look elegant, above all this. Probably trying to imagine she was shopping at Hermès. But she was fooling no one and knew it. Her eyes were cold and hard, steely. Lena recognised the expression from somewhere. Suppressed shame and fury made a heady cocktail.

Lena couldn't bear to look at her anymore and shut her eyes, but the image was still there. Those cold eyes. 'Dirty scumbag,' said the woman next to her. 'Putting her through that. And she's so glamorous. She could find a nice man, like my Barry. Forty and still single, you know. Doesn't chase round with all the girls like that French frog.'

'Swiss,' said Lena, quietly. 'He's Swiss.' She closed her eyes again, ignoring her neighbour's curious look. There was something in François' wife's eyes that seemed so familiar. What was it?

A doctor popped her head around the door and everyone sat up, all eyes focused on her. 'Lena Szarka,' she attempted bravely. It wasn't the worst effort at pronouncing her name Lena had heard, and she jumped to her feet. The others in the waiting room went back to their personal hells. She ushered Lena into the hallway, talking as they walked.

Lena didn't understand much of what the doctor was saying. She spoke quickly and technically and when Lena asked her to repeat herself, she did so at even greater speed. Something about stones and an operation was all she could fathom. She grew impatient at the doctor's jargon.

'Will he die?' she asked.

'No, not at all,' the doctor replied, giving her a strange look. 'Like I said, it's a kidney stone. It will be painful for a few days but he will be fine.'

Lena felt relief wash over her like a tidal wave. 'Then I see him now,' she said. The doctor led her through a long corridor with multiple double doors that each swung back with the violence of an assassin. No one would be able to follow you through this hospital, thought Lena. Not if you didn't want them to.

Tomek was at the end of the ward, lying on the bed while a small nurse fussed around his pillows. He was pale and tired-looking, and didn't even manage a smile when Lena threw her arms around him.

'I'll leave you two alone,' said the nurse, closing the curtains around the bed to give them privacy. 'Tomek, you just call if you need anything.'

'Thank you, Emma,' said Tomek, his voice muffled by Lena's arm around his neck. 'Lena, that hurts.'

She sprung back, ashamed, and sat on the chair next to the bed. Sitting in it reminded her of school. One leg had had a mishap and was a little shorter than the others. Lena found herself rocking slightly. She took Tomek's hand.

'I am so glad that you are OK,' she said. She looked at his pained expression. 'You are OK?'

'I called you seven times when the pain got bad,' said Tomek. 'Where were you?'

'I am so sorry, my phone was off.'

'It rang,' Tomek said. 'At least the first few times. Then it went straight to voicemail, so I know you hung up on me. In the end I called an ambulance.'

'I am sorry,' said Lena.

'I know you are,' said Tomek. 'Were you with him?'

Lena looked down. 'Istvan? No.'

'I didn't mean Istvan. Sherlock.'

Lena flushed, feeling defensive. 'Was it very painful?'

'Yes. It had been building for months. That's what all those pains were, in my stomach.' He shot her a look laden with reproach. 'Not made up after all.'

'And you are better now?' said Lena, pretending not to notice his implicit criticism.

'Sore. But they have broken the stones now so they will come out. But the real relief is having a name for the pain. Knowing it is a condition that can be treated. Not my imagination.'

'I was not very sympathetic,' said Lena, fiddling with Tomek's blanket. 'I am sorry. But I will look after you now.' She wrapped her hand around his and leaned in to kiss Tomek gently on his cheek.

'I wanted you to be with me so much before, when I was in pain,' said Tomek, turning his head so his chocolate-coloured eyes looked directly into hers. 'But when you didn't answer, I realised something. You don't want to be with me.'

'I do,' said Lena, stroking his hair. It was soft, like her mother's prized fur coat. 'I love you.'

'No you don't, Lena,' said Tomek. 'You like me and you feel affection for me. But you don't care as much about me as I want you to. And that's not how I want to live anymore.'

Lena took her hand away from his hair. 'You are overreacting. Just because I did not hear my phone.'

'No,' said Tomek, raising his head up from the pillow. 'Just because you don't love me. I'm sorry, Lena. It's over.' He released his head back with a jolt.

Lena sat back. The chair rocked, tap tap. 'You are confused,' she said. 'Because of the operation.'

'No,' said Tomek. 'It made me see things clearly. You are an amazing person and I love you. For your strength, your determination, your generosity. I wanted to believe you loved me too, but you don't. You can't. And that's worse for me than kidney stones.' Tomek thrust his hand to his heart with a thud. 'It's not healthy, Lena, to live with someone who doesn't love you. It makes you doubt who you are, what you can do. It drives you crazy. And that's not how I want to be.'

'I do love you,' said Lena, reaching for his hand resting over his heart.

'I know you think that,' said Tomek, putting his other hand over hers. 'And I know that you care. But it's not enough. I'm going to move out.'

'No.'

'I want to sleep now, I'm tired.'

'No.'

'Promise me one thing,' said Tomek. 'For your future. You need to give up this investigation. It is an obsession and it will not bring Timea back. You need to let go, so that you can mourn her.'

Lena was silent. Tomek shut his eyes, as if asleep, signalling the conversation was over. She sat and watched him for a while, his stomach gently rising and falling under the sheet. She thought about what he had said. Suddenly it was clear to her what she had to do. She got to her feet.

She passed the nurse on her way out. 'Lena?' the woman said. 'Tomek is very sweet. You're lucky to have a boyfriend like that. Good men are hard to find.'

Lena looked at the woman. She was prettier than Lena had noticed before. 'He is no longer my boyfriend,' replied Lena. She saw a flicker of delight pass over the nurse's features before she took hold of herself and gave Lena a sympathetic look.

Lena let the doors swing behind her as she left.

CHAPTER 26

One of the year's last wasps had found its way into Lena's warm apartment and was dopily thrusting itself against her window. Lena watched its struggles for a moment, before going to the kitchen to fetch a glass and a piece of card. Placing the glass over the noisy intruder and slipping the card underneath, she opened the window and felt a gust of cold swell into the room. She released the wasp into the winter's day and breathed in deeply, feeling the icy air sting her lungs.

Timea had left her involuntarily. Tomek had chosen to leave. Lena closed her eyes; loneliness washed over her like rain. But something at the edge of her consciousness was busy. Lena clung to the edge of the thought, pulling it further into her mind. She didn't want to wallow in loneliness. She wanted to think, to put the pieces together until they made a whole.

Lena heard the bell and buzzed in Cartwright. A minute later he hurried in and caught her up in a short, hot hug that knocked the breath from her. 'I was worried about you,' he said, releasing her awkwardly. 'You got that call about Tomek and haven't answered your phone since. What's happened? Is he OK?'

'Kidney stones,' replied Lena. 'He will be fine. But we are not . . .' Lena broke off. She could feel the words choking her. 'Come look at the board,' she said, pulling herself together. She went into her and Tomek's bedroom and pulled the board out from the

239

wardrobe to bring it to the living room. She propped it up against the television and sat cross-legged on the floor in front of it. Cartwright kneeled down stiffly next to her. Both stared at it.

Finally Lena leaned forwards and took away the Post-it note with 'Yasemin' written on it. Cartwright followed suit, taking down Margery's. Lena took away Faisal, with the black cross through his name, and then Tracy. Cartwright looked at Lena and then took away François. His alibi still stood. They sat in silence for a while longer, looking at the attractive face left on the board.

'It's no statistical matrix or software simulation,' said Cartwright. 'But I think it's pretty clear.'

'I do not want to believe it was him,' said Lena.

'There's no one else,' replied Cartwright.

Lena shut her eyes again, letting memories flood through her brain.

'He has lied to you, repeatedly,' continued Cartwright. 'He had everything to lose if Timea lived. We only have his word that he wanted to be with her, not his wife.'

'There is no evidence,' said Lena.

'It is circumstantial,' replied Cartwright. 'But there is motive. Everyone at the station is impressed with me after Yasemin. Perhaps I can get them to bring him in, scare him a little . . .'

'He has been scared enough recently,' said Lena. She sat back and stretched out her legs to counter the pins and needles creeping up from her feet. 'But I have another idea,' she said, the plan forming as she spoke. 'It might not work, but if it does it could lead us to the truth. Proof of who was really responsible for Timea's death.'

After she had explained her plan to Cartwright and ignored his objections, Lena rang Istvan and arranged to meet him at his rental flat. She arrived before he did and let herself in with Timea's key.

The boxes of toys for Laszlo still sat inside, unopened. Lena wandered around, casually looking at the labels, picking up and putting down boxes like a browser in a shop. She went to the shelves. The magazine with the article on Istvan was still there, plus the little square object she had seen the first time, its red light still flashing. Instinctively she used her sleeve to wipe off the dust, then looked at it more closely. It was as she thought. Good. Nonchalantly, she put it exactly back in place. It seemed like years since she had first cleaned this flat, but in reality it was just three weeks. She had still hoped to find Timea alive back then. She hadn't even known about Istvan and Timea's affair. Or Yasemin's gang. Faisal had still been alive. She had seen her future with Tomek.

No, she thought. That wasn't true. Even before all of this, she had known it wouldn't last. Her relationship felt safe, but she knew that Tomek was right. There was affection, but not love. Perhaps without knowing it, she'd been holding back. Holding him back too. She thought again of the nurse. Of the kindness she had seen in the girl's eyes.

Lena picked up the magazine again and began to flick through it. She paused at Istvan's picture. He smiled back at her from the page, his cheekbones high and his perfect smile a brilliant white. A lustrous lock of black hair hung cutely just above his green eyes. She was struck again by how ridiculously handsome he was. He and Timea would have made a very attractive couple, better than him and Catherine, with her fake smile and her cold eyes. But Timea was gone, and Lena was here.

She said it out loud. 'Lena Szarka and Istvan Nemeth. A happy couple.' They'd been happy together, for a while. But now they had grown so far apart. Would her plan work? She would have to try. 'I wonder if he still loves me?' she said, out loud again. She picked a pocket mirror from her bag and applied lipstick. It was one she had borrowed from Timea's collection. Then she undid a couple of shirt buttons, displaying her modest cleavage.

Lena jumped a little at the sound of Istvan arriving. She was more nervous than she thought. He strode into the room, sat down on the bed and gestured for Lena to do the same. She carefully replaced the magazine and sat down next to him.

'Lena,' he said. 'About Margery. I hope you didn't think I was being rude, but I had to cover up what we thought. You can see how ridiculous I'd have looked if she thought I believed you.'

'You did believe me,' said Lena.

'Yes, but she didn't need to know that,' he said. 'We move in the same circles, you know. I have my reputation to think of.'

'Istvan, shhh,' said Lena gently. She reached out and took his hand. He looked at her in surprise.

'Let's not talk about the past. Not that past, anyway. I want to talk to you about the future.'

'I don't know who else it could be,' said Istvan, misunderstanding. 'Who else could have murdered Timea? Faisal is dead. It wasn't the gang. Margery just had plastic surgery. Who else could you suspect?'

Lena looked at him for a moment before replying. 'Do you remember when we used to climb the haystacks in the fields outside the village?'

'Of course, when Timea—'

'No, not with Timea. Afterwards. When it was just us. When we'd sit on those haystacks, feeling like kings, and watch the sun go down. I miss those times, the two of us. When nothing else mattered.' Lena leaned into Istvan, reaching her hand to push back a strand of his hair that had strayed into his eyes.

'What do you mean?' said Istvan, looking at her. She reached up and touched her hand to his cheek.

'I'm not with Tomek anymore,' she said, feeling his skin soft beneath her fingers. Just a hint of stubble reminded her he wasn't a boy anymore. 'He was not who I wanted.'

'And who do you want?' said Istvan, his voice shaking. He reached his hand to hers, resting on his cheek. As though he wanted to feel if it was really there, if she was really touching him.

'I want who I have always wanted,' said Lena, speaking in English. She turned her face away and cast a glance at the magazine. When she turned back, Istvan's face was close to her own. Then she felt his lips close over hers. It was working.

'I never stopped loving you,' said Istvan, breaking away. 'Even when Timea—'

'Do not talk about Timea,' said Lena, sitting back and taking his hand again. 'Talk about us. What do you want?'

'I thought it was too late,' said Istvan. 'Even now I've made it. I thought it would be too late . . .' He moved forwards to kiss her again, pushing her gently down to the bed as he did so. Lena allowed him for a moment. This had to be convincing.

Istvan was undoing his flies.

'No,' she said, stopping him. 'Not yet.'

'Yes,' said Istvan, kissing her neck. 'We've waited so long,' he mumbled, reaching his hands around her back. Lena found herself pressed into him. 'I can't wait anymore,' he said, the words hot in her ear. It was as if they were teenagers all over again.

Lena pulled back. 'Not like this,' she said, pushing him away and sitting up. She tidied her clothes around her, making sure she was still covered.

Istvan leapt up as if he'd been stung. 'God damn it, Lena,' he said, taking a step away from her. 'What's wrong now?'

Lena took his hand and pulled him back to sitting. 'Really?' she said. 'In this flat where you were with Timea? The room you have filled with toys for the son you had with her?' He looked back at her and then around the room, like he was seeing it for the first time. He opened his mouth and Lena could see in his eyes that he was going to suggest a hotel.

'But that is not the point.' She spoke loudly and clearly. 'I am not prepared to be your mistress. If you want to be with me, you need to leave your wife.'

'Lena,' said Istvan, taking his hands away, still a little breathless. 'You know my situation. Be reasonable.' She noticed a few beads of sweat had developed on his brow.

'I am. You have a decision to make. You don't need to make it now. Think about it, about us, and what you want.' She leaned forward and wiped the hair from his sweaty forehead.

'You know what we could be together. But I will not force it. If you want to stay with your wife, you can. But I will not be your dirty little secret—'

'Lena,' interrupted Istvan.

'Don't decide now,' she said. 'Wait. Think about it.'

'I don't need to think about it,' said Istvan, leaning forwards again. 'I won't make the same mistake again.'

'It is not the same,' said Lena. 'And you must take your time. Send me a text when you are ready and we will meet. But not here.'

'So I'm just meant to go home now?' said Istvan. 'To her, when I feel like this about you?'

'I know you will make the right decision,' said Lena, giving him a final kiss before getting to her feet. She looked back at him as she left. She only hoped that she had done enough.

Back at her flat, Lena sat in Timea's room. After her initial search, she'd avoided it. But now it felt better to be here than in the room she had shared with Tomek. She wasn't sure what they would do when he came out of hospital. Clearly they couldn't share the same room anymore. She could move into Timea's, perhaps. Just for a while, until they each found their own place. Lena couldn't afford to keep this flat on her own and she didn't want another flatmate. And she didn't think that Tomek would be on his own for very long.

She picked up a selfie of her and Timea together from earlier that year. The two of them smiled out at her, Timea's arm caught in the corner of the picture as she held out the camera. It was like a parallel universe, one in which they were both happy. Lena counted back the months. Timea would just have started her secret liaisons with Istvan. She looked more closely at the picture. Had Timea been especially happy? Lena couldn't remember. She had loved Timea like a sister, but she had never been able to read her. It was only when she died that the truth had come out.

What would Timea think of the situation now? Would she approve of what Lena was doing? No. She would have hated having Lena rummage through her life like clothes in the bargain bucket. She would probably rather her murderer went unpunished if it meant her secrets stayed her own.

But Timea had lost the right to make decisions. She had lost that three weeks ago when the last breath had left her body. And Lena was not Timea. She did not like secrets. And she did not like evil going unpunished.

Lena looked at her phone. She realised she had been gripping it in her hand almost constantly since yesterday, waiting for the message to come through. It was sweaty from her hand, and she wiped it on Timea's duvet. It couldn't be long now. Lena put the phone down and went into the kitchen to make coffee. Perhaps if she stopped watching, the message would come.

She would be pleased to leave this kitchen, she realised as she looked around. The veneers were peeling off the cupboards, revealing the cheap plywood underneath. And the mastic that held the Formica together was irreparably stained. The kettle boiled and Lena opened the fridge to see if there was milk. There was not, but instead one of Tomek's sausage rolls looked out at her forlornly. Lena closed the door, not having the heart to check the sell-by date and dispose of the pasty. It could stay there. It was not doing anyone any harm.

Lena heard her phone beep and hurried to where it was sitting, still in Timea's room. She spilt a little coffee on the floor as she went but ignored it, leaving it to merge with the brown carpet. She quickly read the message. It was time.

It was a bitterly cold evening. Lena pulled her coat around her, trying to nuzzle her face further into her collar. Her breath felt warm, but turned to mist as it hit the air and the condensation dampened her collar. She kept moving, partly from the cold but also from excitement at what might happen. The meeting place was about as isolated as you could get in Islington. Twilight was approaching, and the sky had assumed an otherworldly purple. Lena looked around. There were streetlights about a block away, their reflections dancing in the waters of the canal. It would have been romantic, Lena supposed, had it not been so cold. She could smell the canal, fresher here than in other places, but it still had the slight mustiness of a bathroom that was not well ventilated. Lena sighed to herself. Unventilated bathrooms were her nemesis, the mould creeping up the grout, determined to grow no matter how many times she scrubbed with a vinegar-soaked toothbrush.

The sound of footsteps broke her reverie, echoing on the cobbles. Lena looked to the culprit, picking her way carefully in high heels over the slippery cobbles. She recognised her scent, Chanel Cristalle, before she recognised her face.

'Hello, Lena,' said the woman in her familiar, cultured voice. 'I'm afraid my husband couldn't make it. You'll have to make do with me instead.'

246

Lena stepped back. She drew a deep breath. 'What are you doing here, Catherine?'

'I could ask you the same thing,' Catherine replied, walking closer to her. 'But the thing is, I already know. Why were you trying to seduce my husband, Lena?'

'I was not,' replied Lena, edging away from her.

'Of course you were,' replied Catherine. 'You are not the first. Istvan is a very attractive man. I am well aware of that fact. But he is also weak. Easily led by pretty women.'

'Like Timea,' said Lena.

'Indeed,' replied Catherine, turning from Lena to look out across the canal. 'Timea was the worst by far. The first child I could forgive. But then when I found out about the baby on the way. After everything I've done for his career.'

'You could not let her have him,' said Lena. 'What did you do?'

'It was Istvan's fault,' said Catherine, still gazing out at the canal. 'He did enjoy our life together. Fame, success, money. We were quite the glamour couple. So when Timea gave her little ultimatum, he dithered. It was a pity Timea was so impatient. She committed suicide before she even knew who he would choose.'

'Timea did not commit suicide,' said Lena, grabbing Catherine's shoulder to force her to look into her eyes. 'You know that.'

'We were happy,' replied Catherine, casting her eyes upwards. 'Istvan and I. He was grateful for everything I'd done for him, all the strings I'd pulled. His life was pretty seedy in Budapest before I came along. I made his dreams come true in ways a little tramp from his village never could. It wasn't like his acting abilities alone would get him very far.'

'So there was no way you would let him leave you.'

Catherine looked straight into Lena's eyes. 'Never,' she replied. 'Think of the embarrassment. When I see those women, publicly spurned by their cheating husbands, it makes me want to—'

'Loving someone who does not love you back is not healthy,' said Lena. 'It drives you to awful things.'

'It does,' replied Catherine. 'And I'm afraid that directly affects you, Lena.'

'You're not going to let me take Istvan,' said Lena. 'You will do anything to stop me.' Lena took a step back, then realised she was perilously near to the canal edge. She looked around for help.

'You're much more perceptive than your friend,' said Catherine, calmly. 'Much less trusting.'

'You must know I am stronger than you,' said Lena, circling round. She was trying to put Catherine between herself and the canal, but Catherine would not budge. Lena didn't like having the water behind her, where she couldn't see it. 'You cannot hope to overpower me.'

'Of course not,' replied Catherine. 'That's why I brought my rather elegant little gun along.'

Lena watched her. This was more than she had bargained for. 'You are bluffing,' said Lena, trying to sound confident. 'Where would you even get a gun? They do not sell guns at Ottolenghi.'

'These immigrant gangs can get you anything you want these days, for a price,' said Catherine, with a smile. 'And money is not an issue for me.'

'If you shoot me you cannot pass it off as suicide, like you did with Timea,' she said. 'You will get caught.'

Catherine smiled. 'It's not tidy, I know,' she said. 'And you like things clean, don't you, Lena? I watched you in that nasty little flat of Istvan's. Polishing everything. Reaching corners Timea was too busy with my husband to even contemplate. You cleaned my little video camera too. I was half afraid you'd work it out then. But of course you didn't. Cameras are probably still the size of bricks back in that village you all come from.'

'You will not shoot me,' said Lena. 'You do not want to go to prison.'

'You are right, I certainly do not,' replied Catherine. 'But there's no reason why I should. I've already destroyed the tape of you and Istvan. And I hear there's some nasty gangs hanging around these parts who have a penchant for putting bullets in the chests of people who don't matter.'

'Timea was not shot,' said Lena.

'Of course not. Unlike you, little Timea had no idea. She even comforted me when we had our tearful *dénouement*. A tart with a heart, such a cliché, but it did make things much easier. She even gave me a hug.' Catherine shivered at the memory, as though her coat was still dirty from the encounter. 'She didn't suspect a thing when I produced my thermos. Look at me – do I look like someone who drinks from a thermos?' Catherine paused. 'So when I handed her a cup she took it and gobbled it up like it was some kind of peace offering. You're smarter than your friend,' she continued. 'So I came prepared with more than a cup of coffee for you.'

Catherine laughed again, the sound echoing through the tunnel. 'Clearly I'm the one who should be on stage, not Istvan. Ironic, really, that Mother's Little Helper helped me kill that little mother.' Catherine paused to laugh for a moment at her own joke. 'The tranquillisers were not quite enough to kill her, but it did rather put her off when she found herself in the water ten minutes later. I almost wish I'd had a camera.'

'You murdered her,' said Lena. 'You killed Timea.'

'Of course I did,' replied Catherine, sharply. 'Such a pity you'll never be able to tell anyone.'

Catherine reached into her pocket. A gun glistened, catching the flickers from the distant streetlights.

Lena stood stock still. She could feel her heart beating in her throat. It was so loud she thought Catherine must be able to hear it too.

'Go back to where you came from, Lena Szarka,' said Catherine. She pulled the trigger.

Lena blinked. For a second she thought she saw Cartwright's face, panicked and confused. Then all she could feel was pain, burning through her. More pain than she had ever experienced. She realised she was flying. Flying backwards. She caught Catherine's eye for a moment and saw confusion. Then Catherine was gone. Everything was gone. Lena heard a splash. Suddenly she was freezing, colder than she could have imagined. What was causing it? For a second, Lena wondered if this was what death felt like. She thought of how Timea's body must have been, so cold in the mortuary. Cold for eternity.

It was only when she began choking that she discovered she was wet. She was alive, in the canal. But she was sinking. Lena tried to take control of her arms and legs, to drag herself through the water back to the surface. But the cold was overpowering and she flailed her limbs uselessly, the pain in her chest searing through her. Her head was underwater. She could feel the water on her eyes but there was no other sign that they were open. Darkness surrounded her.

CHAPTER 27

She remembered what Istvan had told her, on their childhood trip to the Black Sea. He had said that drowning was the worst way to die. You struggled and struggled, holding your breath until it was impossible. Then you had no choice but to breathe in and flood your lungs with the water that would kill you. Of course, he was only trying to scare her. It hadn't worked at the time, but it did now.

In Lena's mind the years prior to that holiday had been free from trouble. She remembered sitting on the beach, shimmying her feet down until the sand covered them. Lena was thirteen, Istvan fifteen and Timea only seven. It was before Lena's father had left, back when she thought her parents' constant fighting was just normal affection. They'd had more money back then too. Her father had just been made foreman at the factory, and Timea's dad was in steady work too. The girls had learned to swim the year before in the Hungarian sea, really just a big lake, and both families had decided it was time to experience the real thing, salty and immense. They had picked a small resort that was reasonably priced on the Bulgarian coast. At the girls' insistence, they had agreed to take Istvan with them too. He'd stop the girls getting into trouble, they reasoned. And his family could never afford a holiday.

Lena felt contented, staring out to sea, looking at more water in front of her than she'd believed existed in the world. The heat of the day had passed and the sun baked her body with a gentle heat. Back in the village the horizon was always limited by something. A tree or a building or a hill. But here it was like being in a giant upturned bowl, sky as far as you could see, then merging gently into the azure sea. She watched the sea dance and glisten in the sunlight, listening to the waves crash on to the beach, frothing like a rabid dog.

Timea stood at the water's edge, allowing the sea to caress her feet. Every once in a while a wave surprised her with its strength, and the peacefulness was punctuated by a small shriek. The next wave was gentler and Timea regained her nerve, standing firm and daring it to attack again.

Lena looked back to her feet and then leaned forwards to scoop more sand on to the pile that ensconced them. The sand grew colder the further down she burrowed, until she could feel the damp echo of the ocean between her toes.

Istvan was staring intently at a rock pool. Lena thought he was silly for focusing on this tiny puddle when the whole expanse of ocean was so close. Suddenly he leapt forwards and made a grab. 'Got it,' he said, running towards Lena, his arm outstretched. Lena looked. He had something like a hard misshapen beetle, about the size of a conker. She hadn't seen a real crab before and looked at it curiously. Istvan was holding it from behind, and it waved its claw around angrily, unable to reach his finger. He thrust it into her face and waited for a scream.

'Hello snappy,' she said calmly, looking into its beady eyes, held on stalks away from its body like a snail. 'You've got an Istvan on you, I'm afraid. That's what the unfortunate smell is.' The crab wriggled its legs in the air, panicked. 'Let it go, Istvan,' she said. 'It's too small to eat. And I want to see it run away. They run sideways, you know.'

'No way. This took me ages to catch. I'm going to get a scream.'

He crept towards Timea. Lena followed. As he approached he hid his arms behind his back. Lena giggled and Timea spun around.

'What are you doing?' she asked suspiciously.

'I just want a hug,' he said.

'You never want to hug me,' she said, frowning at him. She knew he was up to something but couldn't tell what. He wrapped his arms around her and she hugged him back, giving up suspicion. Then she screamed. Istvan had put the crab into her bathing suit. She jumped around like a goat with fleas. Lena and Istvan burst out laughing as she crashed into the waves, stripping off her swimming costume and shrieking.

'That was cruel,' said Lena, still laughing. She waded into the water and fished out the costume, giving it a shake. 'Put it back on,' she said. 'You'll scare the fish.'

'What was it?' said Timea, awkwardly clambering back into the suit. 'It bit me. Was it poisonous?'

Lena laughed again, wishing Timea's forlorn face didn't give her the giggles. 'It was just a crab. Ignore Istvan and he'll leave you alone.' Both girls could still hear his laughter, ringing out over the crashing of the waves.

'He is horrible,' said Timea. 'I'm not going back on the beach if he is there.' She swam a few strokes.

'I'll go tell him to apologise,' said Lena. 'Stay where it's shallow.' Lena began to wade back, feeling the water resisting her. She tried to scold Istvan, but he did such a good impression of Timea and the crab that she was soon laughing again. She looked back at Timea. The girl was swimming away in a sulk. 'Look what you've done,' she told Istvan. 'You're an idiot.' He responded by dunking her head under. She rose to the surface again with a mouth full of salt water and an appetite for revenge. She spat the water out at Istvan, like the cherub in the fountain back home. He responded by dunking her again, but this time she was ready and dragged him down with her.

When they came back up she looked to see where Timea had got to. The sun was starting to go down, turning the sky egg-yolk orange. Timea was splashing in the distance, then disappeared before splashing back to the surface. At first Lena thought she was messing around. Then she saw the girl's flailing arms and realised this wasn't a game. She caught Istvan's eye. Both started to swim out.

The waves got quickly higher and more fierce a little further out, knocking them back so they ended up further away from Timea than before. Each time Lena looked at Timea she seemed to be getting more distant. Her splashing grew fainter. Lena swam as hard as she could. Now she could just make out Timea's head above the water. Lena could feel fatigue spreading in her arms and legs but she ignored it. She was getting closer and could make out the exhaustion in Timea's eyes.

Then Timea was gone, lost under the waves.

Lena swam the final strokes and took a deep breath, diving down, reaching for the disappearing body. There was nothing. She reached further, and felt something stringy. She prayed it was not just seaweed.

It wasn't. Timea's head was at the end of it. She hauled her up by her hair until she could grip her under the shoulders, Timea gasping and spluttering. She was in time. Lena used her arms to keep Timea's head above water, thrashing with her legs to keep them both afloat. She turned around and looked back to shore – it seemed an eternity away and her strength was failing. Timea was a dead weight in her arms and Lena could feel her own head going under.

Suddenly Timea's body was lighter. Istvan had taken her. He was a slower swimmer than her. But stronger. 'Can you swim back,' he said breathless, 'if I bring Timea?'

'I think so,' spluttered Lena, not sure if that was the truth.

But they made it. The three of them lay on the sand, their bodies made of lead, with barely the energy to cough up the salty water that was invading their lungs.

It was dark by the time they staggered back to the hotel. They'd expected to be in trouble, but the adults had had drama of their own and hadn't noticed they'd been gone, each in a different corner of the hotel, smoking angrily.

Timea wouldn't go near the sea again. She hated the water. When her parents decided to go back to the beach the following year, she stayed behind with Lena's family.

But Timea's parents hadn't made it back to the sea either. On their journey out to the coast, their car had collided with a truck whose driver had fallen asleep at the wheel. Timea had moved in with Lena's family for good.

Lena stopped fighting the water and let it engulf her. She released a couple of air bubbles. It felt good to get the carbon dioxide out of her lungs, but it made her wish for fresh oxygen more than anything. She would delay her watery in-breath as long as she could. Lena distracted herself with a prayer, a prayer that Timea had been unconscious before she hit the water. Lena released the rest of her held breath. She watched the bubbles rise to the surface. They made it look so easy. She didn't want to die like this, in a dirty canal in this still strange city. She made one last thrash with her legs.

To her surprise she began to rise, as if invisible hands were lifting her up. She thrashed again. Her head rose above the water level. She took the breath she never thought she would catch, a breath of air and water combined. She was moving. Floating. Floating to the canal edge. She thrashed again, determined to make it. She wanted to live.

'Stop kicking me, I'm trying to save you.' The voice was breathless but familiar. Lena looked back and saw a sodden Cartwright in the water next to her. Holding her afloat. Lena reached her hand towards him. Then everything went black.

When she awoke, she was lying on the concrete, gasping for breath like a freshly caught perch. There were people all around her, and one of them had a latex gloved hand on her shoulder, pressing down. She called out to tell them it hurt, but no sound came out. She looked down and saw something red on her shoulder, leaking through the latexed fingers. She could feel it, warm and treacly, trickling down over her chest. She realised with horror that it was blood.

Suddenly Cartwright was kneeling next to her, water dripping off him into her eyes. She blinked. He was wrapped in a metal sheet. Lena couldn't help thinking he looked a bit like the tinfoil-encased sandwiches so favoured by her mother. She laughed to herself, but the effort made her choke.

'She confessed,' said Lena. Cartwright looked down at her, puzzled, and she realised he couldn't hear her. She could barely hear herself.

'Don't try to speak,' he said. 'We need to get you to hospital.'

Lena reached up and grabbed Cartwright's shoulder. Pain seared through her, but she had to tell him. 'It was Catherine. She confessed.'

Cartwright nodded. 'I heard it too,' he said. 'And we've got her. You just need to stay with me.'

'You saved me,' said Lena, letting go of him and allowing herself to relax into the pain. 'You saved me again . . .' She began to slip into darkness.

Lena felt Cartwright taking her cold damp hand in his own and squeezing it. Lena squeezed back. 'We did it,' she told him softly, without opening her eyes. 'We caught Timea's murderer.'

CHAPTER 28

Lena liked the hospital bed. She pressed a little button and the mattress raised her up to sitting, and she pressed it again to release her back to the horizontal. It gave her more pleasure than seemed reasonable, moving up and then down again with such little effort. She was on a ward with other patients, but had a curtain that could be closed to give privacy. She preferred to leave it open as she was near a window. With the curtain open the winter sunlight hit her face with a blast of unexpected warmth. And the whole room was so clean and smelt reassuringly of disinfectant. This would be a nice place to work, she thought, and idly mused on the idea of training to become a nurse once her English was good enough. It seemed a long time since she had thought about her future with any optimism, and it felt good. She pushed the button to raise herself up until she had a good view of the ward, and looked around with interest to see if the nurses looked happy. It was hard to tell. She put the bed back down again and closed her eyes, allowing the sunlight to wash over her face. She took a deep breath and began to doze. Although it was still cold and wintry, she thought she could smell spring on the horizon.

'Lena!' A familiar voice drew her back to reality. Istvan was looking down at her, holding a bunch of yellow flowers from the hospital gift shop. A patient two beds down had an identical bunch. 'Oh my God,' he said, looking at her. 'Is it bad?'

'I am fine,' replied Lena. 'It is worse than it looks.' She reached up and touched the tubes coming in and out of her arms, and glanced at the heart-rate monitor, which offered a reassuringly regular beep. 'The bullet missed everything vital, thanks to Cartwright. He rushed out and pushed Catherine as she shot.'

'That's good,' said Istvan. They looked at each other in silence for a moment, then Istvan sank down in the chair next to Lena's bed, wilting like a deflated balloon. The flowers fell to the floor, but Istvan didn't bend to pick them up.

'You spoke to the police?' said Lena. Istvan put his head in his hands. Lena pushed her bed up to sitting. 'Did they tell you everything?'

'I didn't believe it at first. Not my Catherine,' said Istvan. 'But apparently there is no doubt. She has written her confession.'

'What did she say?' asked Lena, leaning forwards. 'Have you read it? Have you seen her?'

'Of course not,' said Istvan. 'I never want to see her again. After what she did to me. To Timea. I can't believe my own wife would do that. And I had no idea. You do believe me, Lena? You have to.' Istvan reached down and picked up the flowers. He began plucking the petals from an unfortunate chrysanthemum and rolling them into little yellow balls between his fingers.

'I should have thought of her earlier,' said Lena, moving the bouquet to the other side of the bed before he destroyed it entirely. 'I saw the video camera in that flat, you know. It did not register at the time, people have so many gadgets. But she was there, the very first time I went to clean it after Timea disappeared.' Lena spoke fast, and in her eagerness to communicate broke into Hungarian. 'I didn't see her but I heard her voice. I suppose she was checking to see if Timea had left any trace of herself behind. Anything that would link Timea to that flat. And then you said that Catherine had never been to the flat. That's when I should have thought about who that woman was. But it wasn't until Tomek said about loving someone who didn't love you, and seeing François with his wife, looking so angry and betrayed. I'd seen that same look in Catherine's eyes . . .' Lena broke off. Istvan was sobbing. 'What's wrong?' she said. 'It's over now. We've caught her.'

'It's all my fault,' he gasped through his tears. 'All this death. Timea and the baby and I almost lost you and my wife is in prison and I had no idea. I am stupid and selfish. My life is ruined.'

Lena looked at him. It was genuine grief, she knew, and yet still he thought more of himself than anyone else. He would never change.

'Istvan, you are not responsible for what Catherine did.' Lena took his hand. He hadn't been a model of good behaviour, but he didn't deserve this.

'Everyone will know. What will they think?'

'Who cares?' she said.

Istvan gave Lena a look of utter incomprehension.

'It's all over for me now,' he said with a wave of his arms. Lena started to feel like Istvan was rehearsing again. 'My wife is in prison. My lover is dead. My career will be in tatters. It will all hit the papers. The evening press will be printing it in hours. It's probably already all over the internet.' He put his head in his hands again. Lena resisted the urge to tut at the melodrama and reminded herself that what had happened to Istvan was traumatic. He deserved her sympathy.

'I do not see how this can hurt your career,' she said gently. 'Your wife loved you so much that she murdered your beautiful young lover. If it wasn't so tragic it would be romantic.'

Istvan ran his fingers through his hair and then focused his piercing green eyes on Lena. 'Thank you,' he said. 'You always know the right thing to say.'

'We have known each other a long time,' said Lena, taking his hand. 'Timea too.'

'You know, even after all of this, I can't believe she is really gone. I feel like she could turn up anytime, with a story to explain it all.'

'That is not going to happen,' said Lena. 'But I know what you mean. I miss her too. It feels like the grief has barely started.'

'I'm all alone now,' said Istvan. 'Timea is dead and Catherine will go to prison.'

'You are not alone,' said Lena.

'You were pretending,' said Istvan thoughtfully. 'When you were kissing me in the flat? That was for the camera, wasn't it? So that Catherine would see and would react. She did just what you wanted her to. We both did.'

'Yes,' admitted Lena. 'I was laying a trap. It was unkind to you and I'm sorry. But it was the only way I could think of to confirm what I suspected.' She looked at Istvan's face. He looked as if he had been hoping for a different answer. 'You were my first love,' she said, wanting to comfort him. 'I think I will always love you, a little.' Lena smiled at Istvan.

'So,' he said. 'So you would like us to be together? Because I would like that too.' Istvan leaned in for a kiss.

Lena pulled back.

'I am here for you,' she said. 'But not like that. Too much has happened for us to be together.'

Istvan looked at her, visibly deflating. 'Then I am alone.'

'No,' said Lena. 'You have Laszlo.'

'Laszlo barely knows me.'

'He needs you to be a father to him. Go home, Istvan. Visit him. Spend some time getting to know your son.'

Istvan sat back in his chair and rubbed his forehead. 'You are right,' he admitted.

'And you can give him a message from me,' said Lena. 'Tell him that his mother didn't abandon him. She wasn't responsible for what happened. That will mean a lot to him.'

'I will,' he said. He stroked her hand.

'And I will come back soon, to visit. I need to take Timea's ashes home. It's time for us to say goodbye to her properly.'

'Where are you going to scatter them?'

'It's up to Laszlo,' said Lena. 'But I was thinking in the Transylvanian hills. There's a spot that the mountain goats like that is covered with beautiful daisies. We used to go there in summer, the three of us, when we could afford to. It was a happy place for us all.'

'That sounds perfect,' said Istvan. 'I would like to think of Timea resting there.'

She only just noticed Cartwright, standing on the edge of the ward watching them. When he caught her eye he waved hesitantly, but seemed unwilling to come any closer. Lena beckoned him over.

'Sorry to interrupt,' he said. He had a potted orchid in his hands that he held up and then down again, not knowing what to do with it. 'I don't want to disturb you, I'm just checking you are OK. Which you clearly are, so I'll get out of the way.'

'Do not be silly, Cartwright,' said Lena as he turned to go. 'Istvan was just leaving. Have his seat.' She looked at Istvan. He smiled back at her, and leaned down to give her a kiss on the cheek. Lena felt his stubble lightly graze her face.

'Thank you, Lena,' he whispered. He stood up and shook Cartwright's hand. 'Let me know when the police have all you need from me,' he said. 'I have a little boy waiting for me in Hungary.'

Cartwright sat down in the chair Istvan had vacated and sheepishly presented the orchid to Lena. She looked at it. The stem was long and elegant. The large white flowers had tiny drops of pink in the centre. It was the most beautiful plant she'd ever owned, more beautiful than the ones she dusted in her clients' houses.

'You've saved my life twice now,' she said to him. 'You pushed Catherine as she took the shot. That saved me. You were so brave.'

'I should have acted sooner.'

'You could have been killed,' said Lena.

'So could you.' They looked at each other.

'I should have guessed it was Catherine,' Cartwright said, breaking the silence. 'But even when I was following you, I still thought Istvan was going to be the person who showed up.'

'I thought it might be too,' admitted Lena. 'And I am so pleased it was not. You have enough evidence?'

'She tried to deny it at first,' said Cartwright. 'Even though I saw her shoot you. Claimed self-defence. But that didn't last long when she realised we knew everything. We got a full confession. I think she's hoping to plead temporary insanity, though even the most expensive lawyer money can buy will struggle to get that one past a judge. Wilson was pretty pleased with me.'

'I am pleased for you too,' said Lena. She smiled at him. 'You deserve it.'

'You deserve it,' said Cartwright. He reached out his hand and gently placed it over Lena's. She felt its warmth on her own. As they sat there, in silence, she began to feel the gentle rhythm of his pulse, beating softly and merging into her own. She looked at his hands and noticed a couple of thin scratches. It must be from Kaplan, she realised. The cat he had rescued for her.

Cartwright's eyes followed her own. He took his hand away awkwardly. 'I don't think Kaplan likes me very much,' he said, running his finger along the scratch.

'No,' replied Lena. She took back his hand, cradling it in her own. 'But I do.'

ACKNOWLEDGEMENTS

First and foremost I would like to thank the fantastic Philippa Pride, AKA The Book Doctor, for her wise advice, immense kindness and enthusiastic championing of Lena and *In Strangers' Houses* from start to finish. I'd like to extend this to my talented friends in the 'Next Chapter' writing group: Tanya, Kelly, Jenny and Elvie, who have supported me throughout and given many excellent ideas and edits.

Special thanks go to my agent Euan Thorneycroft at AM Heath for his insightful suggestions and for finding a wonderful home for the book, as well as Pippa McCarthy and Jo Thompson for all their help. Huge thanks of course to Krystyna Green and the team at Constable for their wonderful support and belief.

I'd like to thank the officers of the Metropolitan police who gave me procedural advice in an area I thankfully knew little about, as well as the numerous Hungarians who helped me with their language and culture, and shared their experiences moving to London. Since my Hungarian grandmother is no longer with us it has been invaluable.

My mother Susan has nurtured my creativity from childhood, and has contributed ideas for this series and some excellent edits. Special thanks go to her as well as my father Roger for his judicious moral assessments and for his attention to logical detail.

Finally, thanks go to my brilliant husband Sui, whose intense messiness inspired me to write about a cleaner in the first place.

Publishing in 2018 ...

A Clean Canvas

Book two from Elizabeth Mundy, featuring Lena, her relatives, friends and clients, in another adventure ...